Of Gods, Flies, and Desperate Lawyers

A Don Julio the Fly Mystery

by

ANNA M. LASCURAIN

Dedicated to Carlos and Rosita Rodriguez

and

Tata BokoKato Endoki with thanks

CHAPTER ONE

East 72nd Street
New York, New York

His eyes were as black and dark as his soul. The stark half-moon that dangled in the midnight sky gave him no final comfort or second thoughts; suicide was the only option for Garland Nowell. The sleeves of his white cotton shirt recently purchased at Neiman Marcus for the tidy sum of nearly five hundred dollars—a Brioni shirt with barrel cuffs, cool and crisp—would shortly devolve into a blood-stained rag. How ironic! But then again, his whole life had been a source of endless irony—the lofty ambitions clouded by unlucky situations and his never-ending poor judgment of his colleagues.

Garland made it to the big leagues, the prestigious New York firm of Boxdell and Lumpton. He was the young man who had wangled his way into the New York social scene, summering in Easthampton and sailing on Long Island Sound where he had met Sissy Blackwood, a buxom blond society miss. She was the perfect arm candy for an up-and-coming soon-to-be partner at Boxdell. Garland Nowell had done all the right things. But as quickly as he'd ascended, he'd fallen from grace.

Garland poured another glass of scotch from the Baccarat decanter after he gulped down the first. The alcohol struck his brain with the gale force of a hurricane. Garland was not used to drinking scotch, let alone a 1937 Glenfiddich he had pilfered from his senior law partner's private stock. The act was thievery of the lowest form.

What did this infraction matter? His career at the firm was over, all because he had advised a high-profile client that it would be cheaper and more efficient to settle a massive toxic tort case than risk a jury verdict. There was lead dripping from the walls of a string of daycare centers! The firm, on behalf of the insurance carrier, took a "no pay" position against the parents who had instigated the lawsuit. Garland explained to the carrier's representative that a jury would not view the insurance company favorably if a jury eventually learned that the insurer knew about the lead paint when they insured the daycare centers. His analysis was spot-on, and the insurance carrier was satisfied with the result of this strategy. A payout of several hundred thousand versus several million from a jury verdict made the concept of settlement all the sweeter.

However, Mr. Boxdell did not agree. Garland knew that his view of the law was money driven, and a consciousness of right, wrong, and fairness played no part in litigation. Once the client desired to settle, the firm's precious billable hours were gone, as was Garland's job.

Everyone watched him pack up his personal belongings at nine-thirty in the morning. Boxdell fired him, then made him do the "perp walk" in front of the whole firm. The young lawyer was paraded down the longest hallway in front of the entire office so other lawyers, paralegals, secretaries, and even the IT technicians knew that he had been fired. If that were not enough, the old man blackballed him with every major New York City firm. Garland figured this out after he received no response to the fifty resumes he had sent out all over Manhattan. He never received a rejection nor request for an interview. Boxdell was determined to ruin his career and did a marvelous job of completing that process.

As he was escorted to the law firm's front door while his colleagues watched, Garland convinced the security guard that his wallet had fallen out in Mr. Boxdell's office. Thanks to nimble fingers, a disinterested security guard, and a box disguised with his personal items, he escaped with the scotch buried beneath diplomas and certificates. He threw his wallet on top of the papers for effect.

"Got it, Louie. It was right here on the floor. Thank God I found it."

"Yeah, that's nice." He yawned. "I shouldn't even be letting you in here. We gotta go." He noticed that Louie looked everywhere but where his attention should have been. The scotch was an easy theft for the depressed lawyer.

So this is what his life had become.

After being fired a few weeks ago, all that Garland had held dear was gone. He was amazed at how quickly colleagues at the firm became strangers. People love to abandon those people they perceive as failures and pariahs. Sissy's promise of eternal love, which manifested in a two-carat marquise-cut Tiffany diamond ring, disappeared. After all, no one wants to be married to a man who's no longer up for partnership at a major New York City law firm. Not only was his lifestyle gone, but hers was also. Garland shook his head. Emotional waves of futility rode over his heart as he recalled her parting words:

"If I wanted to marry a poor lawyer, I would have taken up with a civil servant like a state attorney general or county prosecutor. I expected a good life!"

Now his expectations of life would end in a single deliberate stroke. He would smash the Baccarat glass and slit his wrist with one of the crystal shards. He would be sure to sever the vein with a vertical slice rather than a horizontal cut in order to shred the vein and bleed out faster.

The two glasses of Glenfiddich had their desired effect. He was woozy but still in control. Garland started raising the Baccarat Harmonie tumbler and noticed that a little bit of scotch remained at the bottom of the glass. A flash of Appleton Boxdell went through his mind as he momentarily studied the last sip of scotch.

Old Boxdell never liked waste. Too bad. Waste you old man! he thought as he raised the glass above his head to bring it down in one large smashing motion.

"Are you going to finish that, *señor*?"

"What? Who said that?"

"My question, are you going to *finish* that? The whiskey?"

Garland panicked. He looked around the room…and saw no one. The voice was soft, deep, and rich with the hint of a melodious Spanish accent. "How did you get in here? Look, I can't see you. But I'm armed!" He stumbled over to a drawer in the living room and pulled out a snub-nosed .22 caliber pistol. Garland spun around and pointed the gun, aiming at various areas of empty air.

"Por favor, señor, it will be a waste of time. I am not as fast as a bullet, but I am an acrobat."

Despite the voice's admonition, he proceeded to shoot the empty air. The voice laughed at him. He put holes in the ceiling and the walls but never hit the intended target.

"You are clearly not from Texas, señor. You shoot like a little kid at a carnival shooting gallery."

"Where are you?"

"Right on the counter, señor."

"I can't see you! And stop with the 'señor' stuff! Where are you?"

"Please. Calm down. I am right here on the counter. You can *see* me if you just try."

Garland threw the gun down and gasped. "Okay, I know what this is. I'm hallucinating from the booze. That's it. Delirium tremens."

The voiced laughed. "No, señor. The delirium tremens comes only when you stop drinking the alcohol, yes. No, oh no, no, no, you do not have the delirium tremens."

The thirty-three-year-old man didn't know if he was coming or going…or if he had left already. He felt sweaty, and as he ran his long fingers through his unkempt curly hair, Garland Nowell realized that at this particular moment in his life, he was an epic fail. He had lost his prestigious job, his fiancée, and now he was losing his mind. Hearing voices? It was perhaps the most lost and confused he had ever felt in his life. That had to be the only explanation for the voice in his head asking him if he was going to finish his whiskey right before he killed himself. Psychosis. Pre-death hallucinations. He dropped the gun, then spun around and plopped on the couch facedown.

"Good God. Maybe I'm dead already and I just don't realize it."

"Señor, please get up off the couch and please to sit down where you were at the table near the whiskey."

He turned his face sideways and addressed the air. "Go away and just let me die."

"Ay, yi, yi! Señor, you are not going to die! Just get up and sit back at the table, *por favor.*"

Garland pulled himself to his feet. Grasping his head in both hands, he stumbled over to the table. He dropped into a chair. "Oh boy, do I have a headache. Okay, Mr. Ghost."

"No, señor, I am not a *fantasma*. I am a living creature. Come look and see for yourself. I am on the table."

Garland looked down at the table. He saw the half-empty whiskey bottle and the glass tumbler. There was nothing in front of him but a large fat fly that had landed atop the whiskey bottle. "I see nothing."

"Yet nothing sees you," he chuckled. "You are wearing a white shirt with initials 'GN' embroidered on the cuffs. Handmade, Italy. Very nice. Very expensive. You have good taste."

"Where *exactly* are you? All I hear is a disembodied voice. I see a bottle, a glass, and a white-looking fly."

"Si, si, señor. Then you do see me. I believe that you have a magnifying glass on that counter."

Garland pulled himself to his feet and grabbed an oversized magnifier he'd used to read the fine print on some old deeds he had been researching. Despite feeling nauseated, he asked, "Where should I look?"

"Pass it over the top of me. I rest upon the bottle of whiskey."

With an almost shameful reluctance, the lawyer looked at the top of the whiskey bottle and passed the magnifier over it. He saw a set of large pink compound eyes. A tuft of hair between the two large pink eyes was lacquered down. Gossamer wings poked through a tiny red velvet vest with gold brocade edging that covering the insect's thorax. A small pair of forest-green gaucho pants and a set of tiny black cowboy boots covered the fly's back legs. The fly's front feet were covered in tan leather gloves. A small guitar strapped to the middle of its back between its silvery wings made it look like a wandering minstrel. The fly stood up on its two hind legs, removed its gloves, and winked its large compound eye at Garland.

The last thing the suicidal lawyer remembered right before he passed out was a smiling albino fly dressed as a South American cowboy.

CHAPTER TWO

Revived by the sound of a lively flamenco guitar, Garland had no idea how long he had been lying on the floor. It could have been hours, could have been minutes—for all he knew it could have been days. When Garland opened his eyes, he saw the fly sitting in the middle of his chest. He swatted the insect away and jumped to his feet.

"Get away!" He grabbed his cellphone that was sitting on a nearby counter. "Psychiatrists. Must Google psychiatrists."

"Señor, you do not need a doctor, particularly a psychiatrist. Everyone knows psychiatrists are *medio loco* anyway."

He didn't know what to do. Then it struck him. If he were insane, he would just go with it.

"Okay, I'm willing to accept the fact that I am talking to a fly. That's what you are, right? A housefly? I mean, you're not like an alien from another planet, correct?"

"*Bueno*, we are getting somewhere. Yes, I am a fly. However, I'm not the common housefly."

"No, of course you're not. Most common houseflies don't talk to people. They just land on food or fecal matter."

"Señor, I do not eat fecal matter. While some of my brethren do, I much preferred the rotting garbage at The Sign of the Dove, but once that restaurant closed, I moved over to dining at La Bernardin."

Garland winced. "I thought perhaps you might be more of the Taco Bell kind of fly."

"When I can have the remainder of *canard à l'orange*, why would I eat a gringo's stale tamale?"

Garland placed both hands on the sides of his head. "So this is what a descent into madness is like? Talking to an imaginary friend—a fly. I need to call a doctor. Maybe that scotch was poisoned…"

Before he could complete the sentence, he heard a high-pitched whizzing about the room, yelling at him in Spanish. He assumed the fly was cursing at him. Garland did not understand a word of what the fly said, but he picked up the cognate "imbecile" which seemed to be similar in both English and Spanish. Having an insect call him an idiot was hardly a boost for Garland's battered ego.

Why not? he thought. *Everyone else hates me. Why not a talking fly?*

The fly finally came to rest on an arm of the couch. "I am losing my patience, señor, and we are running out of time."

"Running out of time for what? What kind of schedule does a fly have? Is the garbage dump closing early?"

He heard the fly sigh as though the weight of the world was on his shoulders. "You are an *abogado*, a lawyer? And you just lost your job, sí?"

Garland raised his eyebrows and watched as the albino fly hovered in front of his face. "How did you know that?" He put the magnifier over the insect. The fly, still dressed in gaucho pants, hovered in mid-air standing on its hind legs.

The fly laughed. "You have heard, how you say it, 'be a fly on the wall?' I was on your wall last week, señor. Right when I saw Boxdell give you the boot." He swung his back leg in a kicking motion as if to emphasize the point.

"So you saw me get fired?"

"Was not the highlight of my day or yours, señor. However, the world is a strange place. One door closes and another window opens up, yes?"

"So what do you want from me?"

"Let me see. Private grade school. Rutgers undergraduate with a bachelor's degree in psychology. And Fordham Law School. You are a very bright young man with humble beginnings, yes?"

"I was a scholarship student. My father was a black seal boiler man and my mother disappeared years ago. So what?"

"Have you forgotten where you come from, señor? Is that what happened when you went to the big law firm? You forgot all the little people who helped get you there? Trade in all the old friends from the neighborhood for new rich ones, eh?"

"Stop calling me señor."

"But it is a term *para el respeto*—"

"I don't need respect from a housefly!"

"Do not flatter yourself. You do not have my respect. Not yet, Garland Nowell." The albino housefly shook a gloved foot at him.

Garland looked at the ceiling. The fly's words struck a sour note in the young lawyer's heart. As he recalled his meteoric rise at his former law firm, he realized that he had callously left behind his small-town friends. It was nothing personal. He spoke to them infrequently because in his mind, being an associate at a large firm meant developing a new lifestyle, attending firm social functions even if he despised the people. Garland had a plan and he was determined to rise in certain social and financial circles. It worked…temporarily. Garland rose and rose in the firm's ranks. Then he came crashing down like the waves across a jagged shoreline.

As he looked through the magnifying glass, he found that he had no recourse but to accept the fact that he had lost his mind and was talking to a fly, a fly who knew more about him than he did about himself. Determined to take control of the situation, he started asking the fly questions. He repositioned the magnifying glass over the fly, trying to catch some of the moonlight coming through the window in his apartment. He thought perhaps he could roast him to death with rays of the moon, thereby destroying his winged delusion.

The fly must have sensed what he was about to do. Again, he laughed at Garland. "You know, señor, people do that to ants, but they can't do it to flies. Because we move way too fast." He then proceeded to pilot around the room, diving and rising at breakneck speed. As Garland's eyes tried to follow his movements, his head moved around and around in circles to the point of dizziness.

"Stop flying before I break out a can of Raid! Got a name, fly man?"

"Sí. Julio Javier Hortachea de Lopez. You may call me Don Julio." The fly hovered in front of Garland's nose. Garland placed the magnifying glass in front of the fly and observed him while he spoke. He was still dressed as a gaucho with a tiny guitar strung across his back.

"I was born in Cuba in 1958. However, I was transported to Puerto Rico as a young —"

"I thought flies only lived like twenty days. Transported when you were just a baby fly? Oh, come on..."

The fly jerked his body in what appeared to be an attempt to raise his head in indignation; without a neck, it was hard to tell. "There is no such thing as a baby fly, señor. It is eggs, larvae, pupae, and fly. That is the life cycle of a normal fly. May I finish my story without further interruption from you?"

The young lawyer threw up his hands. "Why not? So you're a sixty-year-old fly. How did you get from Cuba to Puerto Rico? Did you *fly* over?"

"No, I did not. I am not a Boeing 747. I am an insect, or at least partially an insect. I stowed away in a banana crate. Why Puerto Rico needs cratefuls of bananas from Cuba, I have no idea nor do I care. But this is how I came to a village in Puerto Rico and then to a bodega in Paterson, New Jersey." The fly began to pace back and forth before he landed. "But my story is much more complicated than that. So you wonder why I am so old for a fly and how I can talk, yes?"

"That did cross my mind."

"I will tell you, but it's complicated. We must take a look at the past to understand the present, which is why I need to retain your services to help me solve a murder."

"Retain my services? Yeah, right. Got a checkbook?" Garland looked at the nearly empty glass that he intended to use to cut his wrists. Then without saying a word, he shrugged his shoulders and drank the remaining scotch. "Fine. Start talking."

CHAPTER THREE

The Law Office of Julio Lopez
Paterson, New Jersey
1988

Julio Lopez was a newly minted lawyer, a recent graduate of Rutgers Law School, the first in his family to get an education beyond the eighth grade. His law school grades were below mediocre, and one C minus too many landed him on academic probation in his sophomore year. He survived a terrifying legal procedure called an Order to Show Cause as to why he should not be expelled. Lucky for him, showing that his current semester's grades had markedly improved and a promise that he would be a lawyer of the people saved him from expulsion.

He graduated. After taking the New Jersey Bar examination five times, he finally passed and began to build his practice. Julio was not big firm or medium-sized firm material. He had neither the grades, temperament, nor the country club connections for that life. So instead, he settled for as small storefront office on Straight Street in Paterson in a building owned by his Uncle Teofil Lopez, a local santero. Soap writing on the storefront window of the two-room firm offered notary service and car insurance in addition to legal services.

A brand new Cadillac Seville pulled up and double-parked in front of Julio's office as though he owned Straight Street. A short man dressed entirely in white cotton stepped out of the car. Propping himself up with a cane, he made his way into Julio's office. He came to rest on a beat-up chair beside the young man's desk. Julio, as always, was happy to see his uncle.

"Uncle Teo, so good to see you. Would you like a coffee?"

"No, Julio. Drank too much today. If I have any more coffee, I'll sprout wings and fly away."

"Yeah, Teo, I know what you mean. Had like three cups myself." Julio smiled. "Thanks for helping me out with the office. I couldn't have afforded it without you."

"You worked hard to become a lawyer. Your mother and your father would have been very proud of you. They told me in spirit that they were."

"Of course."

A concerned look came across the old man's face. "Listen, I have a luncheon appointment, but there is something I must tell you. I'm very concerned about you. I did a psychic reading the other day and I don't like what I saw."

"Teo, you know I love you. You are the father I never had, but I just don't believe all that stuff that you're into. I respect that you are a santero, but I just try to stay away from all that."

Julio watched as his uncle's face grew dark, the sure sign that a lecture was about to begin. He had a new client coming in about fifteen minutes, and he didn't want his uncle to go on and on about his warnings from the spirit world.

"Julio, I want you to understand something. I did not choose this life. The orishas, the gods and goddesses, chose me. They gave me the ability to see the future, to help, heal, or kill. I would never hurt anyone because I chose the path of light. But when a warning comes your way, you need to listen and put away your ego for five minutes. I read the cowrie shells. They speak of a situation with a woman needing help. They are telling me to tell you to turn her away and pray for her, but do not get involved."

"Teo, is this like a girlfriend or something? I have helped enough broke girlfriends. I'm through with all of that."

"No, nephew, it isn't quite like that. This is a woman who walks into your life seeking answers, and I implore you to turn her away for your sake."

Julio knew that his Uncle Teo was considered a powerful local santero, and while he did not share his beliefs, he certainly respected them. He didn't understand his uncle's world. It was one of Yoruba magic and Catholic saints, Nigerian river gods and St. Joseph. It was a powerful world that was better off left alone.

"Well if I see any strange women with different colored eyes coming in here, I'll have my secretary, Leticia, escort them out the door." Julio looked toward the door. "Uncle Teo, there's a Paterson cop car right behind your Cadillac. You're going to get ticketed or towed if you don't move your car."

He seemed unconcerned. "It's okay. I know that cop. He was having some trouble on the job and I gave him a mojo bag. Next thing you know he gets a promotion." Teo looked out the window and waved at the officer. The police officer smiled, waved back, got into his patrol car, and drove off.

"See? I told you he was not going to bother me. You know, nephew, you are more sensitive than you think. You have the ability to…you know. You have the ability to see beyond the living veil. You have spirits to guide you. Yet you deny this gift." He sighed. "The woman who seeks you has gray eyes and black hair. Avoid her." He leaned on his cane and rose to his feet. "I have to get to my appointment. I have a reading scheduled. A nice young woman is having some boyfriend problems. And I am in the mood for some tacos."

Julio knew exactly where his uncle was going for tacos. "So you're meeting her at the Granny Knockers' Grand Teton Grille? That go-go joint that offers Taco Tuesday with Tanya? Does Tia Rosita know you're going? Besides, the tacos there stink."

The old man laughed. "Please don't tell your aunt. Sí, the tacos are terrible, but the *tetas* are *very* nice. And a young girl needs my counsel." He started walking to the door. "You are a grown man and I can't tell you what to do. But I beg you to be careful, nephew. People are greedy and the world is a strange place; I do not know this world anymore. I worry for you."

"Don't worry, uncle. I'll be okay."

Uncle Teofil walked out the door to his double-parked car and drove off. Julio wondered if the eerie prediction had any legs. He'd long ago accepted his uncle's practice of Santeria; after all, it was his religion. His uncle made quite a livelihood off predicting lottery winners and healing sick people and animals. He made enough money to buy a brand new Cadillac, purchase the building where Julio's office was located, and pay for Julio's law school. Julio would say his business was good; Uncle Teo would say the orishas were generous.

Julio's stomach ached. Something about the prediction made him nervous.

* * * *

Julio was drenched. The heat of the day was the kind that made sweat pour off his body five minutes after stepping out of the shower. The air was a steady and deliberate furnace blast that arose from the bowels of hell and baked the Paterson city streets. Wiping the sweat from his brow, Julio looked at his cheap Timex watch.

"Dammit!" The watch had stopped, and now he wasn't sure if he was late for an appointment. He had overslept after one too many shots of tequila at Granny Knockers. He recalled that his secretary, Letty, mentioned something about a Mrs. Ramos and her daughter coming in, but she didn't say what kind of a case it was. He figured it was probably just another slip and fall. He entered his office only to be greeted by an annoyed-looking Leticia Greenfield.

"Nice of you to show up." The well-dressed, thin African-American woman with long melon-colored talons pointed a pejorative index finger in his direction. "It's ten o'clock. She had a nine o'clock appointment. And she has a sick child. You are late. What were you thinking?" She stood up and ran over to Julio. She sniffed the air surrounding his head and shoulders. "You were at Granny Knockers last night, weren't you? You smell like a damn gin mill."

He shrugged. "Let's discuss this later, shall we?"

"Yes, we shall!" She spoke in a loud whisper through gritted teeth. "Now get your ass in the conference room and talk to that lady and her poor little girl."

A large storage closet had been converted into a windowless makeshift conference room. Julio had bought a beat-up rectangular mahogany clawfoot dining room table with high back chairs from a Goodwill thrift store. Uncle Teo had given him an old chandelier he had picked up at a garage sale to complete the look. With these accoutrements and a coat of fresh paint, a janitor's closet became a lawyer's conference room. It was in this conference room that Julio

Lopez met two people who would inadvertently change the course of his life in a way he could never imagine.

Essi Ramos was a short, chubby-cheeked woman in her early thirties, as round as she was tall. Long, straight black hair cascaded down her back. She wore little makeup save for a coral lip gloss and was dressed in a maid's uniform. An air of weariness and sadness surrounded her. Sitting next to her was a thin five-year-old girl wearing a strange little cap. Taken aback by the sight of the young girl, he took a deep breath. He had recognized the little floral head covering because it was a cap his mother had worn once…to hide her bald head when she had undergone chemotherapy. His heart ached. The little girl looked up, gave him a gap-toothed smile and shyly waved a rag doll back and forth in his direction as a way of saying hello.

He watched as Essi Ramos instructed her daughter to leave the conference room. He noticed Letty was already waiting with a coloring book and a juice box for the little girl. He opened the conversation.

"I am sorry for my lateness. I had a matter before another judge this morning and I was delayed in court. I am so sorry."

"It's okay. I told my boss I would be in at noon. I got your number from my brother, Esteban Ramos. You represented him when he had a car accident."

He smiled and sat down. "Ah yes, Esteban. How is he doing?"

"Good. But other parents and me, not so much, that's why I am looking for a lawyer. There is a group of children in P.S. 578 in Passaic who have all come down with leukemia, including my little Lili." Tears welled up in her eyes. "More children are getting sick and no one seems to care."

"What do you think is the cause of the sickness? Something in the school?"

"Yes." Essi reached into her purse and pulled out a piece of paper with some crude drawings and handed it to Julio.

"What is this?"

"There are a bunch of pipes that run throughout the basement of Lili's school. I think the children are being poisoned from these pipes."

"Do you have anything else besides this drawing?"

"No. I went into the school basement and took a picture of the pipes. A janitor found me, grabbed the camera, and smashed it. He told me I had no right to be in the basement and if I ever came back, he would call the police. A few days later I got this letter in the mail from the school principal, Mr. Robert Van Marcherz." She handed Julio a letter and an envelope, and he read it. "He said if I ever return to the school, he will have me arrested—"

"For trespass." He finished her sentence. "Unbelievable. What I find even more surprising is that old Van Marcherz is still alive. He was *my* principal when I attended P.S. 578." The young lawyer sighed. "What are you going to do if you have to have a parent-teacher conference on behalf of your daughter? Not show up?"

"I'd send my brother or my mother." Her eyes filled up with tears again. "Please, isn't there anything you can do?"

"Have you spoken with old Van Marcherz? How about his boss? The superintendent? Board of Ed?"

"We tried. Some of the parents got together and went to several meetings, and we were told everything is fine. The pipes are old, but nothing is wrong with them. Just an unfortunate turn of luck that our children have cancer. Can we sue?"

Julio felt suddenly flushed. In his mind, this case—if he could make a case by establishing causation between the children's sickness and the water pipes—could be a type of Love Canal, an Exxon Valdez spill, or a Chernobyl disaster. Big firms prosecuted and defended massive toxic tort cases. He was just a one-man law firm, the slip and fall guy with the soap-written advertisement. However, looking at the woman sitting at his conference table, he felt her anger and desperation.

"Let me look into this. I can't promise you anything. I can't file a complaint because I don't have any proof that anyone did anything wrong. At least not yet."

"Talk to the other parents. Some have dead children. That may be all the proof you need." She rose from her chair. "Thank you for listening. I am looking for other medical treatment for my Lili. I don't like her doctor. All the affected children have the same doctor at St. Pancratius Medical Center."

"Why don't you like him?"

"Very businesslike. Treats us like patient number 101." Her tears finally overflowed and fell down her cheeks. "I want to know why. Why did this happen to my child? I want answers."

He put his hand on her shoulder. "Look, I'm not a miracle worker, but I'll look into it and let you know what I learn. You have my word."

Essi Ramos wiped her eyes and looked gratefully at the young lawyer. "Lili and I appreciate anything you can do." She opened the conference room door and exited. Julio watched as she gathered up her daughter and left the office. Letty escorted them out the door. After the mother and daughter left the office, Letty turned to him.

"What a beautiful little girl. Sweet thing, too. And she had gorgeous gray eyes just like her mama."

Gray eyes, just like Uncle Teo's warning. He hadn't even noticed. But how could it be wrong to help this woman?

CHAPTER FOUR

Public School 578
Principal Robert Van Marcherz's Office
Passaic, New Jersey
1988

As Julio walked down the hall of his former grammar school, he realized that twenty-three years later his hatred for the hallowed halls of P.S. 578 had not diminished. His was one of the first Hispanic families in that school district in the sixties when the population of Passaic was largely Polish, Italian, and Irish. It was not easy being Puerto Rican back then, and civil rights was a concept in its infancy. Taunted and teased, he experienced racial prejudice in a way he preferred to forget. In fifth grade, he was in a schoolyard fight every other week. He remembered Van Marcherz did nothing to stop the fights, sided with the bullies, and gave him detention because he defended himself in a fistfight. As he walked down the main hall of the school, he was very happy to see many brown faces mixed in with white. At least that much had changed for the better.

The glass door marked "Principal" had the same black stenciled lettering. Julio wondered how many times it had been repainted over the past twenty-plus years. When the perky young secretary let him in, he immediately recognized Van Marcherz. The principal remained the same, just a salt-and-pepper version of his old self. He still wore his horn-rimmed glasses that had managed to escape from the 1950s. He was about forty-eight now. He put down the documents he was holding and looked at Julio.

"Well, well. Look who's here. Julio Lopez, as I live and breathe. The rebel without a clue, heh, heh. Good to see you." He put his papers down and extended a hand. "Welcome. So what brings you back to the old stomping ground? Have a seat." He gestured for Julio to sit down in an old dried leather chair.

"Thanks, Mr. Van Marcherz." How would he approach this? He had to work his way around old Van Marcherz because if he came on too strong, the crafty principal would toss him out of the office. He needed to walk out with some kind of information. He hated him, but he had to overcome his distaste and get information that would be helpful to developing the cause of action against the school. "You're looking well. Family's good?"

"Oh sure. Everyone is doing really well. A new grandson. And how are you doing? Still living with the crazy voodoo uncle?"

That crazy voodoo uncle raised me and got me through college and law school, you desiccated old man, he thought. *I wonder how your druggie son is doing. God, I still hate this guy.*

"No, I have a small condo in the renovated old Fletcher's Yarn Mill. And Uncle Teofil is doing quite well. He actually bought my condominium and three others. He has places in Florida, and he just got a brand new Cadillac. He and Aunt Rosita are doing quite well."

"Hmmm, pretty good for a witch doctor."

"He is a santero. That is different from being a voodoo priest. But let me tell you why I 'm here."

"Please do."

"A woman came into my office today—"

"What kind of office?"

"I have a law office. I'm a lawyer, Mr. Van Marcherz."

"Really? I'm impressed. Must have greatly improved your grades. Congratulations. So are you here to tell me you're suing me?"

Julio shook his head. "No. I'm looking for information about all the children who have had cancer and are students here. Essi Ramos was in my office a few days ago."

His pseudo-friendly face turned into a sterile wooden plaque. "Yes, Julio, I know Mrs. Ramos very well. She and several other parents have been to see me, complaining that somehow the school has caused their children's cancer. It's absolutely absurd. Sad, but absurd."

"Mr. Van Marcherz, their fears may be unfounded, but has anyone even looked seriously into these people's complaints? That is my question. There could be an environmental issue." Julio tried to contain his annoyance.

"Look, Julio. I don't have to answer your questions. But let me give you the number of the school's attorney. He can help you out.

I'm sorry that you've involved yourself in this. Waste of your time, I'm telling you. Here." He handed Julio a business card. "Deacon Bigelows. Know him?"

Yeah, he thought. *Bigelows was the original ambulance chaser, but highly politically connected. If he tells you it's raining outside, be sure to bring your suntan oil.*

"I've heard of him."

"Call Deac and tell him I sent you. Sorry to rush you out, but I have a meeting in a few minutes. Thanks for stopping by."

"Will do. Thanks, Mr. Van Marcherz." He started toward the door of the principal's office. "I just have one question. What is the source of the water coming into the school?"

He chuckled. "The pipes? The Riverwood Water Authority? I have no idea. Talk to Deac. He has all the answers to your questions." He escorted Julio out the door. "So good to see that you actually made something of yourself." He pointed a playful index finger. "I had my doubts about you."

The young lawyer contained his ire and smiled back. "Never had any doubts about you, Mr. Van Marcherz. Thanks for the info. Have a nice day." He left the office.

Van Marcherz stood by the door until he had assured himself that Julio had left the building. Julio made it half way to the parking lot, when he realized that he had one final question for Van Marcherz. He turned around and went back to Van Marcherz'z office. The door was closed. Julion was about to knock when he overheard the principal having a conversation with someone on the telephone.

"Yeah. We have a new problem." He paused. "Of course, I want you to shut it down."

CHAPTER FIVE

It was three a.m. Garland Nowell was wide awake. Still armed with his magnifying glass, Garland wondered what part he played in a thirty-year-old problem that involved a talking fly. The lawyer looking into the cancer cluster was a Julio Lopez, the same name as his new winged friend.

"This sounds so Kafkaesque. Are you Julio Lopez? Did you get turned into a fly?" Before he finished his sentence, Garland watched as the irritated fly buzzed about the room yelling in Spanish. He realized that he had angered him again, but he wasn't sure why. He waited for the fly to land. "Now what did I say?"

"No, I am not Julio the lawyer! He died in 1988."

"Okay, fine. But I still don't understand what or who you are and why you're here."

"You remember I told you that Julio's uncle was a santero, yes? When his nephew died, he placed a spirit inside me, a simple common fly. I'm here to find out why he died because I think the deaths of those children in P.S. 578 are somehow related. I can't do this alone. I have been trying since 1988."

"I assume it hasn't worked out too well, and that's why you're talking to me. Are you saying it's been thirty years and you still can't find a lawyer?" He laughed. "In my business, that usually means you don't have a good case."

"Nobody wants to listen to a talking fly, Señor Garlando. I have spent thirty years dodging flyswatters. I had a lawyer once, but he drank too much and started talking not only to me, but to pink elephants also. Next thing I see is the men with the white coats, and they take him from me. As they put him in the ambulance all I hear is him screaming, 'Julio the fly, help me! Get me the fly! Talk to my fly! He can explain everything!' So they put my *abogado* in the ambulance a little faster because a screaming lawyer is asking a fly to help him. A lawyer cannot do much from the inside of a mental hospital, particularly after they give him electroshock therapy."

"So what is it that you want me to do?"

"Find out what happened to Julio and those children. You can sue the school, right?"

Garland started to pace. How could he explain the complexities of litigation to a fly? "Look, I am not a magical creature like you. The human world is not quite that simple. Your information is thirty years old. We need witnesses, statements. People die, and even if people are still around, their memories are spotty, especially after this many years. In the law there is something called a statute of limitations. Time has passed, it may be too late to do anything. I just lost my job; I have no money in the bank. I don't have a law firm." He threw up his hands. "I'm not your guy."

"*Sí*, you aren't perfect. The facts are not perfect." He alighted on a table and put his front feet behind his back as he paced. "But it is your imperfections that may save the day. And you need a job. I know where you can find one, Garlando."

CHAPTER SIX

The People's Free Legal Clinic
Newark, New Jersey

Ina Furnstein had established The People's Free Legal Clinic after a wildly satisfying divorce settlement from her CEO husband at the tender age of fifty in 1993. After healing her broken heart by a facelift, a short tryst with her Brazilian repairman, and paying off all her credit card debt, the former Mrs. Ina Stillwater decided that she had more money than she needed. Now it was time to find a way to help others, particularly those clients whose needed legal services who got caught in the middle of a needs test. They were not poor enough to qualify for full the services of the Legal Aid Society yet not rich enough to walk into a lawyer's office. Hence, after the initial fun of being a new divorcee was over, The People's Free Legal Clinic was born, a creation of Ina Furnstein.

The Clinic took the cases law firms and even the Legal Aid Society turned away—tort cases, landlord-tenant matters and civil rights cases. Most cases were losers and not money makers for the Clinic. It didn't matter. Ina paid her staff well and believed that people were entitled to the best legal services they could obtain rather than the most legal services they could buy. She was the ultimate mother hen over both her staff and clients and lived by the liberal principles she espoused.

However, at seventy-five, the tall, thin redhead was starting to tire, and the money for The People's Free Legal Clinic was dwindling. Grants were scarce, donations had nearly come to a halt. Gone were the days of the galas held at the Baltusrol Country Club for fundraising because many of her older, generous donors had either died or left the practice. She had to dip into her savings to pay the last two months' rent. Her staff of twenty-five was now down to three. Ina thought that perhaps this was the time to make a quiet exit, unsolicited, into retirement. She called Liliana Danis into her office, a thirty-five-year-old attorney who had been with the Clinic for five years.

"Come over here, dearest. I want to tell you something. But before I do, I want to know if your divorce was finalized from that bum husband of yours."

The tiny young woman waved the divorce decree around in the air. "Free at last, free at last, thank God Almighty I am—"

"Free at last," both women finished in unison.

Ina lit a cigarette, and Liliana winced. "Boss, this is a smoke-free building. The landlord is going to plotz if he smells smoke."

"Plotz, schmotz, I pay enough rent here he should give me a break. So now are you Liliana Ramos again?"

The young lawyer nodded. "Yes, I am. I'm thrilled to have my name back."

"What did you leave old George Danis with, dearest?" she asked, blowing a large smoke ring. "Just his underwear, I hope."

"It was a two-year marriage, Ina. There wasn't that much to take, particularly when he didn't work. But the main thing is that the cheating, lazy ex-husband is out of my life. Now he can fleece off somebody else."

"Good for you. That's exactly how I felt after Milton left me. But with a thirty-year marriage, I left with a lot more." She paused and looked at her fresh French manicure. "And I'm still enjoying the fruits of his labor. But we have a problem, dearest."

"What's the matter, boss?"

"The Clinic is not doing well. Financially we are nearing bankruptcy, and Lili, I'll be turning seventy-five next week and finally feeling every inch of it. These old bones ache."

"You don't look it."

"Dearest, you are too sweet. And you are a wonderful lawyer. I would just turn the Clinic keys over to you and head to my home on Marco Island in Florida, but you need money to run this joint. And let's face it—the clients we serve can't afford to buy stamps for their own letters." Ina saw tears welling up in Lili's eyes. "Now don't go all soft on me. You're a talented gal. You can work anywhere."

"But I love this place and the people. Ina, I can't see myself going to a firm. We actually help people here. Save their homes, get them medical treatment when they have car accidents or a workers' comp claim. I can't see myself doing corporate mergers."

"But dearest, you could do it. If you wanted to. Top of your class, Rutgers Law Review, a clerk of the State Supreme Court. I still have a ton of contacts and I'm happy to make some phone calls for you. Just tell me what you want to do." Ina leaned back in her chair and sighed. It felt as though she carried the weight of the world on her shoulders.

"What we need to keep this place going is a large case where we can get lots of attorney's fees. That would certainly pump money into this place to cover a few more years, and we would be able to continue helping people who need good lawyers like you. And speaking of needing help," she started as she picked up a new case file and handed it to Liliana, "you have two new clients."

"Two? Is it a couple?"

A delicious smile came across Ina's lips. "In a way. Go see for yourself, a nice civil rights case."

* * * *

Liliana grew tired of hearing people tell her that she could be better places than the Clinic. She absolutely loved what she did and felt as though she was actually helping people who needed help. She was always amazed that when she told people she was working for a human service agency, they assumed she had no ability to work in a private practice. Little did they know about the lucrative job offers she turned down.

She couldn't forget the crafty smile across Ina's face. The last time Liliana saw that look on her boss's face, Liliana defended a bunch of circus clowns who claimed they weren't being paid minimum wage by the Moxie Bros. Travelin' Family Circus. At the time of the hearing, the clown troupe showed up for the hearing in full-on clown suits complete with red spongy noses, white face paint, and large rubber clown shoes. She had that same feelingvnow. As Liliana walked toward the waiting room, "Entrance of the Gladiators," that ubiquitous circus theme song, played in her head.

She looked at her new client with a curious eye. He sat in a chair looking much older than his sixty-eight years. Even though his hair was white, a dyed black moustache spread across his upper lip like bat wings. From the crumpled coat, she could tell that the man shopped in Newark's finest Salvation Army stores. But what caught her attention was a fluffy, rapidly moving object, twirling out from beneath a battered jacket, and a tiny set of eyes studying her.

"Hi, I'm Liliana Ramos, a staff attorney. Mr. Gonzalez? Do you have an animal under your coat?"

"Oh yes." He gave her a cheerful grin as he reached into his armpit and presented her with a small squirrel in the palm of his hand. Liliana watched as it stood on its hind legs. It appeared to have something wrapped around a portion of its tiny body. With a gentle fidgety face, it stared back at her.

"I don't mean to be difficult, Mr. Gonzalez, but unless it's a service animal you can't bring a pet into this building."

"He is not my pet. Señor Pepe, turn around for the nice young lady." At which point, Liliana watched as the squirrel sitting in the palm of his hand turned around. It wore a tiny jacket with the words "Service Animal" embroidered on the back. The squirrel squeaked, then dove back into his armpit, leaving Liliana to look at its hind end and a twirling fluffy tail once more.

I'm in a Fellini movie, she thought. *And no one told me that I was the star.*

"I see." She suppressed a smile. "So what brings you here today, Mr. Gonzalez?"

"I wish to file a civil rights action. Señor Pepe and I were kicked out of the Stardust Diner in Paterson. He is my service animal. I wish to sue the diner under the Americans with Disabilities Act, the ADA."

Liliana started taking notes. She wondered how she was going to tell him that wild animals do not fit either the state or federal criteria for service animals. "Mr. Gonzalez, a service animal is trained to do something for you. A Seeing Eye dog helps a blind person navigate through daily life. That is what a service animal does. Is Señor Pepe trained to do anything?"

"I am lucky to have him. I went to church and prayed for a woman. And *gracias del Dios*, God sent me Señor Pepe instead."

"So you are telling me you prayed for a woman and God sent you a squirrel?"

"Yes."

"And what service does he provide?" She hoped it wasn't a sexual service.

"Thanks to Señor Pepe, I am finally able to leave my house and go places. I don't go anywhere without him. I go to the store, my church, and the supermarket. Everyone seems to like Señor Pepe. Except for that nasty diner owner. He insulted Señor Pepe and me. He told me to go back to the street and take my dirty animal with me. Señor Pepe is not dirty. I bathed him last week. He doesn't smell."

"You give him a bath?"

"Regularly with baby shampoo in a baby bath. I blow-dry his tail and he just he loves it."

Liliana had no idea whether or not squirrels liked baths or if they enjoyed having their tails blow-dried. She had but one job: to determine whether or not throwing a man out of a restaurant with his pet squirrel was a violation of the Americans with Disabilities Act. Ever thoughtful, she needed more information.

"Tell me about yourself."

"I proudly served our country in Vietnam, and I came home after the war. I was," he sighed, "not myself. Had a wife and some children, but they abandoned me." He looked at the floor. "I was a different man back then. I am better now. Treatment at the Veteran's Administration hospital in Newark and Señor Pepe have helped me tremendously."

She nodded. "So you have some…some mental health issues, is that a fair statement?"

He nodded. "Yes. I was seeing a therapist at the Tranquility Harbor program in Paterson, but not anymore. I don't need the program since I began consulting with Señor Pepe. I just go there to get my medication refilled."

"I understand. He talks to you?"

He's crazier than he looks, she thought.

"Yes, he even gave me great advice about where to invest my pension money. I'm a retired janitor. Not bad for an old man pushing seventy." He sighed. "I went to several law firms, and nobody would take my case."

The young lawyer wrote furiously as the semblance of a possible cause of action came to her. It was a quick vision, the kind of case that would give the Clinic headlines…a Vietnam vet with severe mental health issues and his therapeutic companion animal removed from a public place. Okay, so the companion animal was a talking rodent, so what? Whatever his relationship was with the squirrel was irrelevant. The talking squirrel kept him sane, and he probably shouldn't have been turned away from the diner.

"Will you take my case? I have some money. I can pay a little something."

"That would be helpful. I need you to sign a retainer agreement. Our fees are on a sliding scale basis, so if you are on a fixed income, we can adjust our fees."

Without breaking stride, he whipped out a checkbook and began to write. Liliana watched as Señor Pepe poked his head out from under the armpit of the old gentleman and sniffed the air. "I can give you a fifty dollar check to start the process."

"Thank you. Every little bit helps." Liliana didn't have the heart to tell him that launching a case like this would cost several thousand dollars. "Mr. Gonzalez, I have to tell you that we are treading into some new territory here. I think that we have a strong argument that Pepe—"

"*Señor* Pepe. He will get offended if he isn't addressed properly."

She cleared her throat. "Yes, of course. *Señor* Pepe. I think that we have an argument that Señor Pepe is a companion animal and that you shouldn't have been asked to leave the diner. Unfortunately, Mr. Gonzalez, Señor Pepe doesn't really qualify as a service animal because squirrels are considered wild animals."

"But as you can see, there's nothing wild about him. He is calm. And please call me by my first name—Fergal."

"Fergal?" Liliana smiled. "So your mom was Irish?"

"No, she was a *Boriqua* like my dad. Fergal was the name of our old milkman. Right before I was born, he gave her a free quart of milk. She was so excited she named me after Fergal Maccoon, the milkman. My full name is Fergal Jose Gonzalez."

She suppressed a laugh. "I see. Fergal, please explain to me what happened at the diner in as much detail as possible."

"It's a simple story, really. Last Monday at around seven p.m., Señor Pepe and I went to the Stardust Diner. They make good tuna fish sandwiches there. A waitress came over and saw Señor Pepe's tail twirling around under my coat. She asked me if I had an animal under my coat. I showed her Señor Pepe sitting in the palm of my hand, and she ran away and came back with the owner of the diner, Nico Kuklas. Kuklas told me to get out of the diner with my dirty, scummy squirrel. Señor Pepe was very insulted."

"Did he physically touch you?"

"No. He just pointed at the door and kept yelling 'Let's go! Get out! You and your dirty, scummy squirrel!'"

Liliana tried not to laugh at the thought of an angry, tired old Greek giving the gate to some crazy guy and his pet rodent. "Did he see the jacket on Señor Pepe?"

"No. He was too busy yelling and screaming at us. Because Señor Pepe was insulted, he returned to my armpit where he felt safe. To answer your question, no, he could not see his service animal jacket."

"I see. I have to send away for your medical records at the VA and the Tranquility Harbor mental health program. Is that okay with you? You will have to sign a release."

"Sure. I have nothing to hide."

"Well, I am going to recommend to the Clinic director, Ms. Furnstein, that we take your case."

Liliana watched as Mr. Gonzalez stood up. Despite the fluffy tail twirling out from under his armpit, the man's face beamed. He tipped his hat.

"*Gracias*. My generation were fighters. We stood for something. And we never stopped. I am ready to do battle again. Have a nice day." With that, Mr. Gonzalez and Señor Pepe left the Clinic, and as if on cue, Ina Furnstein exited her office, unlit cigarette in hand.

"You know, dearest, I rather like the old gentleman. Don't think it's a case we can win, though. Under federal and state law, squirrels cannot be service animals. You may not win this one."

Liliana smiled. "True. But you know I love the cases we can't win."

CHAPTER SEVEN

Garland decided that it was best to move back home with his divorced father while he figured out what to do. His father was less than pleased to see him back home. Father and son could not have been more different.

Nicholas Nowell was a big man, a black seal boiler man. Patience? He had none. After Garland's mother disappeared with a much younger, wealthier man—an attorney—Nick Nowell had no desire to be around "those bloodsucking lawyers." He had pretty much raised Garland alone and was disappointed when Garland chose to become a member of the bloodsucking leech club he so vehemently despised. Little did Garland's father know that a small, fat parasite rode on the back of his son's collar carefully studying his demeanor.

He lit a cigarette with a slow, deliberate inhale and sat forward in his overstuffed chair. "So the prodigal son comes home. Why did you get fired?"

"I settled a case that saved a company a lot of money. Apparently, I wasn't supposed to do that. My firm wanted me to keep milking the company. And I didn't."

"This is what happens when you get involved with those bloodsucking lawyers."

"Dad, I *am* a bloodsucking lawyer."

"Of all the careers, you *had* to become a professional leech?"

"Do you remember that walk in the park when I was ten years old?"

"No."

"Well I do. When we were walking in Van Saun Park, you asked me what I wanted to be when I grew up, and I told you that I wanted to be an art historian. You pointed to a homeless guy feeding pigeons and said, 'See that bum feeding the pigeons? He was an art historian. Now look at him. Get a job where you can earn a living wage.'"

A half smile came across Nick's face and his eyes twinkled. "Son, I have no recollection of that particular conversation. But here is a question for you. Did you save any money when you were feeding off the law firm's clients?"

Garland shook his head. "I spent a lot on Sissy's engagement ring. Taking her on exotic vacations. Sailing. Trying to impress."

Nick shook his head. "Trying to be somebody you aren't. Sailing, eh? And now you are drifting on the waters of unemployment. She probably forgot your name the minute you lost your job. Were you at least smart enough to get the damn twenty thousand dollar ring back?"

"Not yet."

"What the hell are you waiting for?" His father sighed. "You can live here until you get on your feet. But I'm retired and I don't have the money I used to have. I can't support you forever, Garland. I'm an old man on a pension and social security."

"Dad, it's okay. I just need a place to live until I can get a new job. I think I may already have one."

"Good. Do what you have to do." Nick glanced at his watch. "I'm tired. It's past my bedtime."

"Dad, it's nine thirty. Elementary school children don't go to bed at nine thirty."

"Sweet dreams, son. Dream of a paycheck. Nighty night."

Garland flopped down in his father's chair and waited until he heard Nick's bedroom door close. "You heard everything. What's the plan?"

Don Julio flew off his shoulder and gently landed on a lamp near his father's easy chair. "This is not going to be easy. Your father does not seem happy to see you."

"He isn't. He blames lawyers for all the problems of the world. There is a war in a small village somewhere in Africa. The lawyers caused it. The stock market crashes. Lawyers were behind it. The second-floor toilet overflowed…lawyers. He never got over the fact that my mother left him for a tax lawyer because she wanted a richer lifestyle."

Don Julio jumped from the lamp to the table, then alighted and began to pace. "Garlando, you must live with Papa until you find a job and solve the death of Julio Lopez."

"I can't believe I'm listening to a fly wearing gaucho pants."

"My mother was from Argentina. That is the reason I wear these pants. Besides, the lady flies like them. *Mucho macho, no?* I have buried over 696 wives wearing these pants." Don Julio put his hands on his hips and puffed up his chest.

"How?"

"Garlando, the average life span of a normal fly is about twenty-five days. I have had a new wife each month for the past fifty-eight years." He flew up and buzzed in Garland's ear. "Look, I must be truthful. This number does not count the numerous affairs of the heart I had between dead wives." He pounded his chest. "But this is the way of a man. My father told me that the male fly should have as many lady flies as hairs on his legs."

"Your father? Leg hair? I can't take this!" Garland grabbed the sides of his head. "You know what? You should have just let me kill myself. And I suppose your mother was on the banana crate with you when you got transferred over here from Cuba?"

"No, my mother and father died years ago. But this isn't about me. It's about you."

"So now what?"

He raised a gloved leg and pointed into the air. "First, we must go see the santero, Teofilo."

"I am not going to visit some crazy half-assed witch doctor."

"I do not think that you have a choice, señor."

"That's what you think!" Garland stood up. He grabbed a nearby newspaper and rolled it up.

"Big man trying to kill a poor helpless fly. Have you no shame?" Don Julio flew off the table as the newspaper swung down at the table. He buzzed around the room as Garland swung wildly, striking empty air.

"Where are you, you fat little bastard?" he screamed. "This ends tonight! Where are you?" He swung the newspaper again and knocked over a lamp and his father's favorite ashtray. He heard loud buzzing and laughter. Then he heard the strum of a guitar and a voice singing an old Mexican folk song.

"*Allá en el rancho grande, allá donde vivia, había una rancherita…* Ai-i-i-i!"

"Shut up!" Garland flung the newspaper across the room.

The fly kept singing at the top of his lungs. "*Que allegre me decía, que allegre me decí-a-a..*"

"Okay! I'll do it. I'll see the witch doctor." He dropped the newspaper. "I surrender. Just stop singing."

"He is a powerful santero. You do not want to make him angry. Now go to sleep."

Garland settled into his father's easy chair, closing his eyes and trying to relax. Don Julio landed on Garland's shoulder, strumming his guitar. Garland only felt drowsy at first and then systematically, he began to fall into a deep sleep…until he heard a loud voice yelling from the floor above him that jarred him from sleep.

"Garland! Turn down the stupid TV! A man is trying to sleep up here!"

He jumped, sat up in the chair, and responded to his father. "Okay, Dad. Sorry." He glanced at his shoulder. "I am going to bed. Just buzz around the room and do something with yourself. See you in the morning. I need to sleep."

Don Julio flew off his shoulder and landed on the lamp. He lay on his back and softly strummed his guitar while Garland went to bed.

CHAPTER EIGHT

"Wake up! *Levante, amigo!*"

Garland opened his eyes only to find Don Julio sitting on his nose. "Oh my God, you are still here." He waved him off his nose and the fly landed on the table next to his bed.

"Wake up! We have lots of work to do today. First, we find Santero Teofil. Then we must find you a job."

The young lawyer stretched his long arms. He blinked his eyes several times and squinted.

Garland rolled over in bed and closed his eyes. "What do you know about getting me a job? Are you running an employment agency?"

"No, Garlando. I just happen to know where we can find one for our purposes."

Garland sat up in bed. "There is no 'our' or 'we', my friend. I have no purpose as it relates to whatever mission you are on! Right now, I feel like I have no purpose in life."

"Ah, but that is where you are wrong, amigo. This is all part of the master plan. You need a paycheck."

Garland stumbled downstairs and into the kitchen. His father was already out and about doing his errands. Don Julio flew by a coffee maker and saw a note in front of the coffee pot. He landed on Garland's shoulder and directed his attention to the coffee maker on the kitchen counter.

"Amigo, your father set up the coffee pot for you. He left a note that says, 'All you have to do is press the button.' What a nice father you have. You know how to press a button, yes? They teach you that in law school, sí?"

"Sí. I mean yes! Of course I can press a button." Garland grunted. "Dad's alright—when he isn't telling me to go out and find a job or reminding me that I spent too much money on Sissy's engagement ring."

The fly became indignant. "Your father is correct. You spent all that money trying to impress a woman who doesn't care about you. You need a nice Spanish girl."

"Oh God, no. Please. Let me just drink my coffee first before you start the lecture. Talk to me about the santero. What kind of a person is he?"

"I am not saying a word. You can decide what kind of man he is after you meet him."

* * * *

As Garland left the house, Don Julio sat on his left shoulder. The young lawyer twisted his head to look at Don Julio. He saw that the fly was lying on his back, arms outstretched and wearing sunglasses, his wings gently fluttering. For all intents and purposes, he seemed to be enjoying the ride on Garland's shoulder.

"I like this suit jacket. The shoulder padding is very comfortable."

"It is going to get very uncomfortable momentarily. I have a convertible."

"A convertible what?"

"A car, you idiot. Look." He pointed to a bright red BMW Z4 Roadster.

"Because I am in a good mood, señor, I will ignore your insult. Ah, what have we here?" Don Julio jumped off his shoulder, flew over to car, and landed on the hood of the BMW. The fly hopped up and down on the hood of the car. He flew around in circles and yelled over to Garland, "Isn't this a $50,000 car? You have excellent taste, amigo."

"Yes, I do." He sighed. "And it is a $77,000 car. But enjoy the ride because it is my last. I'm returning it to the dealership tomorrow. I leased it and I can't afford to pay a thousand dollars a month on a car like this now that I'm out of work."

"So no more *coche*?"

"Yeah. More like *adios coche*." Garland used his key fob to open the car door after he gently ran his hand along the canvas roof of the car. He opened the door slowly and sat down in his car, openly frustrated by everything around him. Don Julio flew in and landed on the car's dashboard. Garland rested his head on the steering wheel and sighed. "What am I doing? I lost my job and my girl. Now I'm losing my car and my mind."

"You think too much about what you lost. Do you not see what is before you? The future."

Garland slammed his hands on the steering wheel. "What does a tired old shit fly know about life?"

"I know more about life than you do. I have seen human suffering for decades. I have seen good and I have seen bad. I have looked into the eyes of angels and ridden on the tails of devils. And it is all the same to me. You have yet to learn about life. Maybe the old santero can teach you something. Take your head off the steering wheel and stop whining. *Vamos!*"

* * * *

Garland glanced in his rearview mirror. He was overcome with the sudden feeling of being trapped like a rat on a sinking ship. The whole situation seemed wrong.

This whole thing is a plot by a foreign government, he thought.

Maybe the CIA was following him because the fly was a horrible experiment gone wrong. In moments, the CIA agents would appear to capture the fly and return him to some underground laboratory near the Dugway Proving Ground, a U.S. Army facility where they test biological and chemical weapons. After recapturing the fly, Garland would be executed and his death would be made to look like an accident. He glanced back in the mirror. The vehicle behind him was getting closer and closer, and he could see the CIA agents in the front seat of the undercover vehicle.

In reality, behind him was a beat-up box truck with three men in dirty tee shirts. Unless the CIA was hiding inside a "We Fix You, Cheap Home Repairs" truck, the CIA had nothing to do with him or the whole situation. There was no government conspiracy. Garland was truly alone.

He drove down Main Street in Paterson looking for the address of Don Julio's santero. Garland had his doubts about finding some spiritualist based on thirty-year-old information obtained from a talking housefly. Don Julio told him that he had an address on Main Street in Paterson for the santero's bodega, near St. Joseph's Hospital. Garland was familiar with Paterson because he had a trial in the Passaic County Courthouse. He wondered how difficult it would be to find a Cuban santero in an inner city. Would the name Teofil Lopez appear written with a grease pencil on some storefront windows like the price of a car on a used car lot?

What would he even say to this man when he starts asking questions about his dead nephew? How would he explain who he was? A fly whose head you placed a curse upon sent me? All these thoughts ran through Garland's head as he drove through the streets of Paterson amid the homeless, who wandered aimlessly in its streets. Don Julio navigated from the dashboard of the BMW.

"Garlando, turn here!"

He turned the wheel sharply and looked at the fly. "How sure are you that this guy is even alive, Don Julio? Now what?"

"*Bueno*. I am making progress. You didn't call me a fat bastard this time. You called me by my name."

"Just answer the question."

"He came to me last week in a dream and he was smiling."

"So you had a dream about him? That's what this whole trip is based on? Your stupid dream?"

"Dreams are not stupid. There are messages in dreams that we must interpret. Slow down, there it is! Bodega de Santa Clara!"

Garland saw a parking spot and immediately pulled into the space, which apparently aggravated the truck driver behind him. The driver slammed on the brakes and yelled something at Garland, who simply threw the car in park and turned it off.

"We are here." He sighed. "Let's get this over with." Garland opened the car door. Don Julio alighted on his shoulder. Before they entered the store, Garland paused.

The Bodega de Santa Clara had a colorful window. A small, clean altar held a beautiful statue of the Caridad de Cobre, the Virgin of Charity, which was surrounded by sunflowers, honey, and yellow candles. The face of the statue was serene and calm. As the Virgin of Charity looked out of the window, she appeared to be blessing the world outside of her window. As Garland studied the statue, he was overcome by a sense of peace and serenity…until Julio bit his ear.

"Ow! What the hell!" He grabbed his ear. Garland felt a searing pain course through his body from the tip of his ear straight down to his toes, as if his ear had been jammed into an electrical socket. "Why did you bite me?"

"I needed your attention. We are wasting time."

"I feel like my ear is starting to swell. Are you venomous?"

"You can put an antibiotic on it later. Focus!"

Using the hand that wasn't holding his painful ear, Garland opened the door, which triggered a tinkling bell. The walls of the bodega were stocked with candles, incense, and so-called magical oils. There was a Come To Me oil, a Lucky Seven oil, a Seven African Powers oil, a Sweet Dreams oil, and a list of oils necessary for a variety of mundane and metaphysical purposes. He picked up a vial of reddish liquid with the label Dragon's Blood. Garland tilted his head and whispered to the fly sitting on his shoulder. "Dragons don't exist. How does this guy have their blood?"

"Dragon's blood is a tree resin from special palm trees in southeast Asia. You don't need a fire-breathing reptile to produce such things."

Garland saw no one but heard a sweet melodic voice. "Hello?"

From behind a red velvet curtain, a tall African-American woman appeared, dressed completely in white. Her skin was the color of caramel and her eyes had a hint of some possible Asian ancestry. The woman's head was covered with a white turban. Her eyes were large and portentous, and as she walked, she moved her body with the fluidity of a lioness on the hunt. She studied him. It was strange. Garland felt aroused and terrified at the same time.

"How can I help?" she asked.

Garland felt Don Julio buzz closer to his ear and whisper, "Tell her that you are looking for Santero Teofil."

"I am looking for Santoro Thay-o-fell?"

The woman cocked her head. "Santoro Thay-o-fell? I'm sorry, I don't know him. There is no one here by that name."

Garland felt another nip at his neck and swatted his ear. "Stop that!"

"Pardon me, sir?"

"I'm sorry, there is just this fly annoying me."

Garland felt the angry fly land on his ear again and whisper, "You say it Tay-oh-feel! Tay-oh-feel! Teofil Lopez."

"I am sorry, I probably said his name wrong. I am looking for Tay-oh-feel Lopez."

She smiled. "I bought this place from him. He hasn't owned it in years. If it is a spiritual problem you have, perhaps I can offer you a remedy."

"Do you know how I can contact him? Is he alive?"

The woman's voice became cautious. "Mr. Lopez is alive but he's a very private person. And he does not see clients anymore. He is retired, so to speak. How do you know him?"

Garland cleared his throat. "He and I have a mutual friend, my client, Don Julio Lopez. I am Don Julio's attorney. My name is Garland Nowell."

"Are you looking to sue Santero Lopez? I don't want any part of that." She turned and started walking away.

"Please wait. Here is my number. I am not looking to sue anyone. My client, Mr. Lopez, is ah, ah, sort of a relative, and he wants to contact him. He isn't looking for anything, I can assure you. If you can just have him call me. Please. It is very important."

She turned around and sighed. "Alright, maybe I can help. Give me the number." She walked back toward him and took the telephone number he'd written on a scrap of paper. "I'll be right back." She returned to a room behind the red velvet curtain.

Garland looked at the statuary in the small bodega as he massaged his ear. "Julio, this bite makes my ear look like I have a cauliflower growing out of the side of my head. I am coming after you with a rolled-up newspaper."

Don Julio rested on Garland's ear again. "Calm down. The nice santera is coming back our way."

The store owner smiled and seemed more relaxed. "Well, Mr. Nowell. It seems that Don Teofil has been expecting you and Don Julio for quite some time. Here is his address and telephone number. He suggested that you stop by today." She handed him back the same scrap of paper, but this time written on the back was the address and telephone number of Teofil Lopez.

Garland took it gratefully. The request for information had gone much smoother than he anticipated. "Thank you, Miss..."

"Aintzane. People just call me Zani for short." She smiled. "You must have really impressed Don Teofil. You know, I was one of his students. But you..."

"Yes?"

"You must have really impressed him. He said that he's been awaiting your arrival for years. You must be an especially gifted santero. Did you study Santería with Don Teofil also?"

"What?" With that the fly bit the other ear. "Ow! Yes! Yes! I am gifted and I'm leaving you now. Thanks, thanks for everything!" Garland ran toward the door and turned back to see a confused look on Zani's face. "Adios!" He slammed the door to the bodega shut and stood on the sidewalk, where he yelled out loud and swatted the air. People passing on the street stared at him.

"You bite me one more time and I swear to God I will kill you. I will either spray you with bug spray or buy a flyswatter. I will step on you until your brains pop out of your ass. Then no more Julio! You bite me one more time and I will kill you." Don Julio landed on the center of his nose. In order to see him, Garland had to cross his eyes.

"Okay. I will behave myself. But you are so dense sometimes. I thought lawyers were supposed to be smart. That young lady in there just helped us. Don Teofil said something about you. I bet he told her that you were a santero."

"Oh no." He sighed. "Listen, looking at you from this angle is killing my eyes. Could you please land elsewhere?"

"Okay." Don Julio flew off Garland's nose and landed on his shoulder. "This is much better than your oily nose. I felt like I was about to slide off. My feet wouldn't stick. Maybe it's the leather boots."

"I thought you guys have suction cups on your feet."

"No, it is the tiny sticky bristle-like hairs on the bottom of our legs that keep us steady."

Garland looked at the back of the crumpled paper Zani had given him. "Looks like your santero left Paterson and moved to the Jersey shore. He lives in Ocean Grove, a block from the beach. The old guy must have done pretty well. Those houses go for big money."

"How big?"

"Like a million dollars for starters. How does an old Cuban guy who owned a religious shop make that kind of money?"

"Mr. Teofil is an honest man. He does not do anything that is against the law."

"You sure about that, Julio?"

"Yes. Now we go. We take a ride. I love the ocean." Don Julio lay back and nestled himself in the comfort of one of the shoulder pads on Garland's suit. "Amigo, don't mind me if I take a little *siesta.*"

Seconds later, Garland loaded the address of Teofil Lopez into his GPS. It would be a sixty-one-mile trip to Lopez's house. He was low on gas and he had no answers to questions about his future. His mind raced with of all kinds of thoughts. He was not a spiritual person, but he felt like someone or something was trying to put him on a path. To where? Undetermined. For what purpose? He had no idea. He was completely out of his element. The fact that his companion of late was a talking fly made his journey that much more peculiar. As he pulled away and looked for signs for Route 80 East, he heard gentle snoring coming from his winged companion. He smiled. At least one of them would get some rest.

CHAPTER NINE

He opened his eyes and stretched his long arms across his bed, grateful for the darkness. His bedroom was almost completely dark except for an annoying sliver of daylight that had crept around his blackout shade and reflected off the ceiling. The light bothered him, so he closed his eyes again. Such an intrusion!

Tredd Van Marcherz lived in his father's unfinished basement with only two windows, both of which were covered by blackout shades. He depended on those shades to protect him from the one thing he despised the most—sunlight. Since the age of eighteen, he had managed to live like a vampire, sleeping during the day and working as a janitor at night. The basement was his domain, and he left it only to go to work or buy food.

The walls of his basement apartment were painted a flat black. Lighting was minimal. He decorated his black walls with death scene photographs and reproductions of famous paintings, all of which depicted death or violence. His favorite poster was Goya's infamous "Saturn Devouring His Son", which he hung over his dining area. The largest death photograph was a poster taped on the ceiling, showing Union and Confederate soldiers lying dead on the field at Gettysburg. One soldier, who appeared to have light-colored eyes, died with his eyes open in an eternal stare. When Tredd awoke each night, the first thing he saw was a pair of dead man's eyes looking back at him from the ceiling. Most people would have been bothered by looking at a corpse first thing in the morning, but it had no effect on Tredd. To him, the dead eyes were simply a reminder of what happens to everyone. And he was dead inside anyway.

The walls of his bathroom were also painted black. Poring through sites on the internet, he had managed to find a black toilet and matching bathroom cabinet. This had been an expensive venture, because he had the custom toilet and sink shipped from Michigan. Both the cabinet and toilet cost him over a thousand dollars.

Tredd needed little illumination because his eyes were accustomed to living in the dark. He used incandescent light bulbs or candles when he needed to read or entertain the occasional visitor, like his father. Those were the times he hated…because he had to turn on the lights and look at his father's face.

Robert Van Marcherz was a very tall, heavyset man with a military haircut. He wore expensive clothes and a thick bicycle link chain bracelet of 14 carat gold with his Brooks Brothers suits and starched white shirts. Tredd was tall like his father, but thin and muscular with shoulder-length gray-blond hair parted in the middle. He wore a black tee shirt and black jeans. Unlike his father, he was a man of modest physical appearance and looked much younger than his forty-eight years. With the simple job of a janitor, he had a lot of free time, and he passed that time by lifting weights…in the dark. His physical strength was not to be underestimated by his wiry appearance. And he required strength. In his mind, he was preparing for some kind of battle, he just didn't know when it was coming. He wanted to be prepared. He needed to be physically strong.

When he wasn't working out, he read books. Although this required light—something he despised—he kept it to a minimum with a solitary light bulb suspended by a wire above a kitchen table.

To Tredd Van Marcherz, paperbacks and hardcover books were better friends than people. Books answered questions without speaking and were low maintenance. Humans needed to hear a voice, made petty demands, and were easily offended. Communicating with people required dialogue and interaction, which he found intrusive. It was much better to spend time in the darkness of his basement reading his books than seeking the companionship of his peers. The life of Tredd Van Marcherz was a self-imposed exile, but an exile he immensely enjoyed.

Footsteps on the stairs. Someone was descending. He knew who it was.

"Father, is that you?"

"Who else would it be? Can you put some damn lights on?"

"Put them on yourself. You know I hate the light."

Robert Van Marcherz stumbled on the last step leading into his son's lair. "Dammit, why do you insist on living like, like a mole or a bat in a cave?" He found a light switch and turned on the light that illuminated his son's room.

Tredd grinned, reaching for a pair of sunglasses. "Father, I'm forty-eight years old. I have lived in the darkness since I was eighteen. You know that. And you know the reason why."

The elder Van Marcherz changed the subject and looked about the room, his eyes stopping on a small sign. He pointed to the sign and shook his head.

"I like the scrollwork on the memento mori sign. Victorian, right? 'Remember death'—isn't that what 'memento mori' means? Isn't that all you ever think about? Death?"

"Yes, Father. That is exactly what it means. Remember *death*. And you and I both know that death is quite familiar to me. After all, when I was eighteen, I killed a man for you."

Tredd watched as his father gave him a twisted smile. "Don't ever say that to me again. You killed a man to protect a lot of innocent people whose careers would have been ruined if that nosy lawyer kept poking around. None of this was their fault. You protected the right people, and I protected you. The injured people had lives going nowhere. The fact that you choose to confine yourself to a dungeon surrounded by death images to make yourself feel better is your own choice, Tredd. I mean, look at you. You avoid sunlight and you look like Death, only Death who wears a janitor's uniform. When was the last time you had a date?"

Tredd stared at his father without any emotion. "So nice of you to drop in. Did you want something?"

The old principal sat down on a chair and sighed. "I feel that something isn't right. Something is coming. We may have a problem."

"*We* have a problem? Has something happened?"

"No, nothing like that. Something is...is...I don't know."

"Unless you have something more, you should stop worrying. The case has been closed for over thirty years. The responding officer died of cancer years ago. The guy who fudged the autopsy, Dr. Meadowloc, is demented and in a nursing home. He's about 900 years old. The homicide detective on the case retired and move to a fancy retirement community in Florida. And his was a nice retirement because you certainly paid him enough. He's probably dead by now, too. You took care of the Records Room clerk in the Prosecutor's Office, so those records vanished also. Even if they weren't removed in 1988, they're probably either archived or destroyed. Why are you so worried?"

Robert Van Marcherz drew in a deep breath and released it. "I don't know. Just have this feeling that someone is going to come looking again."

"*Now* you feel guilty about having Julio Lopez killed? A little late, isn't it? And just so we understand each other, if you have any pangs of guilt that would cause you to throw me under the bus for the murder of that lawyer, rest assured that I will take you down with me."

Robert laughed. "Take *me* down, now that's a joke, Tredd. You talk like a big man but you can barely leave this basement. You and your little hairy friend in that cage don't scare me. You're lucky to have a job as a janitor. And may I remind you that the only reason you have that job is because of me." He walked over to a table with a stack of books and picked them up.

"Let's see what your intellectual pursuits consist of. *Invisible Sun? The Arch Conjuror of England: John Dee? The Lesser Key of Solomon?* What are you doing down here? Practicing witchcraft? Jesus Christ. What have you done?"

"What have *I* done? What have *I* done?" Tredd stood up. "You created me. You created this world that I have been forced to live in. But at least I am not alone. I have company. And there she is." He walked over to the other side of the room and gently tapped on the glass of a big terrarium. Nesting in a dark corner was a large Venezuelan jungle spider, *Theraphosa Blondi.* "Wake up, Maria Isabel. Arise, my friend."

In response to Tredd's taps on the glass, the spider began to stretch itself out, one leg, one joint at a time, until it reached its full spectacular glory. Maria Isabel was the size of a very large dinner plate, and it had two-inch fangs. The spider opened its small almond-shaped eyes and turned itself in the direction of Tredd's father. It seemed like the spider was watching, quietly observing the elder Van Marcherz.

"You need help. You need to get out of this basement. And I don't see how you can live down here with that thing."

Tredd shrugged and smiled. He stuck his arm in the spider's tank and the Goliath bird-eating spider jumped on his arm. It crawled all the way up and sat on his shoulder, letting its long legs dangle. "And I don't see how you live with yourself, Father." Tredd turned to glare at his father. "Yet there you are. Is there anything else?"

"No, nothing. As much as I hate to ask you for anything, if, uh, I get wind of something, can I count on you?"

"What is that saying? In for a dime, in for a dollar? If you hear of anything that could implicate us in the murder, please let me know." He rubbed the spider's back. "Isabel and I will take care of the problem."

The old principal sighed. "Thank you. Do you need—"

"I need nothing. Goodbye."

"Alright. I'm leaving."

While Maria Isabel relaxed on his shoulder, Tredd watched his father walk up the basement stairs. *Stomp! Stomp! Stomp!*

"I sense that he may be right. There is a disturbance; I feel it. But it is nothing we cannot handle together. I never liked him." Isabel sighed. "How do you feel about him? He used you."

Tredd continued stroking Isabel's back. "Yes, Isabel. I never liked my father."

"Put me back in my terrarium. And I desire a small rodent tonight." She clicked her fangs together. "For I am very, very hungry tonight," she said as her eyes flashed bright red.

CHAPTER TEN

Home of Teofil Lopez
Ocean Grove, New Jersey
Garland exited the Garden State Parkway. Don Julio gently snored as he lay on one of the shoulder pads of the young lawyer's suit. Garland took the local roads and entered the town between the two famous Ocean Grove pillars. For many years, these two pillars had a chain between them, denying any wheeled vehicles entrance to the formerly religious town from midnight Saturday to midnight Sunday.

Garland pulled up in front of Teofil Lopez's old Victorian house that faced Wesley Lake. From the street he determined that the house appeared to have been freshly painted powder blue with white trim. The landscaping on this property was immaculate. Wisteria vines intertwined with a small evergreen. One small patch of flowers alongside the house had pink roses and lavender plants. Ornate stained glass windows with multi-hued blue glass resembling ocean waves were mixed in with more traditional-style windows. Though it was a narrow home, it had multiple turrets and towers and a slate roof. The home of Teofil Lopez was a gingerbread house from an old English fairy tale.

In the center of the main garden stood a large statue of a mermaid rising from the sea. Her face had a serene yet penetrating look. At the base of the statue a plaque read "Queen of the Sea." The mermaid was surrounded by seven silver dollars, seven cowrie shells, and an unopened bottle of white wine strategically placed in an arrangement of blue and white impatiens in the shape of an ocean wave. Garland reached down and picked up the bottle.

"I can't believe this. A bottle of 2012 Jadot Louis de Montrachet Grand Cru, and he's letting it boil in the sun?"

Don Julio awoke from his nap. He stretched and yawned. "Amigo, we are here, yes?"

"Yeah. Look at this, Julio. A five hundred dollar bottle of wine, and this guy is letting it boil in the sun."

The fly panicked. "Are you crazy? That is an altar offering. Would you go and take the wine off an altar from a church? Put it down, you imbecile!" The unnerved fly scanned the area. "Look around. Do you see storm clouds? She may punish us with a hurricane or a tsunami or something. *Ay, Dios mío!*"

Garland put the bottle of wine back where he found it. "Okay, okay. Calm down. Look, I put the wine back. Relax, Julio, there isn't a cloud in the sky." He sighed. "Let's get this over with."

"Why are you always so negative? You will never get the *chicas* that way. Women like happy men. Trust me, I know. I am a happy fly."

"Shut up! I don't need a woman right now, and I'm not interested in taking love advice from a fly. I need a job and some answers."

Garland walked up the steps to the house and knocked on the door. From out of nowhere, a strange, sweet-smelling breeze surrounded them. He inhaled deeply. It was the fragrance of ginger and sweet almond. "Wow, Julio, what is that? It smells so nice."

The fly sniffed the air. "Incense, my friend, it is incense. Almond, ginger, and jasmine, I think. It is for the goddess, the Great Mother."

"And who might that be?"

The fly laughed. "You will see shortly."

Garland gently knocked on the door again. Finally the door opened slightly and a single eye looked at him. "Yes, can I help you?"

The young lawyer swallowed. "I am looking for Mr. Teofil Lopez."

The door opened wide. A gentleman dressed completely in white and leaning on a cane greeted him. He did not have a single gray hair upon his head. "And I have been looking for you, Mr. Nowell, for a very long time. How has my little friend been treating you?"

"How do you know my name?"

"I heard your name on the wind, Mr. Nowell." He laughed. "Actually, old people know lots of things."

The fly interjected. "I call him Garlando, Teo."

Teo pulled out a magnifying glass. "Don Julio, my old friend. I have missed you. It has been a long time. You have put on a few pounds, Gordo."

The fly reached into the pocket of his brocade vest and pulled out a cigar. "I cannot complain too much. My life hasn't been terrible. Even though I have been avoiding bug spray and fly swatters for the past thirty years."

A tiny puff of cigar smoke encircled the fly's head like a wreath. Teofil said, "I recognize that rich aroma. A Cohiba from the old country?"

"You still know your cigars, amigo."

Garland rolled his eyes. "You know, Mr. Lopez, I am glad that you and the fat fly here have been reunited, but I need to know what the hell is going on." Garland found his voice rising with each word he spoke. "Who are you?"

The santero looked up with gentle eyes. "I know that this must be very confusing for you. Let's take a walk to the sea."

"I don't want to go for a walk. I want to know why I am here. I want to know why I am stuck with him." With his thumb and forefinger, he flicked Don Julio off his shoulder. The fly yelled as he and his cigar went soaring through the air. He landed headfirst inside a bluebell flower.

Garland studied Teo's face. He did some quick mathematical calculations in his head. He didn't know how old the late Julio Lopez was when he died, but if Julio had gone straight through college and law school like he did, he would have been about twenty-four or twenty-five when he graduated. If Teofil Lopez was his uncle, he may have been in his mid-forties in 1988. It was now 2018. He estimated that Teo was roughly in his mid-seventies. It was strange. Garland thought that the man standing before him looked much younger.

"I want some answers!"

The man leaning on the cane remained calm. "I can do that, Mr. Nowell. I will give you all the answers you want. But first, we need to get Don Julio out of that bluebell. And we must walk to the sea. It isn't far."

Garland took a deep breath. "Sorry for raising my voice, Mr. Lopez. It has been a strange couple of weeks."

"Please call me Teo."

The santero opened the door all the way and came out of his house. He tore open the bluebell and released Don Julio, who shot out of the flower like a cannonball. Garland saw that that Don Julio was less than pleased. He hovered in front of Teo's face and started to yell.

"Teo! See how this idiot treats me? He treats me like garbage. I will find another lawyer!"

"Amigo, it took you over thirty years to find this one. Time is short. Come, both of you. Let us walk."

Teo shut the door to his house. This time Don Julio sat on Teo's shoulder. The heat of the day bounced off the sidewalk, but the breeze coming off the ocean kept their walk to the beach cool. Teo started talking as they slowly walked toward the beach.

"My nephew Julio Sanchez was a young man, just like you. He had started his law practice in 1988, when one day a mother came in with a little girl who had suffered from leukemia. As it turned out, this little girl was not the only child suffering from blood cancer. Over thirty children from this one particular school came down with the same disease. My nephew took the case of the woman and the little girl and started to investigate the school these children attended. The little girl's mother thought there was something in the water pipes of the school. Next thing you know, my nephew turned up dead in the school's basement surrounded by bags of cocaine."

Garland interrupted. "Did he have a drug problem?"

"No. My nephew was a straight arrow. He may have grown up in an inner city, but he stayed away from drugs, gangs, and trouble with the law. The whole thing was a setup. The killer was never found. The police were so busy with gang shootings back then they didn't pay much attention to a dead lawyer surrounded by cocaine."

"How did he die?"

Teo stopped walking. "The medical examiner claimed his heart stopped from the drugs. A suicide. But I can assure you, Garland, that is not what happened. My nephew was not suicidal or a drug addict."

"And what about the schoolkids?"

"Many died. Some lived. And the name of my nephew has been dirtied up for no good reason. Julio was a good man whose life was cut short for trying to find out the truth." Teo stopped on the board-walk at the entrance to the Ocean Grove beach. "Ah, we are here at the foot of the Great Mother."

Teo gestured to Garland to take off his shoes. With Don Julio still planted on his shoulder, Teo walked down the beach barefoot and stood close to the water. The waves gently drifted in and swirled around his feet. He inhaled deeply. Teo turned to Garland.

"Raise your hands above your head and reach up to heaven. Stand quietly. Don Julio, you too."

The fly kicked off his cowboy boots, stood on his hind legs and raised four of his legs above his head and closed his eyes. Teo threw seven pennies into the ocean and began to speak.

"Yemaya, great goddess, Mother of All, protector of women and children, and Queen of the Sea, accept our humble offerings, bless us with your wisdom, and give us peace. Allow your presence to be known, give us a sign. We ask for your love and your blessing in what we are about to do."

"Can I put my hands down now?" A small wave in the shape of a hand with long foamy fingers swept over Garland as if to answer "No!" Garland jumped back. Even though his face and shirt were soaked with seawater, he kept his hands up. "I'm okay."

The fly landed on his back and laughed. "See, Teo? Even the Queen of the Sea hates him. Yemaya just slapped him in the face." Don Julio continued to hover in midair in front of Teo.

"Be quiet, both of you, and listen. The Great Mother is speak-ing, and she is happy to see us. She has questions." Teo inhaled. "Garland, do you believe in that which you cannot see?"

"I don't know what you mean. I believe in proof. I believe in truth. That's why I went to law school. To seek truth. Can you ask the Queen of the Sea if I can put down my arms now?"

Teo closed his eyes and threw his head back. He brought his head forward and when he opened his eyes, his eye color had changed from brown to a bright green. "She has granted permission. You may put down your arms. But the Queen has more questions."

"Thanks." He dropped his arms.

"She wants to know if you believe in spirits."

"Not until I met a talking fly when I was about to kill myself. And I still wonder if I have not been hallucinating this whole time."

"The Queen of the Sea tells me that I should explain the World of Spirits to you."

"Alright. I'm listening."

Teo's head fell back once again. He moaned slightly as his rich baritone voice began to change into a gentle woman's voice, a voice that was soft and musical. It was the sound of a chorus of angels combined in a single voice. Garland shook his head and blinked his eyes. He watched Teo's body begin to change and shift. His hair turned from short and dark to long, bright red locks that flowed in the wind. The body of a man with black hair and a moustache became a young, vibrant woman cloaked in a shimmering white gown. She had large glowing green eyes and spoke in gentle tones. Garland looked down and saw that a fish's tail flowed out from under the gown.

"Hello, my children. I am the Star of the Sea, Yemaya. I thank you for your offering. I love my children. What do you seek?" She looked at the fly hovering in the air. "Hello, Julio. I know it has been some time that your soul has not seen the inside of a human body. But remember it is your spirit that carries on for an eternity, not your body."

Garland looked at the hovering fly. "You were once a human being?"

"Oh sí, a long time ago."

"How old are you?"

The goddess spoke. "He is an old spirit. And he is here to help you so that you can help him. Don Julio cannot be free until his work here is done. Garland, life presents us with strange gifts. You have long sought truth and justice, yes?"

"Yes, that is right."

"And have you found it yet?"

"I...I don't know. I mean, I have tried to find truth for others."

"That is a noble endeavor. But you must find truth for yourself. You must continue in your work, Garland. Always seek truth and justice, especially for those who cannot seek it for themselves. Be careful. Truth has many dark enemies. Where there is light, darkness will try to overcome it. But it must never prevail. Oh, and one more thing..."

"Yes, ma'am?"

"I love Jadot Louis de Montrachet Grand Cru. Thank you for putting it back."

Without warning the image of Yemaya began to fade. The long red locks of her hair receded into Teo's head and changed back into his black hair. Her shimmering gown faded. Teo's eyes returned to their normal color, but he looked weak. His white cotton clothes were soaked by his own sweat. He leaned on his cane.

Garland felt a chill come over him. "Are you okay, Teo?"

"I need to eat something. I need to ground." The santero smiled at Garland. "It is always exhausting when the gods enter you. What you saw was a rare occurrence for a human to be possessed of a godly spirit. And she spoke to you directly." He pointed his index finger at Garland. "You should heed her warning."

"This is too much. I can't handle this. First, a talking fly, and then a man changes into a mermaid in front of me. Look, I cannot even begin to understand what's happening here, what's happening to me. I'm not your guy."

"Do you believe in something beyond this world?"

Garland raised an eyebrow. "I don't know what I believe anymore. I'm confused."

Teo smiled. "Welcome to the world of magic, my friend."

CHAPTER ELEVEN

The trio decided to eat in a restaurant in Asbury Park, off the beaten path. The tiny eatery was run out of the back of an old house owned by the Corazon brothers—Jorge, Miguel, Jaime, and their mother, Mama Linda. The food was as good as any of the more expensive restaurants along the boardwalk in Asbury Park, but their prices were reasonable because the Corazon brothers had Mama Linda in charge of the kitchen. The restaurant didn't need a cook or a cleaner. Mama Linda cooks and cleans for free.

They called their underground restaurant Los Tres Gatos. "Gatos" was the nickname created by the local people for the three Corazon brothers. Prior to becoming "restaurateurs," the brothers were the local cat burglars who broke into apartments, stealing flat-screen televisions, money, and jewelry. After a few stints in the Monmouth County Jail for multiple burglaries, the three brothers gave up their lives of crime, only because Jaime, the eldest brother, came up with a better idea to make some quick money. Jaime convinced Jorge and Miguel that there was more money in running an illegal restaurant out of the back of their ramshackle house than breaking into other peoples' homes in the middle of the night. Jaime, a short, fat man with a sweeping moustache, greeted Garland and Teo wearing a large white apron as they walked in the door.

"My friends, welcome to Los Tres Gatos! Don Teofil, my mother has made her famous pork and clams dish. She rarely makes that." He shook a playful finger at him. "You must be psychic. You knew Mama Linda was cooking today."

"Jaime, your mother is chained to the stove. That poor woman cooks every day whether she likes it or not." Teo tapped Garland on the shoulder and pointed in the direction of the kitchen to a short, chubby, gray-haired woman who looked a lot like Jaime, minus the moustache.

"Wave at her, Garland. Hola, Mama Linda!"

Garland smiled and waved. The woman with the red apron smiled, waved back, and returned to preparing the restaurant's food.

At first, Garland was not excited about eating, but he would force himself to have a little something just to keep the peace. After all, he was confused, a little frightened, and tired. He wondered what he was doing with Teo and Julio. How did his life get so crazy? While sitting on Garland's shoulder in Los Tres Gatos, Don Julio decided to talk.

"Garland, I wasn't always a housefly, you know."

Garland shook his head. "So once upon a time were you a spider? And then God got angry with you and downgraded you to a fly?" Garland looked at Teo. Both men both laughed.

"Must you always insult me? No, my life was a bit more complicated than that."

"You told me you came from Cuba in a banana crate and wound up in a bodega in Paterson after living in Puerto Rico. You never mentioned that you walked the earth as a living man."

"When we met, you had enough trouble believing that you were talking to a fly."

Garland turned to Teo. "Does he ever get to the point of a story? Does he? We'll be here all night."

"Calm down, Garlando, I knew Don Julio sixty years ago. If you asked him what time it was, he would tell you how to build a clock. But he was a good man back then. And he still is today."

"Okay, okay. I will be quick in my story. Teo and I lived in the same village in Cuba, Cabo de Cristobal. I was a spiritualist who read tarot cards and conducted séances. Villagers used me to contact their departed loved ones, for a small fee. But my real love was music. In the spring and summer, I would play my guitar at the local bars and serenade people. I was content because the villagers not only consulted me for spiritual advice, but my music made them happy. I knew Teo back then. In fact, I even played at his wedding. I watched him grow into a fine young man. In Cabo—"

"Wait a minute. Had I been good at algebra, I would have gone to medical school rather than law school. But I can do basic mathematics. What year were you born?"

"As a fly or a human?"

"Human."

"1910."

"So you are 108 years old?"

"I guess." He flew off Garland's shoulder and hovered in front of his face. "But I was reborn as a fly in 1988, so in reality I am only thirty years old. Garlando, you and I are almost the same age. We are, how do you call it now, millennials. You and I are young guys!"

"Okay, sure." Garland turned to Teo. "I may be sorry I asked this, but just how old are *you*?"

Teo chuckled. "Does it matter? I was born in 1938."

"You look pretty good for an octogenarian. Let me get this straight. I am talking to an eighty-year-old man who barely looks fifty, and a one-hundred-eight-year-old fly. Do they sell booze in this place?"

"I am afraid not, my friend. They have no license for alcoholic beverages..."

"Teo, they have no license to run a restaurant."

"But Garland, I can unofficially get a drink." Teo asked a waiter to come back over to the table. "Jorge, give us two specialties of the house."

The waiter responded with a wink and a nod. He disappeared into the kitchen and returned with two Styrofoam carryout cups with plastic lids. Garland took the lid off his cup and sipped the drink. "Rum?"

"Yes, one hundred and fifty-one proof, simple syrup, fresh mint, lime, and club soda. A mojito! Goes great with chicken and rice, yes?"

"Sure does." He licked his lips. "I have had a few mojitos in my day but nothing as good as this one. Kind of makes me wish I was sitting under a palm tree on a beach in the Caribbean." He turned his attention to the fly. "Julio, you're still hovering in my face. Finish the story. How did you become a fly?"

Julio landed on the table and began to pace. "As I started to tell you, I was a spiritual advisor. There was a woman in Cabo de Cristobal named Dona Maria Isabel. She, too, was a spiritualist, but she walked a different path—a dark, sinister path. At first, I did not know this. She convinced me to use my psychic abilities for power, greed, and to harm others. When I finally realized that what I was doing was wrong, it was too late for me. I tried to break free from her. Then one morning I woke up with six legs and a set of wings. She was about to kill me, but Teo saved my life by turning her into a spider. I flew away before she could catch me."

"Look, I'm no magician, but Teo, wouldn't it have been easier to change Julio back into a man?"

"The rules of magic are complicated and not always fair. Julio was cursed by the witch Dona Isabel. One curse cannot always undo another. I prayed to the orishas for a solution. The wisdom I was given was this: if Julio can do one good deed, he can pass on to the next world and finally rest in peace."

"So that's why you need me? For the salvation of a housefly?" Garland pointed to the fly. "Jesus Christ."

Teo nodded. "Garlando, if you walk away from this table tonight and never speak to Don Julio and me again, we would understand."

"No, we wouldn't!" Don Julio yelled back.

Garland was torn. He quickly realized that this was something much deeper than he expected. "So what is it you want me to do?"

"I want you to find the murderer of my nephew Julio Lopez. I want you to find out why the children in that grammar school died from cancer. If the scales of justice are to be balanced in heaven and earth, truth must prevail. Isn't that what lawyers do? Search for the truth?"

Garland looked at Teo's face. For a split second, he thought he saw the real Teo, a sad, frail, eighty-year-old man who never recovered from the death of his nephew. Garland felt helpless. He wasn't a god. He wasn't a magical creature. He was a thirty-three-year-old unemployed lawyer who had basically lost everything.

"I don't know what I can do. My own life is a disaster right now. But you have my word, I will try to do something."

Teo smiled. "Thank you, Garland. Now we must get to work."

CHAPTER TWELVE

arland did not remember how he got home that night. He woke up in bed wondering if the prior day had been a dream. He stretched his arms above his head and glanced over at the alarm clock hoping it was noon, but it was only eight o'clock in morning. Rolling on his side, he closed his eyes until he heard his father gently tapping on his bedroom door.

"Going to the store. Do you want anything?"

He rubbed his forehead and muttered, "How about a new life?"

"What did you say, Garland?"

"Nothing, but thanks anyway, Dad."

"Okay. Just push the button on the Mr. Coffee. I set it up for you and it's all ready to go. A bunch of us old men are going to meet at Dunkin Donuts to discuss how much we hate our ex-wives and lawyers. No offense meant to you, son. I'll be back later."

"Thanks, Dad. No offense taken. Enjoy your coffee with the guys." He listened to the sound of his father's boots stomping heavily across the floor, then becoming quieter and quieter as he walked farther and farther away from Garland's room. The last sound he heard was the front door closing. There was silence for about twenty seconds until Garland heard a familiar buzzing in the distance. He braced himself. He was not alone. Don Julio was flying around the bedroom…and apparently, he had plans for the young lawyer.

"Listen, amigo, I have a lead on a job for you. Not as much money as New York, but at least it may be a possible paycheck."

"How did you find out about this job? A little birdie told you?"

"No! Little birdies like to eat creatures like me. Another fly told me, my friend, Nuno."

"You have little fly friends? Nuno, eh? An Italian?"

"No, Nuno Gandarez. He is from Portugal. He lives on top of the garbage dumpster near a popular restaurant in the Ironbound section of Newark. We have to meet him in the back alley of O Montanha Deserta Café."

"I have to meet a fly by a garbage dumpster? What has the world come to? I wonder if Harry Potter had these problems." He jumped out of bed and started to pace back and forth across the floor. "No, he was a wizard. He had wizard friends, a broom he could fly around on, and a magic owl. He didn't have to meet Portuguese flies by garbage dumpsters. So does old Nuno run an employment agency?"

"No, but he saw something in a newspaper."

"He reads newspapers?"

"Do you want a paycheck or not?"

"Of course I want to work."

"Good, then just do as I say. And one more thing. You need to get that ring back from Sissy Blackwood, your ex-fiancée."

"Impossible. I never want to see her again, and I think the feeling is mutual."

"This is no time for false pride. You paid twenty thousand dollars for that ring. You need to get it back so you can get the cash for it."

"No, I need never to see that woman again. She broke my heart. And anyway, I paid for it by credit card and paid off the card. That money is gone."

As Garland looked in Don Julio's direction, he noticed a very small spot hovering in the corner. He squinted his eyes. This time he did not need a magnifying glass to see him.

"Julio, are you putting on weight?"

"Do not call me fat again. I grow tired of being insulted."

"No, no that's not what I meant. I mean I can see you a little bit. I think you're getting larger."

"Larger?" Julio drifted over to a dresser that had a mirror attached to it. "Ay Dios mío, I have gotten a little larger. This is not good."

"Why?"

"I cannot be seen by others. This isn't good, Garland. It means we have to work faster."

"Why?"

"The magic is wearing off. It's Dona Isabel. She is here some-where. We have to work quickly. If I become noticeable and she finds out I am still alive, I am as good as dead."

"Do you want me to call Teo?"

"No, don't bother him. I don't think he can do anything any-way. We need to go to Newark today and see Nuno."

"Whatever. Let's go see Nuno the fly." Garland went into the bathroom. Leaning over the sink, he turned on the faucet and splashed cold water on his face, hoping it would wake him from a dream state. He then looked in the mirror and saw the beard growth on his face. He had to face facts. This wasn't a dream, and the day had not yet begun.

*   *   *   *

O Montanha Deserta Café, the Deserted Mountain Café, was a charming little restaurant located on Ferry Street in the Ironbound Section of Newark, New Jersey. The owners blended cuisines of Brazil, Portugal, and Spain, knowing that most American patrons wouldn't know the difference between a Brazilian feijoada and a Spanish Paella Valenciana. Whatever Chef Jose prepared tasted good, and that was all that mattered to the patrons of O Montanha—fine cuisine at reasonable prices.

Garland parked the car right in front of the café. As he exited the car, he stared at his pathetic-looking vehicle. Oh, how the mighty had fallen! He had gone from a brand new BMW to a three-year-old Ford Fiesta with seventy-five thousand miles on it. As he stood on the corner, Garland inhaled the air outside of the café while Don Julio sat upon his collar.

"Hmm, I heard this place has amazing food."

"Too bad we have no time to eat any, ha ha. Follow me, Garlando!"

Don Julio hopped off his collar and flew in front of him. As he followed the fly, Garland's brisk walk down Ferry Street turned into a jog. He had difficulty keeping up with the flying insect because Don Julio weaved in and out of the crowds like a sewing needle through cloth. Garland yelled at empty air space, telling Don Julio to slow down. The people on the street reacted to Garland's conversation with his invisible friend. Some shook their heads. Others turned away from him. Garland bumped into an old man walking with a cane, causing the gentleman to stumble. He stopped his fall onto the pavement by grabbing onto a nearby telephone pole for support. After he collected himself, the old man shook his cane in Garland's direction and yelled, "Go back to the mental hospital!"

Garland kept up his mad pace. He turned the corner from Ferry Street. Seconds later he found himself standing in a narrow alleyway behind the café, facing a small yet fetid dumpster. Between the summer heat and the smell of rotting fish, he felt nauseous.

"Garlando, knock on the top of the dumpster."

Garland rolled his eyes. "Why not?" He made a fist and pounded on the dumpster. He watched as a large green insect flew out of a hole in the lid of the dumpster. Don Julio flew right behind him. Garland followed the two flies. He watched as they landed on a pile of newspapers lying next to the dumpster. The two flies faced each other, and it appeared that they were communicating. Then Nuno flew away.

"Garlando, Nuno says to move the trash and lift up the second newspaper. Go to the third column where it says 'The People's Free Legal Clinic.' Nuno says he put a red circle around the job you should take."

Garland noticed a small stack of newspapers off to the side of the dumpster. A large green fly rested atop a banana skin, empty soda cans, and the contents of an ashtray. Garland tried to hide his look of disgust as he pushed aside the rotting banana peel, soda cans, and cigarette butts to reach the small pile of several papers hidden underneath the garbage. The large green fly returned to his dumpster. Garland picked up a filthy copy of the *Jersey Legal Journal of Law and Government* and spotted the ad with a big red circle around it. His blood pressure rose. His face grew red with anger as he yelled at Don Julio.

"Are you serious? I need money. This legal clinic is looking for volunteers, preferably ones still in law school." He threw the paper down and began walking out of the alleyway. "I am out of here."

"Garlando, wait!" Don Julio flew in front of him. "I know this is not the job you wanted. But it is the job you need."

He pointed a finger at the fly, who was hovering in the air. "No! I need a job that pays. I can't afford to volunteer in some poor man's clinic. And how does all of this help you find who murdered a lawyer in 1988?"

"You will see. Look, you are not working now? What is the harm of volunteering somewhere until you find the job you want? Nuno says it is easier to find a job when you have a job."

"Nuno says? Nuno says? Sorry, not taking advice from another stupid fly. By the way, why can't I hear him?"

"Because you can't. And even if you could, you don't speak Portuguese. You have to do something while you wait to get the job you want. And once you get that money back from your ex-fiancée—"

"What part of 'no' don't you understand! I never want to see Sissy Blackwood again!"

"Stop yelling!"

"I am not yelling!"

At this point, a man carrying restaurant garbage came out of the O Montanha wearing a white chef's uniform. The man looked at Garland...strangely. He saw the filthy newspaper in his hand. "Can I help you?"

Garland hit his palm with the newspaper. "No, just leaving. Lost my newspaper. Found it just now, thanks."

"That paper is yesterday's news. Can't you afford to buy today's paper? And what the hell are you doing in the alleyway of my restaurant?"

"No worries, I was just leaving."

"Good. Now get out of here before I call the cops."

* * * *

It had been a long, exhausting day. Between putting furniture in storage and closing out various aspects of his New York life and moving to New Jersey, the day could not have ended soon enough. Don Julio buzzed in his ear. The fly convinced him to send a resume to the Clinic in Newark. With bills piling up, the last thing he wanted was to be a volunteer lawyer, but at least it gave him something to do while he looked for a paying job.

As Garland pulled up to his house, he noticed that his father's car was in the driveway. Part of him felt like venting to his father; the other part was depressed and wanted to go to bed and forget the day had ever happened. He decided that the best thing to do was to forget the day and go to bed. He told Don Julio to leave him alone for the evening.

As he lay there, his thoughts turned to Sissy Blackwood and how he would handle her when he saw her. Don Julio had told him that the ring was a gift in contemplation of marriage and he was entitled to have it returned to him. Garland smiled to himself. He knew the crazy old fly was correct in his legal analysis.

I guess all those years of hanging onto the walls of lawyers' offices taught you something, he thought.

Would she give him the ring back or tell him to go to hell? Would he be forced to sue her? Garland knew who Sissy Blackwood was inside and out. Their separation had not been friendly. In fact, it had been downright ugly. Perhaps if he tried to get her to remember their better days, when they spent summers working at the Easthampton Watersea Club and making love on the beach, she would be kind to him. But he knew what kind of person she really was, and it did not paint a pretty picture.

Sarah Selene Blackwood was, at least in her mind, American royalty. She was nicknamed "Sissy" by her little sister who could not say "Sarah Selene" without stuttering. Her life was a finished product of Miss Porter's School, an elite, private all-girls boarding school in Farmington, Connecticut. After Miss Porter's, she went on to Wellesley for an undergraduate degree in fine art. Despite her Ivy League credentials, she was unable to find a job in her field until her daddy made some phone calls to New York politicians. One senator with connections to the art world through his wife introduced her to a wealthy heiress, owner of Le Galerie du Joie, "The Gallery of Joy," on Fifth Avenue in Manhattan.

Le Galerie was a pretentious interior art and design firm run by a woman named Vienne du Soleil. A self-proclaimed French baroness, her real name was Dorina Fleebash. As luck would have it, Dorina worked as an airline stewardess on a fortuitous Pan Am flight headed for Paris in 1968. That was a turning point in her life. It was on that flight that Dorina Fleebash of Harrison, New Jersey met a wealthy French businessman, the so-called Baron Henri du Soleil. An ancient widower, the baron fancied buxom blonds and *young* American women. They married quickly and the old buzzard died while they were having sex. His death left her enough money to pursue whatever she wanted to do in the art world. She recreated herself as the Baroness du Soleil, complete with an affected British accent. From her inherited wealth, Le Galerie was born.

The furnishings in Le Galerie were expensive. A plain wood chair that looked like it came from a flea market could easily cost a buyer five thousand dollars. A red spray-painted plastic bucket with the words "Love me, Love my dog" painted on the front cost at least several hundred dollars. Vienne's own artwork, which had the quality of an inebriated high school student with a fondness for Jackson Pollack, sold for thousands of dollars.

Sissy was Vienne's favorite "design assistant." She spent her days at Le Galerie moving furniture and art from one side of the showroom to the other, depending on Baroness Vienne's mood in the morning. Sissy would plan cocktail parties, inviting New York's creative elite to Le Galerie simply to celebrate recently acquired works of art. While it was very quietly known through artistic circles in New York that Vienne's taste in art was horrid, the cocktail parties were always fun and lavish, so people came to them. Le Galerie made money in spite of itself, making the Baroness Vienne du Soleil a successful artistic entrepreneur.

A phony rich baroness, lousy art, and overpriced furniture? Sissy Blackwood fit right in.

* * * *

He took the Path train from Newark's Pennsylvania Station to Manhattan at 33rd Street. From there, Garland took a cab over to Le Galerie du Joie. He stood outside and took a deep breath, trying to calm the knot in his stomach. Don Julio had insisted upon coming, which hadn't helped his anxiety at all. He sat hidden beneath the collar of Garland's jacket.

"Do you see her, amigo?"

"No. But I have to be let into the building. Make sure you stay hidden."

"Okay, okay relax. This collar is so wide, I could put ten more of my fly brothers underneath here."

He rang the bell. A cheerful British-sounding voice over the intercom said, "Bonjour! Welcome to Le Galerie du Joie! And whom shall I say is calling?"

"Umm, good morning. My name is Garland Nowell. I am here to see Ms. Blackwood."

"Do you have an appointment?"

"No, I'm sorry. I was in town and I just thought I would drop in and say hello."

The cheery voice changed. "Well, sir, Designer Blackwood is quite busy cataloging our recent acquisitions. I shall see if she can see you. One moment, please."

Seconds later he was buzzed in. He looked around. The walls of Le Galerie were stark white with artwork scattered over them in no particular order. An older woman approached him wearing a simple black dress and a string of pearls. Her blond-streaked hair was severely drawn off her face in a tight chignon.

"Good morning, I am Baroness du Soleil, owner of Le Galerie." She opened her arms wide. "So what do you think of my art?"

Garland stuttered as he looked above his head. He saw a mobile dangling from the ceiling, composed entirely of used plastic paint spatulas. The paint spatulas were individually suspended by thin fishing wire tied to a rubber chicken hung from a coat hanger. The whole monstrosity was attached to the art gallery's ceiling by more fishing line.

"Very unique. I've never seen anything like it."

Don Julio whispered, "I have landed on better art in the city dump. This art stinks."

The baroness smiled proudly. "Yes, I know. Anyway, please look around. If you need assistance, Ms. Blackwood will assist you. Ah, here she comes now. I will leave you two alone." With those words, the baroness left the room.

Garland heard the *click click* of high heels moving across the wooden floor. Sissy wore a similar black knit dress and a set of pearls. Her hair was tightly drawn off her face like the baroness. She was not smiling.

"I see why you liked her, amigo. She is very pretty. Nice tits."

"Hello, Garland. To what do I owe the pleasure of your company? I'm very busy."

"Look, Sissy, I don't want to waste your time or mine. I'm here for a reason."

"Did you get a new job in New York City?"

"There have been offers, but I am undecided right now as to what firm I want to go to."

"Still blacklisted, eh?"

"Don't know. Don't care." He looked at her finger. She was wearing a diamond ring, but it was not the diamond he had given her. "Gee. I see you didn't waste any time after you dumped me."

"What can I tell you? Jackson Blillefy is a full partner at Criley Renshaw. He didn't get fired and ruin my dream wedding. I was humiliated."

Garland raised his voice. "So let me get this straight. You never loved me. The only reason you wanted to marry me was so that you could be the wife of a partner in a large firm and a have a big stupid wedding? Oh yeah, and then you could decorate your mansion with crap art like this?" He pointed to the ugly spatula mobile.

Julio whispered. "Ay, what a *bruja*! It is a good thing she left you."

"Lower your voice before the baroness hears you!" Her tone softened. "It was more than that. I did love you, but I felt like, well like, I just needed more. I was scared, especially when you were fired."

He half smiled. "It seems like you have 'more' with your new fiancé. Well, here's the deal. Now I need something *more*. When you loved me, or so you said, I gave you something as a sign of my love for you. A twenty thousand dollar Tiffany ring, a marquise diamond. I want it back. You don't need it. You have a new one." He pointed at her hand.

She cocked her head. "And what if I don't want to give it back?"

He shook his head. "Easy. I'll sue you for it. Hey, your new future husband can defend you for free. Doesn't matter to me. I gave you that ring as a gift in contemplation of marriage. You broke up with me, the ring comes back. That's the law."

"Way to go, amigo," Julio whispered.

"You would sue me? Me?"

"Yes. I don't want to, but I will."

"Can I think about it?"

"You have until the end of the week. It's Monday, so you have a good four days. If I don't have the ring by Saturday, you will have a lawsuit by Monday." He looked at her face. "Hey, Sissy, you have the same look on your face that I had when you told me you wouldn't marry me."

"I should have expected this from you."

"Yes, you should have, but you didn't. Now I'll leave so you can get back to work for the Baroness of Rotten Art. I'll see myself out." He turned and walked away.

"Bravo, amigo! You are stronger than I thought," Julio whispered. "I am proud of you."

"Wait, Garland."

Garland didn't turn around. He just kept walking toward the door.

"I said wait!" she yelled, then her voiced softened. "Please."

He stopped to turn around. "Yeah?"

"I don't know where you live anymore. You moved out of the apartment on 73rd Street."

"Send it to my father's address. He can get the ring to me. Goodbye, Sissy. Have a wonderful life with Jack the Blowfly or whatever his name is."

Garland smiled and Don Julio laughed because the last words they heard as the door slammed were, "It's Jackson Blillefy!"

CHAPTER THIRTEEN

Liliana Ramos sat at a small antique ladies' writing desk she had purchased in a local thrift store. The old wooden desk had been scratched and stained. She paid ten dollars for it but spent over five hundred dollars restoring it to its original Victorian beauty. It was now an important part of her home, and she was proud of her thrift store find. She placed the desk in front of the bedroom window of her Broad Street condominium. From there, she looked out at the City of Newark when she worked at home.

She loved to observe the changing of the seasons from her bedroom window. During spring she watched flowers bloom in large metal pots outside of tall Newark office buildings. Summer nights were lively and filled with music. While businessmen occupied the streets during the long days of July and August, artists, musicians, and food vendors took over the streets on hot summer nights. In October Liliana watched colorful leaves drop from the trees in the park, then swirl in circles around streetlamps in the fall. Winter was Liliana's favorite season, and she was happy to enjoy it from the warmth of her apartment. The streets were empty, devoid of cars and people. Blankets of snow floated down from the sky, purifying the air and the dirty city streets. All seemed peaceful and silent.

Newark, like Manhattan, was a city that never sleeps. The sound of frequent police sirens and ambulances did not bother her; it was something she was accustomed to hearing. Having grown up in Paterson, it would have been a miracle if she didn't at least hear ambulances during the night.

As she sat at her desk, she took a deep breath. Ina had given her the tedious job of finding volunteers for The People's Clinic. A pile of unopened envelopes lay in front of her containing resumes. She opened the envelopes one at a time. It was a painful process. Each cover letter that came with a resume started the same way:

"I am a first year law student seeking experience and feel that The People's Clinic serves my important desire to engage in public service..."

"I am extremely interested in serving the needs of the public and gaining experience in litigation as a first year law student. I would require a modest stipend..."

"I am a first year law student..."

"I am a second year law student..."

Liliana sighed. The last thing she needed was another law student who she would have to train and who would be unable to make court appearances. First year law students were about as useful as a young goldfish. They could do research, interview prospective clients for the agency, and not much else. The Clinic had only four full-time lawyers, and Liliana was not excited about training another law student. She continued to open up the envelopes on her desk. The same story repeated itself:

"I am a first year law student seeking a summer internship..."

"I am a first year law student seeking part-time employment..."

Then at the bottom of the endless pile of first year law students, she saw a resume that actually piqued her interest. "Finally," she stated. "Hmmm. I wonder."

"Dear Ms. Furnstein,

I am writing in response to your advertisement in the Jersey Legal Journal of Law and Government for a volunteer attorney. I have been a member of the New York and New Jersey Bar for over a decade, where my practice consisted of state and federal litigation in both New York and New Jersey. After a decade of private practice, I have decided that I would like to devote time to public service. I believe that my vast experience in commercial transactions would be useful in assisting the needs of your clients in consumer fraud matters as well as landlord/tenant litigation. I understand that this is a non-paying position..."

She smiled. This resume belonged to a practicing lawyer who could help move The People's Clinic's cases. He could actually do something beyond legal research. Liliana looked at his bar admission dates and did some quick mental mathematics. They were almost the same age. Very interesting. She assumed that he had probably made a lot of money practicing law at a large Wall Street firm and grew tired of the long hours. Having made a lot of money, he could take a pay cut and work in a public service position. That was one possible story.

Then, of course, there was always the other scenario.

He was fired from a major law firm and couldn't find a job. Needing something to do, he could take a public service job while he looked for a job in another big firm. But even if that was the case, it was of no consequence. Having another attorney to share the caseload, even for a short time, would be worth it to Ina. Liliana would recommend him and demand that Ina call this Garland Nowell first thing in the morning. The other resumes would get a gracious rejection letter, and Ina would be thrilled they had a *real* lawyer this time and not a law student.

Suddenly her bedroom grew cold. It was as though the setting for the air conditioning had been turned down to freezing. Rubbing her hands together, she blew warm breath onto them as she walked across the room to check the thermostat. It was a steady 68 degrees. No cold air was blowing, but the room was still frigid. It was strange. She would call the building manager in the morning. Glancing at a wall clock, she saw that it was after eleven o' clock. Time to go to bed. She was done for the night.

When she returned to the desk and looked out the window, she saw a shadowy figure near a street lamp. She studied the figure. It was a tall man with broad shoulders wearing a long dark coat and a large-brimmed hat. She could not see his face. The figure looked somewhat lopsided because one shoulder appeared to be slightly higher than the other, as though the figure were either deformed or had something sitting upon his right shoulder.

She kept looking. As she studied the dark figure, she noticed that something had shifted. Whatever was positioned on the right side of the shadow's shoulder shifted to the left side. It was moving back and forth, back and forth across the tall figure's shoulders.

Living in Newark, she was used to seeing street people. After all, Newark was a big city with a large urban population. The Father Nelson Shelter for the Homeless was on Mulberry Street, only three blocks away from her condominium. Liliana saw street people all the time with their bags and shopping carts but this, this shadow figure was different. His presence frightened her.

She was cold and uncomfortable. She became nauseous staring at the shadow man, yet she couldn't stop looking at the figure. Finally, the dark figure slowly backed away into the darkness and out of her view. Clutching her chest, Liliana sighed with relief. As soon as the figure was gone, the temperature in her bedroom returned to normal, and she no longer felt sick.

CHAPTER FOURTEEN

Home of Nicholas Nowell
Totowa, New Jersey
"Hey, Mr. Attorney! You have a package," the elder Nowell announced. "What did you do, buy some lousy piece of art from some New York gallery? You don't even have a job, so how is it you're buying art?"

"I'm not buying art, Dad!" he yelled back.

Garland lay in his bed with half-closed eyes as he listened to his father yell from the first floor. Don Julio lay on his back on Garland's dresser. Upon the sound of Garland's father's voice, he flew upward. Hovering over Garland's head, Don Julio said, "Garlando, I think that your papa is calling you."

"Yeah, yeah, I heard him." He hopped out of bed and trotted downstairs. Garland saw his father holding a cup of coffee in one hand and a padded yellow envelope in the other.

"Dad, is that for me?"

"Yeah. From some art gallery in New York. Hey, is this the gallery where Sissy? That snake. She dumped you when you got fired." Nicholas Nowell was clearly irritated. "You didn't buy anything from that saggy bag of bones, did you?"

Garland smiled. "No, Dad, I didn't buy a thing." He opened the envelope and dumped the contents into his hand. "But I did get something that I bought returned to me." A crumpled piece of toilet paper fell out. Inside the tissue was the twenty thousand dollar engagement ring and a note from Sissy Blackwood.

"Well, Dad, what do you know? Sweet Sissy wrote a note to me, and it says, 'Here is the ring. I hope you choke on it.'"

Nicholas Nowell grinned. "Looks like she choked on it. You got the ring back. I'm impressed. How did you do it?"

"I went to the gallery and told her that I wanted the ring back. She broke the engagement. According to the law, the ring belongs to me."

Garland's father slapped him on the back, nearly knocking him off his feet. "Well done, Garland. You got a set of acorns. You've made the family proud."

"Acorns? Dad, what are you talking about?"

Don Julio flew in and hovered near the refrigerator. "Garlando, he is referring to your *cojones, sus huevos, bellotas.*"

Suddenly Garland's father looked in Don Julio's direction. "What have we here? Look at the size of that fat fly. Man, that is one fat little bastard." He began rolling up a newspaper.

A look of panic came over Garland and he began frantically waving his arms, blocking his father. Don Julio took off and headed out of the room as quickly as he could.

"Dad, stop! Leave the fat fly alone!"

"What? That's one of those big shit flies. They bite. Where's the bug spray?"

"Dad, leave him alone. He isn't hurting anyone." With those words, he removed the newspaper from his father's hands. "Live and let live?"

"Since when did you become a Buddhist?" He pointed a finger at Garland. "That fly better not be the reincarnation of my ex-mother-in-law, your Grandma Joyce." He yanked the newspaper out of Garland's hands. "She was 101 years old when she died. Survived cancer, diabetes, and two heart attacks. An atomic bomb couldn't have killed that miserable old bat, but she finally croaked when she choked on a potato chip. But if she's alive again in the form of a fly—"

"Dad, calm down. That fly wasn't Grandma Joyce. It was just a fly. Don't you have something to do? Don't you have a lawyer to insult?"

"Yes, I have better things to do than sit here and fight with you over an insect. Give me back my newspaper. I'm leaving."

Garland handed him the newspaper as his father started to walk toward the front door. Papa Nowell was obviously really annoyed by his desire to save the life of a fly. "Have a nice day, Dad."

His father stopped and turned around. "So what are you going to do today? Save a mosquito? Hug an earthworm?"

"No, Dad. I am going to get the cash for that ring. If I get some cash, I can help out around here a little more until I get a job."

"Good." Nicholas Nowell exhaled. "It's okay. Look, you're doing the best you can." Then he raised an index finger and pointed in Garland's direction. "Just don't let your acorns change into flan over some woman!"

* * * *

Garland took a shower and dressed. He had an interview with The People's Clinic at ten o'clock. From there he and Don Julio would go to a pawn shop. Nuno the Portuguese fly knew someone with a connection to a pawn shop that would pay good money for the ring. Garland wanted nothing to do with Julio or his friend Nuno, so he tried to return the ring to the retail store where he had purchased it. The store was uncooperative because time had passed and he lost the receipt for the ring. After elevating his complaint to the highest authority in the store, the district manager, the most Garland could get was store credit—something he didn't need. He wanted money. Cash.

Julio rode inside the collar of Garland's suit. Garland parked the car in a public garage in Newark and then walked down Broad Street, heading toward a building that used to be the First National Bank of Newark. The bank had closed a decade ago, and a wealthy businessman converted the entire bank into a series of doctors' and lawyers' offices. Garland knew the building well; he had taken many witness depositions at 3500 Broad Street. He knew exactly where the Clinic was located.

After passing a disinterested security guard, Garland entered a dirty elevator and pressed the button for the twelfth floor. He wondered if it would be a panel interview, where three or four lawyers employed by The People's Clinic would fire questions at him all at once in order to see if he was a good fit for the Clinic. Perhaps he would have several one-on-one interviews with different staff attorneys. Either way, he felt calm and prepared. He had been on so many interviews in his professional career. This would be easy…he hoped.

He was greeted by a secretary who reminded him of his Grandma Joyce. A chubby, matronly lady with long painted fingernails that looked like they belonged at the end of a grizzly bear, she directed him to sit in the same room with The People's Clinic's clients. Garland looked around. The clients seated in the waiting room did not resemble the type of clients he would find sitting in the waiting room of his old New York law firm.

A Hispanic mother with an infant in one hand chased after a set of three-year-old twin boys who couldn't sit still. An elderly man sat quietly muttering to himself, appearing to engage in conversation with a person only he could see. He noticed that a long fluffy tail extended out from under the man's coat and draped across his lap. Garland thought it was odd and that the poor man was probably mentally ill. What was he hiding in his coat? But how could he judge the man? His companions for the last few weeks were a santero who communicates with spirits and a talking Cuban fly who could play a flamenco guitar.

He had no right to judge anyone's sanity when he questioned his own.

"Mr. Garland Nowell. My name is Mrs. Jones. I am Ms. Furnstein's secretary. Ms. Furnstein will see you now. Follow me." The large woman rose from the chair and gestured to Garland. He followed her down the hall into a large conference room. There inside sat Ina Furnstein and Liliana Ramos.

"Ms. Furnstein, Ms. Ramos, may I introduce Mr. Garland Nowell." Mrs. Jones looked him up and down and gave him a savage grin, as though she were about to eat the young lawyer for lunch. "Good luck." She slammed the door and left the conference room.

Garland felt a strange knot in his stomach. "Hello."

Ina smiled. "Please, Mr. Nowell, have a seat next to Ms. Ramos. And don't let Mrs. Jones worry you. She's a pussycat once you get to know her. Would you like coffee?"

"No thanks, Ms. Furnstein. Had my share this morning. If I have any more, I'll be flying around your office."

She smiled. "Okay. So then let's get to it, shall we? Ms. Ramos, who is a senior attorney here, and I have reviewed your resume. You have impressive credentials. I'll get to the point. Why are you here?"

"I'm sorry. I don't understand."

"You were at Boxdell and Lumpton for several years. You were probably earning about two hundred thousand a year plus bonuses. The fact that you are sitting here tells me that either you didn't make partner and the firm asked you to move on, or you just got sick of working eighty hours a week. So. Which one is it? I'm not judging you, but I am curious."

"I ended an insurance case by offering a settlement that saved an insurance company, our client, a lot of money. The firm preferred not to settle the matter but engage in protracted litigation to keep the money coming in to Boxdell. I didn't realize making the firm money superseded my ethical obligations. I settled the case and I was asked to leave the firm."

"Did L. Sanden Boxdell blacklist you in the City? No firm in New York will give you an interview or even take a phone call, right?"

Garland nodded. "Yes. How did you know that?"

"I played golf with him. Sandy was a cheat and liar twenty years ago. He bragged how he worked behind the scenes to ruin people's careers, and they would never know that he ever had anything to do with their problems. A blackhearted bastard, he is." She leaned across the table and looked at him with big green eyes. "I'm sorry for two things. Number one, that you had to work for such a greedy lawyer like Sandy Boxdell. Number two, while The People's Clinic would love to have someone with your skillset, we have no money to pay you what you are worth. In fact, I can't pay you at all."

"Ms. Furnstein, I understand that. I'm not here for the money."

"Good, because right now we have none." She continued, "I established this clinic decades ago based on grants, donations, and my own personal funds. Everything is running quite low, but we nevertheless persist. The People's Clinic has one goal: serving the poor. There are no corporate mergers or acquisitions here. We help people in the areas of civil rights, landlord-tenant matters, and family court. Your clients are not bankers or wealthy businessmen. They are poor souls, welfare recipients, the disabled, and homeless people. Still interested?"

"I am."

"Well, Mr. Nowell, you are either kindhearted, crazy, or desperate."

"Would you hate me if I told you I was all three? Please call me Garland. I can give you references at Boxdell and the contact information for the federal judge I clerked for."

"I have an investigator here who handles background checks. Mrs. Jones will give you some forms on the way out. Fill them out and return them to her." Ina turned to Liliana. "I've been doing all the talking. Liliana, do you have any questions for Garland?"

She smiled and shook her head. "Not really." She shook Garland's hand. "Welcome. We can really use the help."

"And Garland, one more thing. If, and this is a big if, we landed a big case where the Clinic is awarded substantial attorney's fees, it would help to keep the Clinic alive to serve its clients. In other words, this place will provide you the opportunity to bring in cases that are noteworthy. If you bring in a case that generates a lot of attorney's fees, maybe then we can talk salary in the future."

"I understand."

"We also work very closely with the local county Prosecutor's Office, the Public Defender, and other law enforcement agencies. Keep that in mind. So when can you start?"

"Whenever it is convenient for you."

"Great. How does tomorrow sound? Be here at nine o'clock. You will need to prepare for a mediation with a Judge Frances on the Gonzalez matter on Wednesday. Oh, and by the way, Garland, your old firm Boxdell and Lumpton was retained by the insurance company on this matter. Does that bother you?"

No wonder she wants to hire me, he thought. *She is a shrewd old girl.*

"No, not at all. I welcome a good fight with my old firm. What's the case about?"

Ina stood up and reached down to grab a very large Louis Vuitton shoulder bag. "Well, *heh heh,*" she chuckled. "It involves a man with a squirrel that offers investment advice. Claims his squirrel was a service animal. He and Señor Pepe were thrown out of a diner, and now he is suing for violations of his civil rights."

Garland's eyes widened, he leaned forward and placed his hands on the conference table. "Talking squirrel? Does the squirrel talk back? I mean, does anyone else hear him besides the guy?" He suddenly felt the pit of his stomach twist into a knot.

Ina turned to Liliana and laughed. "I think I am going to like you, Garland. You have a sense of humor. You fit right in. Liliana, get him up to speed on the Gonzalez matter. I have a luncheon date with a partner at Eliswell Smythe to scare up a donation or two."

Liliana nodded. "Will do, Ina. Garland, why don't you come with me? Mr. Gonzalez is outside and I can introduce you to him."

"Sure. Can you tell me where your men's room is?"

"Down the hallway to the right."

Garland made a quick exit and headed for the Clinic's bathroom. The bathroom had a singular toilet, and the small space was pleasantly decorated with paisley wallpaper and Victorian pictures. Garland was surprised to see such a well-decorated bathroom in a public building. He entered and locked the door, then looked into the mirror above a pedestal sink.

"Did you know about the talking squirrel, Julio?"

Julio flew out from under his collar and hovered in front of the mirror. "No, I am not too friendly with the rodent population. I am also not a psychic."

"Don't you think it is a little strange that I am here talking to a fly, and now I have to go out and meet some guy who talks to a squirrel? Who do you people think I am? Dr. Doolittle? The Squirrel Whisperer? St. Francis of Assisi?"

"You are neither a doctor nor saint. You are a lawyer who must help me solve a crime. And I know nothing about this man and his talking squirrel." He raised several of his legs and pointed at Garland. "You are overreacting again, señor."

"Okay. Shut your mouth and go back under my collar." Frustrated, Garland washed his hands, then took a deep breath. He opened the door to the bathroom. Outside stood a line of men, probably clients from the clinic, waiting to use the men's restroom. Garland assumed they heard the one-way conversation he was having with Don Julio. From the expressions on their faces, Garland thought they looked pretty annoyed, confused, or both. He offered a few words to placate them.

"Sorry. I was rehearsing an oral argument for court tomorrow." The men did not respond.

* * * *

Liliana Ramos waited for him outside the conference room. She escorted Garland to a different room, then stopped short before they entered the room where Mr. Gonzalez and Señor Pepe were seated. Liliana turned to Garland.

"Okay, here's the deal. Mr. Gonzalez ate in a diner a few weeks ago. He entered the diner with his squirrel, claiming it was his service animal. The owner of the diner, Mr. Kuklas, threw him out, and now he is suing under the Americans with Disabilities Act—"

"I am familiar with the ADA."

"Not like this, you aren't. Mr. Gonzalez was a decorated war veteran at the tail end of the Vietnam War. He received a purple heart, but he suffers from post-traumatic stress disorder. He gets upset when he thinks about the 'children'. We could never determine if he meant his own family or something else."

"Like what else?"

"Ina assumes he must have witnessed a children's massacre in Vietnam and just went crazy. He worked as a janitor for years and took an early disability retirement when he tried to attack the principal of the school with a mop."

"Jesus."

"His family wants nothing to do with him. Very sad. Fergal is a nice man but a lonely man. Since he befriended the squirrel, he is actually much more...I don't know..." she raised her arms, "sane? Not as crazy?"

"I didn't know that we play psychologists here."

"We don't." She sighed. "But sometimes we have to. Let me finish."

"Okay."

"The Clinic handled a lot of things for him in the past—Medicaid appeals, landlord-tenant issues—but nothing like this. He wants half a million dollars for himself and Pepe the squirrel."

"For being tossed out of a diner? He really is nuts. The case isn't worth that much. No way Boxdell and Lumpton will permit the insurance carrier to pay that much money to a crazy man and his pet."

"I don't disagree with you, but we have to try. I've done some legal research. I think we have a weak argument."

"Weak arguments do not work well with Judge Frances."

CHAPTER FIFTEEN

The midnight hour approached. The light of a clear full moon flooded Teofil Lopez's prayer room as he knelt before his altar dedicated to Yemaya. While he was respectful of all the orishas, he dedicated most of his work to her. Yemaya was the great mother of the sea, who often extended many kindnesses to those less fortunate when he asked for her intervention. The santero believed that when he was touched by the goddess, she had given him the gift of clairvoyance and the ability to talk to spirits. The veil between the worlds of the living and the dead were very thin, yet the average person could not pierce the veil. Ancient philosophers believed that those who crossed over into the spirit world came back stronger, became insane, or died in the process.

Teo was a special man. He could walk between the worlds in order to perform good deeds on behalf of Yemaya. For the most part, dealing with spirits, even malevolent ones, never took a toll on him physically or mentally.

He had prayed to the orishas for justice for his nephew Julio. With the return of Don Julio the fly and his newly found lawyer friend, he had hoped that the killer would be found and his prayers would be answered. The spirit of his nephew could be laid to rest... finally. But there seemed to be something more, something worse. A pair of dark, perilous eyes watched him. He knew who those eyes belonged to: Dona Isabel. She was lurking somewhere in the night, like a demon seeking a vacant soul to inhabit. Teo knew he would have to prepare himself for spiritual warfare.

His senses told him that Dona Isabel was not working her magic alone. She enlisted the aid of something dark. It was a bad energy and a type with which he was unfamiliar. This worried him. In order to fight a spirit enemy, he would have to identify it by name and know its weaknesses. Teo had no idea what he was up against. He wondered if he would be strong enough to fight Dona Isabel as he had done so many years ago.

He would read the cowrie shells and ask the ancestors for help. He would also call upon St. Michael for protection and guidance. As Teo sat quietly, he heard a voice.

"Come to the window, come and see. Come to the window, come and see," a voice repeated.

Teo stood up and walked over to the window. He looked outside. In the darkness he saw a tall male figure standing in the middle of a quiet street. He wore a long black coat with a wide-brimmed hat. From a distance, Teo saw that the figure had a very large spider sitting upon its shoulder. The long legs of the arachnid draped across the man's shoulder like a ragged old woman's shawl. It didn't take long for Teo to figure out who the spider was. He knew that Dona Isabel would find him eventually. He just wasn't expecting her to be accompanied by a new friend.

Teo envisioned wrapping himself in a cloak of white light. He envisioned St. Michael's sword in his hand. Though no words were spoken aloud between him and Isabel, a conversation occurred between their minds.

"I was expecting you, Isabel."

"You knew I was coming. I see that you have someone poking around trying to reopen an investigation into the death of your nephew."

"And what business is this of yours, Isabel?"

"You are still protecting the fly. Julio is *my* business, Teofil. Who knows? Maybe I had something to do with your nephew's death. That poor drug-addicted boy."

He realized Isabel was trying to draw him into a fight. He must end the conversation. "My nephew was not involved in drugs. Go in peace, Isabel. Or I will be forced to kill you."

"Peace? Don't make me laugh, old man. And once I have taken care of Julio, you are next."

"If you challenge me, you challenge and disrespect the orishas. That would be most unwise."

Isabel released a deep, guttural laugh that sounded as though it rose from the bowels of hell. "Your orishas? You think they'll protect you? Your sacred little African river gods? Chicken sacrifices? Herbs?

You are nothing more than a tired folk magician. You do not know real power. But we do." She lifted a leg and pointed to the man whose shoulder she sat upon.

"Who is the *we*, Isabel? Are you in charge of him?" He pointed to the man. "Or is he in charge of you?"

"We receive our powers from a greater source. Something you clearly do not understand."

"There is nothing I want to know from you. Time for you to go, Isabel. And take your little friend with you." Teo raised his arms, placing his palms out. He gave the empty air a shove as though he was pushing a person away from him. With that motion, the man and the spider fell hard onto the pavement. Losing no time, the man got back on his feet, then bent down to pick up his hat. He then raised his hands in Teo's direction.

"No! Not yet." Isabel hissed. "Pick me up." The man reached for the large spider and gently placed her back on his shoulder, stroking her as he did so. The pair stood defiantly.

"Is that the best you can do, Teo? Knock me off my feet?" Isabel hissed. "I expected better from you. You will see us again. And I won't be so merciful." Just as passing clouds blocked the moonlight, the man and the spider faded into the darkness.

Teo felt weak. The encounter had drained his body and spirit— this was something he wasn't used to feeling. When the goddess had taken over his body down by the sea, he walked away tired yet energized. This time when he stepped away from the window, he flung himself on the nearest chair. He needed to catch his breath. He felt warm fluid flowing from of his nose. Blood. Teo rolled his head back. He pulled out a handkerchief and wiped away the blood.

He could not battle Dona Isabel alone, and he knew that she would be back. He needed help.

CHAPTER SIXTEEN

Garland and Liliana spoke for hours trying to come up with a strategy before they appeared at the mediation before Judge Frances. This case was difficult on so many levels. Mr. Gonzalez was not settling his case against the Stardust Diner and its owner, Mr. Kuklas, for less than five hundred thousand dollars. Premier First Insurance Company refused to pay a single penny on the case. They took the position that squirrels were wild animals, therefore, they could never be service animals even if Fergal Gonzales trained Señor Pepe to play poker. Judge Frances followed the letter of the law. If The People's Clinic attorneys had no argument, he would dismiss the case on motion. The case of Gonzalez v. the Stardust Diner would be over. In the privacy of his bedroom, Garland and Don Julio discussed Mr. Gonzalez's case.

"Don Julio, I hate to be negative, but I don't know if this is a case I can win," said Garland.

"Amigo, I do not see what choice you have. You must fight for this poor man. Sometimes in life we are meant to lose things."

"Yes, but I am going up against the partner who blacklisted me and fired me from Boxdell and Lumpton. Sandy Boxdell is a bastard."

Don Julio flew in front of him and hovered. "So you be the bigger bastard and be more fierce."

"It's easier said than done." He sighed. "Speaking of big, Julio, look in the mirror."

Don Julio flew over to the mirror, his expression becoming horrified. He was now two inches long, making him more visible than ever. "Ay Dios mío! No wonder your father could see me. This is not good." He landed on the bureau and stood on his legs, looking up at Garland.

"Why?"

"Because it means she is coming closer."

"She who?"

"Dona Isabel. She is coming to kill me."

Garland felt sad for the fly. He sensed that Don Julio was truly frightened. "Julio, I don't understand any of this. I still don't know why you are here and why, of all the possible lawyers in New York City, you chose me. I'm still trying to process everything—where you came from and what you are. My only dealing with flies was at the end of a flyswatter." He bent down. "But I promise you this. I won't let anything happen to you."

Julio landed. "Thank you, Garlando. Now let's get to work."

*　*　*　*

It was decided that all parties would meet in a neutral setting near the Essex County Courthouse. For Garland and Liliana, this was a walk of only a few blocks from The People's Clinic. Garland offered to carry her litigation bag, which had an extensive file on Fergal Gonzalez. This included about three inches of documentation related to his psychiatric history. Briefs were written by both sides that explained to the mediator, Judge Frances, the merits of their cases. However, as in most civil litigation, the bottom line was who was liable and who would write the check for the wrongdoing. Premier First Insurance Company had made what they considered a generous offer to Mr. Gonzalez: nothing.

"Hey, Liliana, it feels like you're carrying bricks in this litigation bag. I won't have to go to the gym tonight."

She smiled. "I think when all this is over, I'm probably gonna go to a bar rather than a gym. Care to join me for a cold one?"

For a moment, Garland actually felt a twinge of something he hadn't felt in years. Don Julio, who was riding under his collar, started singing a Julio Iglesias song, "To All The Girls I've Loved Before.", and this really started to annoy him.

"Would you please shut up for five minutes?"

"Excuse me? Did you just tell me to shut up?"

"I'm sorry. I wasn't talking to you."

"Oh, great. I'm working with somebody as crazy as the squirrel guy."

"Wait." Garland stopped dead in his tracks. "I-I-I have a neurological problem. I have this constant buzzing in my ear—"

"Like tinnitus?"

He stumbled. "Yeah, that's right, tinnitus. Sometimes it sounds like muffled speech or music. But I am not crazy. Sometimes I just get annoyed with myself and express it out loud. But please, Liliana, it has nothing to do with you."

Garland and Liliana's eyes locked Had he been too obvious, just now. Even if he had, Liliana's gaze was soft; she must of known how he felt. He thought he saw the same interest in her eyes. Suddenly Garland didn't care about Don Julio's guitar playing. Instead, he was staring into the eyes of a woman he was very attracted to. She blushed.

"Well, I guess I can accept your apology. I hope I didn't do anything to irritate your neurological issues. By the way, this issue is not going to affect your ability to enter discussions today with Judge Frances and Sandy Boxdell?"

"Not at all."

"Good. Because I'm going to need you to back me up."

* * * *

Judge Frances had the largest and the most dramatic courtroom in the Essex County Courthouse. The walls were covered with hand-painted murals of events from American history such as George Washington crossing the Delaware, the signing of the Declaration of Independence, and Abraham Lincoln delivering the Gettysburg Address.

The courtroom had many elaborate gilded columns and cornices. Two very large Doric columns were strategically placed on either side of Judge Frances's bench, and the top portion of the columns had the faces of King Solomon and Socrates carved into them. Lawyers or litigants walking into Room 1A of the Essex County Courthouse thought they may have entered the wrong room, because Room 1A looked like the throne room of a king rather than the courtroom of an old judge.

Liliana and Garland ran into the courtroom. The had been delayed by elevators and crowds. The pair raced to counsel table just in time to hear Judge Frances' court clerk announce, "All rise!"

A small man, as round as he was tall, entered the room. Were Judge Frances wearing a red suit and not the black robes of a superior court judge, he could have passed for Santa Claus. Beneath a meticulously groomed white moustache and beard was a ruddy complexion and a constant smile.

Judge Frances was a man of gentle demeanor. When he pronounced sentence for a defendant for serious crimes, his manner of speech was pleasant. It was not until the defendant heard handcuffs lock around his wrist that he realized it would be thirty years before he saw the light of day. Such was the temperament of Judge Frances. However, over time he grew tired of hearing criminal matters, so he'd asked to be transferred to the civil court.

Today was his first day presiding over a civil matter. As luck would have it, Gonzalez v. Stardust Diner was the first case on his calendar. He put on his reading glasses and looked down at the stack of papers before him.

"Enter your appearances, please."

"L. Sanden Boxdell for Mr. Nico Kuklas and the Stardust Diner. Your Honor, Mr. Fred Angelo, insurance claims supervisor from First Premier Insurance, is present in court today. And I'd also like the record to reflect that Mr. Kuklas, owner of the Stardust Diner is present."

"Liliana Rivera-Ramos of The People's Free Legal Clinic on behalf of Mr. Fergal Gonzalez. I would like the record to reflect that Mr. Fergal Gonzalez is present today with his service animal."

"Garland Nowell of The People's Free Legal Clinic on behalf of Mr. Fergal Gonzalez."

"Please be seated, counsel." Judge Frances glanced over the top of his eyeglasses. "Ms. Ramos, can I assume you and Mr. Nowell are representing not only Mr. Gonzalez, but Pepe the squirrel as well?"

Before she could respond, Gonzalez stood up. The squirrel's head popped out from under his armpit. "Mr. Judge, with respect, it is *Señor* Pepe. He gets very insulted when he is not addressed properly."

Garland looked at the floor and tried not to laugh. He saw that Judge Frances was smiling. But as he glanced to his left, he saw that his old boss, Sandy Boxdell, was not amused.

"Your Honor, this whole matter does a great disservice to disabled people who have real service animals. First Premier is in the business of addressing claims of the injured, car accidents, and people who lost their homes to hurricanes. We serve individuals who have real injuries. The fact that this whole matter is even brought before Your Honor is a travesty of justice."

"Well, Mr. Boxdell, I think Ms. Ramos and Mr. Nowell would disagree, wouldn't you?"

Liliana stood up and addressed Judge Frances. "Yes, Your Honor, we most profoundly disagree. Mr. Gonzalez is entitled to accommodation for his disability. He is entitled to eat his sandwich in peace. Despite what Mr. Boxdell thinks, this is a matter of grave concern because what happened to Mr. Gonzalez could happened to other disabled people with service animals who are asked to leave restaurants for no reason."

Mr. Gonzalez piped up. "Señor Pepe and I agree."

Garland watched as Judge Frances shook a playful finger at Mr. Gonzalez. "Now, now, Mr. Gonzalez, you have attorneys, two very fine young lawyers. You cannot address the court. Ms. Ramos and Mr. Nowell will address the court on your behalf. Please remain silent."

Mr. Gonzalez stood up. "On behalf of me and Señor Pepe, we apologize."

Judge Frances smiled. "No worries, sir." He looked at the lawyers standing before him. "I would like everyone to please go into my conference room so we can begin this mediation. Perhaps we can all resolve our differences. Let's take a five-minute recess."

* * * *

All the litigants were escorted by Judge Frances' law clerk into a large conference room. L. Sanden Boxdell was a tanned, well-groomed sixty-plus man prepared for battle with The People's Clinic. He brought an equally well-dressed legal army of lawyers and attorney assistants from Boxdell and Lumpton. It was his attempt to use big firm tactics to "shock and awe" the public servants of The People's Clinic into dismissing the case through a show of force by intimidation. Boxdell, the most senior lawyer, a managing partner, one senior associate, a junior associate, an investigator who was a retired FBI agent, and three legal assistants filed into the conference room one by one. Liliana, Garland, Mr. Gonzalez, and Señor Pepe trailed behind them. The team from Boxdell and Lumpton sat on one side of the conference room; Liliana, Garland, Mr. Gonzalez, and Señor Pepe sat on the opposite side of the table.

Garland looked at the man who silently ruined his career opportunities in New York.

I know what you did to me, Garland thought. *This isn't over.*

Judge Frances sat at the head of a rectangular conference table waiting for his litigants. When everyone was seated, he spoke.

"My, my, we certainly have a lot of people here today. So, here is what I am going to do. Talk among yourselves. Call me if you need me. I'll be right down the hall, but try not to need me. I think we have some fine attorneys here and you can work it out." With that remark, the smiling judge left the room.

Garland watched Liliana's face as she whispered, "I can't believe Judge Frances left. What kind of a mediator walks out of the mediation? He ran out the door."

With the exit of Judge Frances, Garland knew this was Boxdell's chance. He would waste no time.

"Garland, can we talk outside for a minute?"

"Sure, Mr. Boxdell." He turned to Liliana. "Let's go out in the hallway."

"No, Garland. Just you. We can deal with this."

Garland smiled. "Sorry, Sandy, it doesn't work that way. Ms. Ramos is the lead attorney on this case. I'm her assistant."

"Of course you are," he muttered. "Very well. Both of you join me in the hallway, won't you? Clayton, please join us. This will be an interesting discussion."

Liliana, Garland, Boxdell, and his junior associate, Clayton Briggs, stepped into the hallway. Garland felt his blood pressure rising. Sandy Boxdell was a hungry tiger salivating for something or someone to eat, and Garland knew that he was on his menu.

Boxdell set the tone. "Let's get to the bottom line. This is a Mickey Mouse case. First Premier isn't paying a dime." He folded his arms.

Liliana spoke first. "I expected you would say that. If that's your position, that's your position."

"Ms. Ramos, it is clear to me that you haven't spent time reading the case law. That dirty squirrel is a wild animal. It is not a service animal under the law because it provides no service for his disability." His voice raised. "And I don't give a damn if he can teach that thing to play the piano."

Garland chuckled.

"You find wasting my client's time funny, Nowell? No wonder my firm got rid of you."

"No, Sandy that's not what I find funny."

"So, what then?"

"Sandy, you keep talking about this being a waste of time because the squirrel is not a service animal. Our position is that he provides a service. He is a companion animal."

"Give me a break."

"Companion animals give people comfort and help enable them to engage in the activities of daily living. Señor Pepe, whether you like it or not, is Mr. Gonzalez's companion animal." At this point, Garland reached down into his litigation bag. He removed about three inches of documents and a small jewelry box.

"Sandy, this is large stack of documents that I will give you with the permission of Mr. Gonzalez. These are all his psychiatric records for say, oh, the past twenty-five years approximately? It seems that our Mr. Gonzalez proudly served our country during the Vietnam War as a platoon leader and came back with a bad case of post-traumatic stress disorder. PTSD was called 'shell shock' in World War I—"

"I don't need a damn psychology lesson from you, Nowell."

Garland ignored the interruption and kept on talking. "PTSD was fully defined in the psychiatric manual called the DSM-III in 1980. His treatment, which was quite extensive, included things like first generation anti-psychotic drugs and electroshock therapy." Garland shook his head. "Poor man. He still has shrapnel in his body as a result of being shot in the back by the enemy in 1968." He opened the small jewelry box and showed Boxdell Gonzalez's Purple Heart medal. "He was in a hospital for eight months in a full body cast."

Garland continued, "Poor fellow! As if getting dosed with Agent Orange in 1967 wasn't enough, right? Now mind you, Sandy, this is back in the early 1970s when we didn't know as much about psychotropic drugs and PTSD as we do now. However, in reading his therapist's recent notes, the psychologist noticed that since he has had the company of Señor Pepe, my client is a changed man. He attends workshops during the day, he goes to church, and he isn't depressed or psychotic. He is even thinking of getting a little job. These are all improvements in his life that didn't happen prior to his acquisition of the squirrel."

"Yeah, yeah, so the rat makes him happy. What's your point?"

"Quite candidly, I think we do have a good case. Because your diner owner had no right to remove him from a public place simply because he didn't like his companion animal. And Sandy, if we survive your motion to dismiss our case, which I think we will, a laughing bunch of jurors will award this man five hundred thousand dollars once they see his Purple Heart and hear about his psychiatric history. Think about it. The negative publicity against First Premier will be incredible. I can see the newspaper headlines now. A military veteran with no family and PTSD was kicked out of a diner because his only friend, his companion animal, was a squirrel."

The older lawyer's face grew red. He looked like a tomato that was about to explode. While he completely despised the man who had tried to ruin his career, Garland made sure that his face had no expression. He trapped Sandy in a corner that the old lawyer couldn't get out of, and Garland enjoyed it immensely.

"What do you want? And don't get ahead of yourself. Be realistic. Even you have to know that this case is not worth half a million dollars."

Garland rubbed his chin thoughtfully. "I'm sure that we could persuade Mr. Gonzalez to be more reasonable. But I can't see him being reasonable for less than ten thousand dollars. Ah, but I have been rude. Ms. Ramos, I have been doing all the talking. Have I forgotten anything?"

Liliana smiled at old Boxdell. "No, Garland. I believe you've covered all the points. Do you want to talk to your client? I see that Mr. Angelo from First Premier is here."

Boxdell shook his head. "This is ridiculous." He started to walk away. "If, and I say if, my client agrees to pay something today, we will need a confidentiality agreement. I don't want any press coverage on this."

"I don't really see how that's your decision, Mr. Boxdell," stated Liliana.

"And you have no idea who you are talking to, Ms. Ramos. Getting press on this case and embarrassing my client would not be helpful to your career as a young attorney." Once again, Boxdell's face grew red, but this time he clenched a fist. He was absolutely infuriated. "I'll go talk to my client." Boxdell walked back into the conference room.

Liliana looked at Garland. "I don't want to inflate your ego, but I have to tell you I thought you were masterful."

"Thanks. I don't know how masterful I was, but I hate that guy. It was my pleasure to ruffle his feathers. But my question to you is, do you really think that Mr. Gonzalez will settle this case for ten thousand dollars?"

"Let's go in and find out."

* * * *

Mr. Gonzalez had been left to sit in the conference room with Boxdell's legal team. When Garland and Liliana entered the room, Señor Pepe sat on top of a Black's Law Dictionary while Fergal fed him pistachio nuts one at a time, much to the amusement of the people in the room. Boxdell opened the door and gestured to Mr. Angelo to step outside.

Liliana addressed Fergal. "Mr. Gonzalez, would you mind coming with us for minute? Garland and I would like to speak with you."

"Yes, of course. Señor Pepe is just about done eating lunch anyway." The whole room chuckled.

Mr. Gonzalez and Señor Pepe were escorted into a small room adjacent to the larger conference room. The room was far less elaborate than Judge Frances' conference room and much, much smaller. Señor Pepe hid inside Gonzalez's jacket, and the three sat down. It was a cramped space, and they all sat elbow to elbow.

"Fergal, I am pleased to tell you that we have a settlement for you."

"Did you hear that, Señor Pepe? We can move back to the Dominican Republic after we help the children."

Liliana looked at Garland. "Fergal, what children?"

His face grew dark and his eyes became watery. It looked as though he were about to cry. "The ones who died years ago."

"I see. Perhaps we can talk about that another time. Focus on me for a minute. The insurance company on behalf of the Stardust Diner put ten thousand dollars on the table."

"Señor Pepe, did you hear that? Ten thousand dollars? What do you say?" he asked. The squirrel poked its head out and squeaked.

"Señor Pepe says no."

The two lawyers looked at each other in disbelief. Liliana spoke first.

"Fergal, this case is not open and shut. There is a very large legal question as to whether or not Señor Pepe is a service animal. He does not perform a service, like a Seeing Eye dog who guides the blind through busy streets."

"That is not true. I consult with him on many issues of finance and people. He gives me very good advice. Isn't giving advice a service? The government has been paying psychiatrists for years so they can give me advice. Señor Pepe advises me for free. He is saving taxpayers' money."

"Yes, Fergal, but the problem is that receiving advice from squirrels on any level is not considered a service under the Americans with Disabilities Act. And Garland and I can't prove that he's a service animal under state or federal law. It's just a crazy—"

"You think I am crazy, yes? That is why you want me to take nothing and go away. You think because I talk to a squirrel I belong in a mental institution? Just because I talk to him and you can't hear Señor Pepe, doesn't mean I am insane. He can talk. I swear it. And he advises me not to take your insulting offer of ten thousand dollars."

Liliana sighed and looked at Garland. "Jesus Christ. Now what do we do?"

Garland looked back at Liliana, then at Gonzalez. "You know what, Mr. Gonzalez? You're right. I believe you. I believe you can talk and understand a squirrel because I talk to and take advice from a fly named Don Julio. Isn't that right, Don Julio? Don Julio says 'yes.'" He looked up into the air as though he were speaking to an invisible spirit.

Julio, who had been napping under his collar at the time, woke up and whispered, "What, what? Who are you talking to?"

"Yes, that's right Julio. That's right. I can talk to you the way Mr. Gonzalez talks to Señor Pepe. It's a gift we have, you and me, the ability to talk to each other. And Mr. Gonzalez has that gift, too. But it's a terrible burden we carry because no one understands us. No one understands that I can talk to a fly and my client, Fergal, can talk to a squirrel. No one understands the magic."

"Ay Dios mío!" Don Julio whispered. "This is not a magic. Just look at him. Your client is crazier than a drunken woodpecker on a metal roof."

Garland saw that Liliana looked completely stunned. "What are you doing?"

He ignored her and kept talking. "People like you and me, Fergal? Nobody appreciates our brilliance. But Don Julio is telling me that you're better off taking the ten thousand dollars and enjoying life. Oh sure, we can go to trial, but the insurance company will play off your psychiatric history and put our esteemed Señor Pepe through hell. It wouldn't be right. I know because I wouldn't do anything to hurt Don Julio, my pet fly."

"I am not your pet fly, amigo!" he whispered.

Gonzalez smiled and turned toward Liliana. "Now this young man makes a lot of sense. It would be difficult to put Señor Pepe through a trial. I think I can talk to him. I still think that the money is low for being humiliated, but to protect Señor Pepe, I will accept this less than generous offer." His face grew dark again. "Perhaps I can use the money to help the children. Anyway, I accept the offer."

Garland left the room. As he entered the hallway, he ran directly into his ex-boss.

"What did your client say, Sandy?"

"You first."

"Mr. Gonzalez is interested in resolving his issues and moving on for ten thousand dollars."

Garland watched as Boxdell's eyes narrowed. He knew that Boxdell would not be able to end the conversation without insulting him.

"Okay. Angelo, the head claims supervisor, is here with First Premier's checkbook. For some reason I cannot understand or support, they are willing pay your crazy client ten thousand dollars. They want this over with. I tried to tell them that this case was a winner and we needed to litigate it. Angelo wasn't interested."

"We often have to do what is best for the client, Sandy."

"They want to give your client the money today. And I will expect no publicity on this matter by The People's Clinic."

"Confidentiality would cost a great deal more than ten thousand dollars. Moreover, I don't make those decisions. You need to talk to Ina Furnstein, the Clinic's director."

"Old Ina is still around, huh? My understanding is that the clinic is running out of money and it's on the verge of closing its doors to the public."

"Doesn't seem that way. Lights are still on and clients still come through the door every day. Oh, Sandy, there's the issue of the attorney's fees for even having to bring this action against First Premium."

Boxdell appeared to be extremely agitated. Garland didn't really care. He was enjoying the moment. What was Boxdell going to do? Blacklist him again? His former boss did not like losing a case. Boxdell also looked rather foolish, having brought an army of lawyers to mediate a case against a harmless mental patient. Boxdell brought a cannon to kill a mouse, or in this case, a squirrel. He had wasted First Premier's money on a losing litigation strategy: twenty thousand dollars billed to a case that would never see a courtroom. At least the defendant insurance company had the common sense to know when they needed to walk away from a litigation, even when L. Sanden Boxdell did not. He had spent decades pushing people to litigate hopeless cases just to put more money in his pocket. Boxdell's hubris had just taken a beating in front of his client.

"So, this is what has become of your career, Nowell. What's the matter? Couldn't get a job at Cadwallader? Patton Boggs? Criley Renshaw? No big firms wanted you? How the mighty have fallen." A sadistic smile came across his face. Even in the face of a crushing defeat, the man was arrogant.

"When you blacklisted me, no one responded to my resumes. I couldn't even get a foot in the door of those law firms to water their plants."

"I had nothing to do with that. All I know is that you just didn't work out at Boxdell and Lumpton. I'm just surprised you lowered yourself to work in a failing public service firm."

Garland did not respond. He kept the conversation professional. "Liliana will handle the check and prepare the releases. There is also the issue of attorney's fees. Since you stated that you read the case law, I know that you are aware of the fact that I am entitled to them. Should I submit my application for my legal fees to you or your associate, Mr. Briggs?"

Boxdell glared at him with eyes filled with revulsion. He then turned his back and began walking away. "Send it to Briggs."

CHAPTER SEVENTEEN

Garland thought it would be nice to take Liliana out for dinner. Don Julio, who had spent the better part of the day trapped under his collar, suggested that they have dinner at the O Montanha Deserta Café. The fly reminded Garland of how spectacular the food was in this small, unpretentious Newark restaurant. Julio suggested that it would be a nicer place to get to know Liliana better, since it was more intimate than the louder, bustling restaurants in Newark's Ironbound.

Though he longed to see Liliana, the young lawyer was nervous. He didn't know what to expect. Was this a date? Was this just dinner with a colleague to celebrate a legal victory? He was unsure, but Don Julio was ready to give poor Garland plenty of advice on how to handle Liliana. The fly also asked Garland to pick up a dish of O Montanha's famous paella for the ride home.

"While you are busy with the romance, I will be in back of the restaurant with Nuno discussing business."

"I'm almost afraid to ask. What business do flies have to discuss?"

"None of your concern. Fly business. When you are finished having dinner with Liliana, just come around the back and look for me."

"No! I'm not going to chase you around by a garbage dumpster again."

"Garlando, I don't exactly own a cell phone. How am I going to know when you are ready to leave the restaurant to go home? And I am tired of hanging around under your shirt collar all day. It's been hot and sweaty."

"Look, when I'm done with dinner, I'll walk around the back of the restaurant. Find me there. Maybe you could tell Nuno to look for me. You guys are born with two or three thousand eyes, right?"

"We have only two eyes made up of several thousand simple eyes. And we can only see a few yards, but we are better at detecting motion than humans. Anyway, I will find you. Don't forget my dinner."

* * * *

By the time Garland arrived at the little restaurant, Liliana was already seated with an open bottle of Dao Alfrocheiro. When Garland entered the restaurant, he was greeted by the same man who had seen him picking up a newspaper by the garbage dumpster a few weeks earlier. The two men looked at each other but said nothing.

Liliana had found time to change out of her business suit and was now wearing a simple knit dress. Seeing her outside of the Clinic, Garland noticed that Liliana had a certain beauty about her with her fair skin, hazel eyes, and deep chocolate-brown hair. Hers was not the not the sophisticated look of a fashion model, but it was a wholesome attractiveness, complemented by what he perceived was a woman with a very kind heart.

"You're late." She laughed. "But only by ten minutes."

He grinned. "Sorry. I ran back to the office. Caught a little more crosstown traffic than I expected."

"So what did you think of your first day at The People's Clinic?"

"Interesting. I loved it."

She leaned across the table. "I was so impressed by how you handled Mr. Gonzalez. You convinced him to settle. Loved that whole story about your pet fly. You played right into his delusion and it worked."

Grabbing his tie, he chuckled nervously. "Sometimes in jest there is truth."

Liliana sat up. Her eyes widened. "You mean to say that you really have a pet fly?"

"*Heh, heh.* Only in the summer." He laughed, then changed the topic. "I read the mediation statement you submitted to Judge Frances. You are an excellent legal writer. Ina says that you graduated top of your class, you were on the Rutgers Law Review, and you clerked for the New Jersey Supreme Court. I don't get it. Why are you working in a legal clinic for soup kitchen wages?"

She rolled her eyes. "Why are you? I believe in helping those less fortunate. I came from humble beginnings. My father walked out when I was born. My mother was a maid in a hotel chain and supported me through some difficult times. In fact, she supported many people with her kindness. No one gave her a break, a chance to better her life. She was sick, yet she took care of me when I had cancer, childhood leukemia."

"I'm sorry, I didn't know—"

"It's fine. Most children don't survive it, but I'm still here and in remission twenty years later. I figure that God is trying to tell me something. Mama is looking down from heaven and she wants me to help others. I made a promise to God and my mother that I'll always help those less fortunate. Poor people need good lawyers, too, not just big corporations."

Suddenly, something struck a familiar chord. "Where did you grow up?"

"Passaic, New Jersey. Why?"

He wondered if she knew Julio Lopez, Teo's murdered nephew. He did some math in his head and figured out that Liliana would have been a little girl at the time.

"A nephew of a friend of mine was murdered back in 1988. He was a lawyer in Paterson. His name was Julio Lopez."

"Julio Lopez," she whispered softly. "I remember him. I was at his office when I was a little girl, I had just come out of St. Joseph's Hospital in Paterson. I remember my mother telling me that he was going to sue on behalf of the families who attended my school. Several of my friends and I all came down with leukemia. My mom had this theory that the source of the problem came from the school's drinking water."

"What happened?"

"The case never went anywhere. Our lawyer committed suicide by a drug overdose. Mom couldn't get anyone else to take the case. Do you know something?"

"No, but I do know that my friend believes that his nephew was murdered because he started looking into the school's drinking water."

"Dear God." Liliana looked around the room as though she wanted to avoid anyone listening to her next choice of words. "I want to do something. I hear that children are still getting sick."

"Leukemia?"

"No, thank God. But kids have stomach issues, allergies, and rashes."

"Okay, I'm in. What do we do?"

"First, we need to talk to Ina to see if she'll let us bring this case in. And we'll need money. And an investigator."

"And right now, I think we need to order some food."

Laughter and smiles passed back and forth between the pair. The two-hour dinner seemed to pass in only minutes. They exchanged life stories. Garland told her about his broken engagement to Sissy Blackwood, and Liliana told him about her divorce from her chronically unemployed artist husband, George Danis.

"Yeah, he was hoping to be the next Pablo Picasso."

"Was he any good?"

Liliana looked sideways, then back at Garland. "Ha! If you think art that looks a second grader's finger painting is acceptable, then yes, he was the best. Couldn't make a single dollar selling his paintings, though. I know because I paid for enough expensive wine and cheese receptions. People came to the receptions, ate up all the appetizers, and left without buying a thing."

Garland laughed. "I'm no artist myself, so I probably shouldn't laugh. My ex-fiancée works at Le Galerie in New York. I stopped in there once and saw some strange-looking pieces. It's hard to believe what passes for fine art these days."

She cocked her head. "I have a question. Where did you get a name like Garland?"

"It was my mother's maiden name. I think it's old English and has something to do with a person who owned a triangle-shaped piece of land, so it was really Gara-Land."

"And Nowell?"

"Dad was born in America, but I think it was a French name, "Noel," as in Christmas. Put it all together and you have an English

Frenchman who owns a piece of land in the shape of a triangle. What about you?"

"Liliana Rivera-Ramos? Liliana was my grandmother from Spain. Rivera was my mother's maiden name and Ramos was my Puerto Rican dad who walked out on us."

"Yeah, me too."

"Me too, what?"

"My mother, walked out on my dad and me to marry a wealthier man. She hung around until I was about eight. I was raised by a single-parent father. Family, right? Can't live with them, can't shoot them."

It appeared as though the conversation became too intense for her because she knew exactly what he was talking about—abandonment. Liliana looked at her watch. "It's late. I have an appearance in landlord-tenant court tomorrow at nine in the morning. We better get the check." She gestured to the waiter to bring over the bill. The waiter placed the bill on the table and started to walk away.

Garland, ever the gentleman, reached for it.

"I got this." He called the waiter back. "My friend! I need a paella to go."

"Don't get the check. You're working for free at the Clinic."

"You have to start somewhere." He looked through a series of credit cards. "This one should work." Garland looked down wistfully at a black American Express card, threw it on top of the check and handed it to the waiter.

"Wow. You must have had an impressive salary at one point in time."

"Yeah, but those days are gone, and I'm going to dump this card because of the annual fee. Paying way too much and making way too little."

"I'm sorry. That was rude of me."

"No, it was the truth." He reached for her hand and squeezed it. "And it was my pleasure to have dinner with you. Where did you park?"

"Around back."

"So did I. I'll walk you to your car, but I have to wait for the takeout."

"Sure. Paella? Bringing that for lunch tomorrow?"

"No, no." He hesitated. "Bringing it to my dad. He likes Spanish food."

The pair left the restaurant and walked to the small parking lot directly behind the back door of the café. Garland walked Liliana to her car. They spoke for a moment. When Garland saw that she had driven far enough away, he proceeded to the back of the O Montanha looking for Don Julio.

"Julio, Julio, where are you? It's dark back here. I can't see you," said Garland. "Come on, man, I want to get out of here. Your dinner's going to get cold."

"I don't want to come out."

"Julio, I don't have time for this. What are you doing?"

"Please just go home."

"Julio, what is going on? C'mon, come out and let me see you."

Because of the darkness, Garland couldn't see him at first. Then came the buzzing; Julio was close by. He had become used to hearing this sound since he had met the fly, but now the buzzing seemed much louder. Garland felt that something wasn't right, something was amiss.

As he stepped back from the café's back entrance, a bright full moon lit up the Newark streets. It was right at that moment that Don Julio emerged from the darkness. Garland gasped.

"Oh no. You've grown bigger. I can see you, your pants, your glasses. Oh crap, I have to hide you." He snatched the fly midair and shoved him into the paper bag with the paella. He then ran to his car and started the engine. He wanted to get home and hide Julio as quickly as possible.

"Julio, how big are you going to get?"

The fly's response was muffled, partially because he was stuck inside a paper bag and partially because he had a mouthful of paella. "I don't know. How big am I now?"

"A Barbie doll measures about eleven and a half inches. You are about half that size."

"The size of a churro? Five inches?"

"Slightly less. About four and a half inches, a small churro. Julio, it's going to get harder to hide you. You can't ride under my shirt collar anymore."

"What am I going to do?"

"Look, it's late and I'm exhausted. I think we need to call Teo."

"I agree. Call him tonight."

"No. Tomorrow. I can't even think straight right now. Eat some paella, you'll feel better."

"Call Teo tonight. What if I wake up and I am the size of dog? Then what?"

CHAPTER EIGHTEEN

It was a typical night.

Tredd Van Marcherz had janitorial responsibilities for P.S. 578 and 728. Each night he would leave his home in Haledon, arrive in Passaic at eleven thirty, clean both grammar schools, return home and sleep through daylight. It was a routine to which he was accustomed, and he rarely deviated from this pattern.

Though he had no formal education, Tredd was not a stupid man. He was well-read and could have attended college with a little effort. He could have been something more than a janitor, but that implied that Tredd would have to interact with people. This was never going to happen. He despised society and enjoyed his solitary life surrounded by esoteric books. Books speak to you without talking. People required a lot of work, and he did not understand them. The whole concept of having a conversation, exchanging word for word, emotion for emotion with individuals irritated him.

The simple life of a mundane maintenance man working the night shift was perfect. He did his job well. When there was nothing to clean, he read his beloved books on the occult. The knowledge he obtained from his books gave him a freedom and power that he had never felt before. In time, Tredd would make sure that the father he hated knew of his power, real power beyond the comprehension of his dear old dad.

He always began his night's work at P.S. 578, starting with the principal's office. When he went in to mop and clean this office, he always looked at his father's various awards such as "Teacher of the Year" or the plaque he received from the Parent Teacher Association in recognition of P.S. 578's academic scholarship under Principal Van Marcherz's stewardship. It disgusted him. His father was no hero. Tredd knew that his father liked the power he wielded as a school principal because he could control lives. But the children's well-being? He couldn't have cared less about schoolchildren, and this was reflected in the way Tredd was treated growing up. Verbal degradation coupled with the end of his father's leather belt created a sociopath. Nettie Van Marcherz, his mother, just stood by and watched. She was weak and didn't protect him.

The Van Marcherzes never cared about their son. After all, what mother doesn't protect her child? What kind of a father enlists his son to commit a murder? But it didn't matter anymore. He didn't need his father or mother. Tredd had someone he truly loved and loved him: Dona Isabel.

Sometimes Tredd would take Dona Isabel to work with him, sometimes he would leave her at home in her terrarium. Now she was someone he could talk to, someone with whom he shared his ideas and his innermost thoughts. Tonight he brought the huge Amazonian spider along to keep him company. The two had plans to make for their future.

"Teo is weakening. I feel it, Tredd. He is old and tired."

"Good. What happens next?"

"The santero must die along with the fly. He has been searching for you for thirty years, and he still seeks to avenge the death of his nephew."

"Not worried about it. That whole crime was covered up. Thirty years later it will be hard to put all that together."

The spider stretched her long, segmented legs. "Yes. But the few who were complicit are still alive. The doctor. The file clerk in the Prosecutor's Office. They need to be dealt with. Along with the cancer survivor."

"We paid her a visit the other night, remember?"

"Yes, and we did nothing. If a memory is triggered within the girl, she may do something about it. Remember, she is working with Julio's new friend, a lawyer."

"What would you have me do?"

"In order to bring things full circle, a blood sacrifice will be required. Then I can get out of this exoskeleton," she whispered softly, "and slip into something more comfortable. Something more *human*."

Tredd reached into Dona Isabel's cage and stroked her large back, feeling the softness of her hairs. He was on his way to work and took her out of her cage. She immediately hopped on his shoulder.

135

"You know, my love, I have had you for over fifteen years now. I long for you to become human so we can share our life together. I can't believe I ever found you."

"Yes, how our paths crossed always amazed me. Who'd have thought you'd buy me from an underground pet shop in Manhattan?"

He smiled at her. "Yes, you were an illegal import with other creatures from the Amazon. I rarely leave the basement during daylight, but that day I just so happened to come out of my lair and find you. What a fortunate man I am."

She lifted one of her legs and stroked his cheek. "Enough reminiscing," she whispered. "A deal has to be made and the sacrifice must occur. Your skills as a necromancer are incredible and you have mastered the black magic I have taught you. But we need more so that I may be renewed."

"Blood magic. Yes, the spirit who will transform you will be Betel, an infernal corporal in hell's hierarchy."

"Hmm, I was hoping for someone a little higher such as an infernal duke like Dantalion or a prince such as Vassago. Someone with more power."

"Dantalion commands thirty-six legions in hell, teaches arts and sciences, and can control the human race. Vassago rules over twenty-six legions in hell and can declare things past and present."

"Very good. Taken right from *The Lesser Key of Solomon*. You have been studying and preparing. You know your demons. What do you know about Betel?"

"Betel is a corporal in their infernal legion and commands many. He has strength to command the elements and restore the dead to life. But a magician must bind him to a magic circle in order to get the truth out of him. And then provide him with a blood sacrifice."

"Good. We have to move quickly. Time is short."

"I don't understand."

"The body of this spider is my mortal shell. As I have always said, magic is a two-way street—we shall be attacking Teo, and other forces exist to attack us. That is how the universe works," she sighed. "And I am aging. My youth can only be renewed once the blood ritual is completed."

The janitor and his spider pulled up in front of P.S. 578 first. Tredd stretched his back in the driver's seat, looking around to see if anyone was watching him. "We have quite a bit to do. The ritual of transformation must be performed within sixty days on the eve of a Blood Moon. Where do we start first?"

"Let me think about this." Dona Isabel open her jaws as if to smile. "The santero dies last. His blood will be my gift to the infernal ones. Now, my darling, go about your work tonight and dream of our future together."

*   *   *   *

It was eleven thirty at night.

When his telephone rang, Teo was in the middle of watching a Mae West movie from 1935 called *Goin' to Town*. He inhaled deeply and shook his head. The last thing he wanted to do was talk to anyone. He'd read Tarot cards for the entire evening, finishing his last client at about ten thirty. Feeling the psychic energy of his clients was draining. Teo felt their physical illness and their emotional pain. After being exposed to this over four and a half hours, he'd had enough for one night.

Teo had just reached his favorite part of the movie where Mae decides to go to Argentina to chase down her British lover played by Paul Cavanaugh. In Buenos Aires, Mae was surrounded by men who want to date her, jealous women who want to ruin her reputation, fast race horses, and tight-fitting evening gowns. Who could ask for more? The old santero enjoyed this movie, each time reliving his twelve-year-old-boy crush on Mae. As he heard each ring of the telephone, Teo sensed who was calling. He put the DVD on pause to answer it.

"Hello, Garland. I was just watching Mae West. You know, she believed in spiritualism. I did a reading for her once in Buffalo, New York in a place called Lily Dale, summer of '52. She was a lovely—"

"Teo, we have a problem."

"I thought as much. What is wrong, amigo?"

"It's Julio. He's…he's growing, becoming bigger."

ANNA M. LASCURAIN

"I feared this. It is not going to stop as Dona Isabel gets closer to us. We have to find and destroy her. What are you doing tomorrow?"

"Working at The People's Clinic."

"I want you to meet some people. Can you go to work a little late?"

"I can. And I have some other news for you. I met someone who knew your nephew, Julio Lopez."

"What?"

"Yeah, another lawyer I work with met Julio Lopez when she was a little girl. She's a cancer survivor who went to that school in Passaic. And here's the best part. She wants to help. Her mother had retained your nephew to try to sue the school, but then he died."

"We can use all the friends we can get. You must go to a meeting tomorrow."

"I said I would be there. Do you want me to bring Julio with me?"

"Of course."

"Who is going to be attending this meeting?"

"You'll see when you get there. At ten tomorrow morning, I want you to go to the history department of Edward Williams College in Hackensack."

"Okay. I know where it is."

"You will want to ask for Dean Nettlebrook. He is a nice old English gentleman, and he's head of the history department at Edward Williams."

"Okay. What about Julio? He's growing out of his clothes."

"I have a lady friend who is a seamstress. I'll tell her that I need her to make some doll clothes for my grandniece. I am sure she can come up with something by the end of the week. What size is he?"

"Size? I don't know. Picture a fat churro with six legs."

He laughed. "Garland, any more questions?"

"No, why should I have any more questions?" From the other side of the telephone, Teo sensed that Garland was throwing his hands up in disgust. "I surrender, Teo, I surrender. I have a talking fly outgrowing his gaucho pants, I'm trying to solve a thirty-year-old murder, and now I'm meeting with a college professor and others

138

who you won't identify. Why should I have any questions? It doesn't matter. Nobody answers my questions anyway."

Teo chuckled. "Good night, my son. All will be well. I will see you tomorrow."

CHAPTER NINETEEN

Edward Williams College
Hackensack, New Jersey

It was an unusually warm day for early January. No students walked around Edward Williams because it was still the middle of winter recess. The empty college campus with its pale building, barren trees, dead vegetation, and peculiar yellow sky made the area look like summertime…in hell. Garland pulled into the parking lot of the Edward Williams campus. Julio lay across the top of his dashboard, looking completely bored, nibbling on the remains of a fried egg sandwich. Garland looked at Julio.

"Do you know this Professor Nettlebrook? What's he all about?"

"I have heard of him," said Julio as he wiped his mouth.

"He's human, right? I mean, he's not a cockroach disguised as a man?"

"No, he is not Gregor Samsa. He's an old college professor who has known Teo for decades. Nice man, still has a bit of an English accent even though he's been in America for a long time."

"How long do you think this meeting will take?"

"Oh, not long. You can be back to work by noon."

"Who is going to be here? At this meeting?"

The fly shrugged four of his legs. "I don't know."

"Oh, great. Let's go and get this over with." Garland pulled out a small insulated canvas lunch bag and opened it. "Sorry about this, Julio. Get in the bag so I can carry you into the building." The annoyed fly reluctantly hopped in the lunch bag and Garland sealed it.

As Garland walked into the building, he could not help but notice a very tall man, a construction worker, standing outside of the building. The man, who had been carrying lumber, stopped what he was doing to look at Garland. A lit cigarette dangled from his lips as he stared. His look was not friendly.

He wore jeans with a gray-and-blue plaid shirt, which he had tucked into very tight-fitting jeans. There was not an ounce of fat on this man, who looked anywhere from twenty-eight to forty-eight years old. He was about six foot three and built of solid muscle. His hair was light brown, shoulder-length and parted in the middle. The man kept looking at Garland with a penetrating gaze as he walked into the primary hall of Edward Williams College. Garland glanced over at him and then looked away.

Once inside the college's Great Hall, Garland approached a security guard whose desk was stationed before two elevator banks. Upon seeing Garland, a security guard instructed him to sign in.

"Who are you here to see?"

"We—I mean, I have an appointment with Dr. Nettlebrook, dean of the History Department."

Without looking up, the security guard prepared a name tag, then handed it to him. "Are you a student here?"

"No."

"Open the lunch bag, please."

"What? Why?"

"I need to see what you have in there. I can't let you into the building if I can't look in the bag."

"It's nothing, just a turkey sandwich."

"Then you won't mind if I take a look at it."

A lump rose in Garland's throat. There was nothing in the canvas bag but Julio. This was going to be awkward. He needed a way out of this.

"You know what? I'm just going to go put my lunch back in the car. I'll be right back."

"No time for that, I'm afraid."

An old white-haired gentleman in a three-piece suit that looked older than him walked down the hall. He looked at the bag and then back at Garland. He extended his hand to Garland and smiled.

"Dr. Brogan Nettlebrook," he stated with a handshake. "And you must be Garland. Ah, very good. I see you brought my lunch." He grabbed the lunch bag and turned to the seated security guard.

"No worries, Mr. Shed. This nice young man was kind enough to bring me a sandwich. Tuna fish, of course?"

"Uh no, turkey."

"Very good also. Follow me, Garland. Mr. Lopez has already arrived."

With a lively spring to his step, Dr. Nettlebrook trotted down the hall. Garland followed him into a large conference room. Teo was seated at the end of the table. Next to him was a young man, appearing to be late teens early twenties. He was clad entirely in black. His hair matched his clothing, except for a wide lime-green dyed strip across one side of his partially shaved head. He played with a handheld Nintendo DS that completely occupied him. The young man ignored everyone until Dr. Nettlebrook called him to attention.

"Leopold Stremnik, please turn that off for five minutes. I would like you to meet someone. This is Mr. Garland Nowell, an attorney."

The young man looked up. "I knew you were coming."

Garland looked somewhat surprised. "Really? How?"

He pointed to his head. "Gnosis."

"That means knowledge in Greek." Dr, Nettlebrook smiled.

Garland turned to Teo and pointed to Leopold. "Why is he here?"

"Be calm. Everything will be explained momentarily," Teo reassured.

That sinking feeling returned to Garland's stomach. Garland watched as the door to the conference room opened and other people entered. It was a colorful assortment: a middle-aged woman dressed in a white nurse's uniform, a light-skinned African-American woman with long dreadlocks and fashion model looks, the construction worker Garland had noticed outside of the building, a man wearing a priest's collar, and a well-dressed, dignified Asian businessman in his early forties. Before sitting down, all of them walked over to Dr. Nettlebrook one at time and exchanged hugs and friendly greetings. Suddenly he heard an angry voice yelling from inside the insulated lunch bag that Dr. Nettlebrook had dumped on the conference table.

"Let me out of here! There's no air in here! I am going to die!" Julio's muffled voice yelled from inside of the bag.

Garland grabbed the bag as if to protect Don Julio. Teo looked at him and placed his hand atop Garland's. "It's okay. You can let him out. No one will be shocked." Garland nodded and opened it. Julio poured out on the table.

"Look at me! Look at me! This is humiliating!" His gaucho pants were now ill-fitting men's gym shorts, his feet poked through his cowboy boots, and his brocade vest looked like a crop top that belonged on a pre-pubescent girl. His size had increased again. Julio was now about six inches tall and quite visible to the naked eye.

Garland watched as everyone seated at the table chuckled. Teo was right. It was as though the people sitting around the table didn't think there was anything unusual. Garland didn't know what to make of it until Dr. Nettlebrook began to speak.

"Mr. Nowell, thank you so much for joining us today along with our dear friend Teofil. I know this must be overwhelming for you, but let me explain that there will be no human sacrifices today."

Garland's face froze. "What is this? Some kind of a coven?"

Dr. Nettlebrook laughed. "The human sacrifice line was a joke, Mr. Nowell. Is this a coven of witches? The answer is yes and no."

Garland glared at Teo. "What have you involved me in?"

"Mr. Nowell, please give me the opportunity to explain why you're here. There is a grave danger among us, which you have unfortunately been dragged into. We are here to help and protect you, not to cause you any harm. I would like to begin by having the people seated around this table introduce themselves and explain why they are here. But before we begin, I have some ground rules. What do they say—what happens in Vegas stays in Vegas? Nothing here today leaves this room. So let us begin."

Dr. Nettlebrook stood behind the young man dressed in black and cleared his throat. "We shall start with the young gentleman, who will shut off his video game for five minutes and explain who he is. From there we will go around the table."

The young man in black exited his video game and looked over at Garland. "Leopold Stremnik, professional gamer, math geek, psychic intuitive, and follower of the teaching of Austin Osman Spare, chaos magician."

Dr. Nettlebrook interjected. "Mr. Stremnik also failed to mention that he will be leaving Edward Williams for a full mathematics scholarship to Stevens Institute of Technology. He will hopefully use his scholarship for better intentions than merely improving the quality of his silly video games. This young fellow believes that many disciplines of magic can work together. Mr. Stremnik is also an expert on sigils, symbols that can be used in magical outcomes. Now, the lovely lady to my right, I like to call her the Mistress of the West."

Garland watched as the woman in the nurse's uniform glanced over in his direction. She was a petite blond in her thirties with a cheerful face, big blue eyes, and a short pixie-like haircut. She was the kind of nurse who would make you forget the pain of a tetanus injection with her infectious smile. Garland felt a certain calm and gentleness about her.

"Garland, my name is Bridgette, but most people just call me Bea. I work the nightshift at the Hillview Medical Center here in Hackensack. I'm an oncology nurse. I see a lot of death. Gee, there's a surprise, right? It comes with the territory. But I have another ability, something I've had as a child. I see and communicate with spirits. I have watched many souls leave the body at the moment of death. Now I work with another to help them enter the afterlife. Together we help the dying exit this world peacefully. Most people, if they have led good lives, leave peacefully. Others who led bad lives? Well, that's another story." She glanced at Dr. Nettlebrook. "Dr. Nettlebrook calls me the Mistress of the West after Hathor, the Egyptian Goddess who escorts the dead into the Underworld. This is something I do. Help to sort out the dead."

Garland cocked his head. "Who did you say you work with?"

Bea smiled. "A story for another day." She pointed to the construction worker to her left. "Your turn."

"Can I smoke in here, Doc?" he asked as he pulled out a pack of Camel cigarettes.

"Dreadfully sorry, Mr. Einarsson. The college is a smoke-free zone."

"Too bad." He put the cigarette pack away. "It's kind of hot in here, Doc. Can you adjust the heat?"

"Dreadfully sorry again, Viktor. Heat and air are centrally controlled by the college. Faculty and students at Edward Williams either sweat or layer their clothing for warmth depending on the season."

Garland watched as the big guy smiled. "If I have to get naked in here because it's too hot, Doc, it's your fault." He removed his heavy plaid shirt, revealing a black tee shirt and a sleeve of tattoos on his left arm. Garland's eyes widened as he took particular notice of one tattoo on the man's large bicep.

"Teo, I'm surprised this guy is even sitting here talking to you. He has the mark of the Aryan Nation. They don't talk to brown people."

Viktor's face grew dark. He slammed his fist, which was the size of a small picnic ham, on the conference table. "That was my past life. It was a prison tattoo. What of it, pal?" He stood up.

Garland stood up. He looked at Julio who, upon hearing the shouting, dove back into the canvas lunch bag and sealed himself in. Garland looked at the shivering lunch bag and shook his head. "Coward."

The two men faced off across the table. Garland figured if Viktor attacked him, he was dead; Einarsson would crush him like an empty soda can. Garland's blood pressure was rising and he didn't care.

"I don't like Nazis, living or dead. My grandfather fought against people like you in World War II."

Viktor raised his fist. "People like me? People like me? You don't know nothing about people like me, you son of a bitch!"

The two men continued their staring contest until Dr. Nettlebrook interrupted with his calm British aplomb. "Gentlemen, gentlemen, hostility isn't welcome here. We have more important problems. Focus." Dr. Nettlebrook looked back and forth between the two men. "Please be seated. Viktor, perhaps you'd like to explain."

Viktor Einarsson threw himself back in his chair and looked at Garland. "You must know the consequences of laundering drug money, particularly if you're part of a gang. Did ten years in a federal pen in upstate New York. I was only nineteen when I entered and thirty when I got out. Sitting in prison, I managed to get a bachelor's degree and found religion. An old religion. I got to know the Nordic gods, which changed my life. I dedicate my life to Odin and I worship the Old Ones, the ones that are the subject of the Icelandic Eddas." He paused. "I left the Aryan Nation, and I can assure you it wasn't easy. Nettlebrook knows my whole story." He pointed to the African-American woman. "Next."

She rose like a lioness and started to walk around the room. "I need to walk about a bit, stretch my legs. Mr. Nowell, my name is Izilda Montague. I'm an editor for DeLyse, a fashion magazine in New York. But what is relevant to you is that my mother was an Obeah woman in Kingston, Jamaica, and Papa was from Haiti where he practiced Voodoo. Mama Mavis could heal you and curse you all in the same breath. What we worship is similar to that of your friend, Santero Teofil. Like the others, I am here to help." She turned to the priest. "Father Hearn?"

The priest looked at Garland sympathetically. "Son, you must be so confused."

"That's an understatement. I'm listening to everyone's personal history, but I still don't understand what any of this has to do with the fly and me. I'm a Catholic, so at least I'm familiar with one religion in here."

"I am Father Hearn from St. Morand's in Hackensack. I don't worship pagan gods; after all, that's against what I do and what I believe. But I have learned over time that evil must be dealt with. While everyone here believes in something different, the one thing that binds us together is our belief in the power of good."

Garland looked around the room. "If this is some kind of metaphysical Justice League or Harry Potter club, that's all well and good, but here's the deal. I'm not interested. I have enough problems. All I know is I find myself with a talking fly who wants me to solve a thirty-year-old murder." He stood up and started to pace. "And since I've met him, every day brings me some new little presents. Today's gift? Sitting in a room with a bunch of people telling me fairy tales and a six-inch fly growing out of his clothes."

The Asian man spoke. He was a tall, lean gentleman with a broad face, large eyes, and short military-cropped hair. He had observed the entire dialogue between the parties with an expression of the same amusement a cat has right before he eats the mouse he has been tormenting.

"Typical arrogant lawyer. There are no fairy tales here. None. Zero."

Nettlebrook cut in. "Garland, may I introduce Mr. James Yao. Yao is in the import/export business and a Master of the Art of Gu, Chinese Black Magic."

"I thought black magicians were the bad guys."

Yao looked down at his fingernails. "Let me ask you this. The law is neither good nor bad, correct? It is, in fact, neutral. Words on paper, words in a law book. However, when someone uses the law to find loopholes to evade justice, does that make the law itself evil?"

"No, Mr. Yao. But finding a technical loophole that lets a client back on the street who you *know* committed a murder? That is unethical. That is evil."

He yawned. "You completely missed the point. The statute, the court rule or whatever law that was used to set that defendant free is neutral. Magic is neutral energy unless used for bad intent."

Garland leaned across the table. "What exactly is your intent, Mr. Yao?"

The Asian man smiled. It was one of those smiles that appeared to be friendly on the outside but was actually meant to cut open your soul. "I am neutral. I don't care about good or evil."

"That sounds fairly vague. And what about you, Dr. Nettlebrook? What's your specialty?"

"Student of the Kabbala, ancient Hebrew mysticism. I used to work with a group called the Golden Dawn, but that was many, many years ago. So you asked why we are here. I will tell you. But first you may want to let your friend out. He seems a bit upset."

The canvas lunch bag rolled across the conference table. Don Julio spewed profanities in English and Spanish from inside the bag. Izilda reached for the bag and coaxed him out.

"Hel-looo my little friend. Come out. Don't be afraid of us."

Julio stumbled out of the bag. He stood on the table, looked at Izilda, and blushed. He slicked back his hair with one of his legs, twirled his moustache, and winked at her. "Hello, negrita."

"Are you flirting with me, naughty fly? Once a man, always a man."

Julio twirled his moustache again and laughed. "Perhaps someday I will be a man again, and then we can share a little wine, a little steak between us?"

"Yes, my darling, but now we have business to discuss." She gently scratched Julio's back between his wings. His wings fluttered. "You like that?"

"Oh yeah, mami. Keep it up."

Garland noticed Leopold had turned his video game back on. He had been playing throughout the conversation. Even as he spoke, he still played with his Nintendo. "So I work with magical symbols, right? I had a vision of a symbol that I've never seen before. Nothing in any of my books or ancient manuscripts. I think it's a demon of some sort trying to cut through from the other side to this world. That's a problem."

"What does that have to do with the fly and me?"

"Look, it's like this. Teo basically took an evil witch named Isabel and turned her into a spider. Ships her off to the Amazon jungle, and like wow, she finds herself back in New Jersey." Leopold pointed to the fly. "Then he turned his friend into a fly to save his life. The fly found you, Mr. Nowell, so that you could find out who killed his nephew." He looked at Teo. "I'm impressed. That is some powerful magic through Santeria."

Much to Garland's annoyance, Teo grinned and nodded.

"Okay. So now what?" asked Garland.

"It seems that the spider wants to break the spell. She's also trying to open a portal to a spiritual world that should never be opened. Not a good thing. I don't think the person she's using even knows that he's part of her plan. Or worse, if he does know, he doesn't care. And that spider-lady and her magician are coming after the three of you." He pointed to Teo, Garland, and Don Julio. "That is the vision I had."

"It's even a bit more complicated than that," said Dr. Nettlebrook. "The symbol in Mr. Stremnik's vision contains infernal markings. We don't know what or who she's trying to bring forth. But we cannot, whatever it is, permit it to enter this world. Isn't that right, Father Hearn?"

"Yes. For many years, Dr. Nettlebrook and I have seen strange things, some of which are not good. The veil between the worlds of good and evil, living and dead, must be kept separate. At certain times of the year the veil becomes thinner, but it must never be torn open. Things from bad places desperately want to get into this world to assert influence over humanity. The group of people around this table are those who can walk between the worlds. We prevent the spillover from their worlds to this one."

"I don't walk between the worlds. I can barely walk down the street. And now some crazy spider from hell is coming to kill me?" Garland rose from his chair and started to pace. "This is lunacy."

Viktor gave a hearty chuckle. "Hey, man, I'm happy it's not me she's after."

"Dr. Nettlebrook, what am I supposed to do?"

"You are to do nothing. We will deal with the more, how shall I say it, metaphysical aspects of the problem. Just worry about finding Julio Lopez's killer. And take comfort that we are all watching. But I must caution you. You don't have a lot of time. Take a look at our little friend here. Julio is growing and will become more difficult to hide from the public. And would you be so kind as to get the dear boy some proper clothing?"

CHAPTER TWENTY

The meeting was over in precisely forty-five minutes, although it seemed like he was at Edward Williams for hours. As Garland drove back to Newark, he felt dazed. Everything was moving way too fast. Julio sat atop the dashboard, chattering away about his need for better fitting clothing. Garland's thoughts were much farther away.

"Teo told me that he had a seamstress making me some clothes. I told him that she should prepare the clothes as though she were sewing for a rapidly growing child."

"Uh huh."

"Are you even listening to me?"

"Yes. I have to go to work and try to function as though nothing happened this morning. I am trying to get my head around the little discussion we had back at Edward Williams."

"Look, let them worry about it. We have to find out who killed Julio before I get so big I wind up as a sideshow in a circus somewhere. Do me a favor. Drop me off at home. I need a break from this lunch bag."

*   *   *   *

The last thing Garland saw as he pulled away was a large fly lying on his back, legs up in the air, sleeping on a window sill. He almost felt relieved as he drove to The People's Clinic. But he had a feeling it was not going to be an easy day. As Garland entered the Clinic, eager eyes awaited him. Liliana grabbed Garland in the hallway.

"Good news."

"I could use some."

"Ina is willing to let the Clinic take the case."

"We can't investigate homicides. That's the job of the Prosecutor's Office."

"No, not that. Finding out about why half the people in my first grade class died of cancer. She hired an investigator for us and everything."

"Really?"

"Yes. I think she's hoping that if we bring this case, we can get some attorney's fees. The Gonzalez case gave us just enough to keep the Clinic up and running for the moment. Ina's wealthy, but she is tapping into too much of her personal money to keep this place going."

"Right. So what do we have?"

"Let's talk to the investigator. He's a former homicide detective. He worked in the Essex County Prosecutor's Office. Retired from law enforcement in 1988."

"They can retire at forty. If he retired back then, this guy is like seventy years old?"

"Seventy-one, to be exact."

"A spry senior citizen? What's he going to do? Chase the perpetrators in a motorized wheelchair? Beat them to death with his cane?"

Liliana slapped him on the arm. "Stop that! This is serious. He's supposed to be really good. They worked together years ago. Ina worked a homicide case with him. She says he's the best. He's in the conference room."

The two lawyers heard the sound of laughter. Ina and her new investigator must have been reliving their past victories.

Liliana opened the door and peeked inside. An ever-cheerful Ina waved her in. "Come in, my darlings, I want you to meet Detective O'Connell."

Garland looked over Liliana's head to see the detective. This was not the seventy-one-year-old man he had expected. He was anything but an old buzzard.

O'Connell stood up when Garland entered the room. He was quite tall and carried himself like a military man. He had a full head of thick white hair that complemented a set of piercing blue eyes. The man's body was in terrific shape. He wore his gun holster on his left side. Garland thought he could have been the father of Viktor Einarsson.

"You two must be the lawyers," he said. "Pete O'Connell." He stuck out his hand to Garland and then he turned to Liliana. "And you must be the lovely Liliana. I'm looking forward to working with you. Ina tells me you are brilliant."

Liliana blushed. "Thank you. I'm hoping that we get to the bottom of what happened here, even though it was thirty years ago."

"There was a lawyer involved, but I hear that he overdosed and was found dead in the school. Shame."

Garland interjected. "Maybe he didn't kill himself. Maybe he knew something and…" He made a slashing motion with his index finger across his throat.

"I understand the murder case was closed. But if we come across evidence that this wasn't an accidental overdose, that's another issue. For now I would like to focus on this business of a cancer cluster. Liliana, do you remember the names of any of your dead classmates?"

"All too well." She reached into a file folder. "Here's a list with the names of all the kids who died in my grade. My mother had some idea that it was caused by water being piped into the school."

"What made your mother think the water had something to do with it?" O'Connell asked.

"My mother recalled that the principal before the current one had bottled water brought in. We were only allowed to wash our hands with the tap water. I recall that we had water coolers throughout the school until I was in first grade. Then Principal Van Marcherz came in and he said that bottled water was too expensive and that there was nothing wrong with the tap water."

"And then what happened?"

"After that we all drank the water. And I guess about a year or so after that, my classmates and I came down with cancer. I was one of the few survivors. My mother tried to get a lawyer to sue the school and prove there was actually something wrong with the water, but you know what happened there."

The detective looked thoughtful. "This all happened in 1988, correct? That was a long time ago, but there have to be records somewhere. I also know a Passaic County detective, an old friend of mine, who worked on the police force at that time. He's retired now and lives in Florida, but might be worth having a conversation with him."

Ina interjected. "What do you think he knows?"

"The police force knew everything back then. It was quite a network."

"Does this have to be an in-person conversation or can we do it by phone?"

"I can make a couple of phone calls first. At some point, it may require a trip to Florida. But let's not get ahead of ourselves. Gary, can you get records from the school?"

"The name is Garland."

"Gary, Garland," he laughed, "whatever your name is, can you get records from the school?"

"No. We have not filed suit against the school, so we can't ask them for anything. But what we can do is maybe use something called the Open Public Records Act. Keep in mind though, we are asking for records from thirty years ago. We don't know what the record retention policy is. Those records may be destroyed."

Peter put his hand on Garland's shoulder. "Come now, Gary, let's not be negative."

* * * *

The day at The People's Clinic seemed much longer than usual. Garland had worked on several landlord tenancy matters, and he had worked on a child custody issue. He had to be in Union County Court the next day in Special Civil Part in order to try to prevent a man from being evicted from an apartment for the fourth time. He knew that the case was an exercise in futility because the man hadn't paid rent in four months. Garland would simply go before the judge and beg for a thirty-day extension in order to give the man time to find a new place to live. The People's Clinic truly did the work of the angels.

When Garland got home, he immediately noticed that there was another car in the driveway. He did not recognize the other vehicle. As he walked down his driveway, he noticed a Subaru Outback with two children's car seats parked in front of his father's Cadillac. Garland sighed. He was not in the mood for any of his dad's lawyer-bashing friends tonight. He would make a quick run to his room upstairs without being seen by anyone.

He put his key in the lock and opened the front door. Immediately, he was greeted by a little boy and a little girl about six years old. He wondered why these children were running around his father's house until his father appeared behind the children. The little boy appeared to have something in his hands. He ran upstairs giggling while the little girl followed him.

"Some guy named Teo dropped by and left you a box. I left it outside your room. Garland, in case you're wondering who these kids are, they're not mine. You're still an only child."

"Thank God for small miracles. I don't think I could take any more shocks to my system today."

"No, these kids belong to my girlfriend. They're her grandchildren."

"Girlfriend?"

"I'm entitled to have a life, you know. After all, your mother took off with that bloodsucking lawyer."

"Dad, I can't listen to this tonight. It's been a long day."

"You don't have to listen to anything. Hey, Betty, come in here a minute. I want you to meet my son, the attorney. He's one of those bloodsucking lawyers I always complain about. But he's actually a good guy."

"Thanks for the compliment, Dad. I feel so much better," he stated as he rolled his eyes.

A plump middle-aged woman with flaming-red hair and a very pretty face emerged from the room and extended her hand. "Hi, I'm Betty. The twins are my grandchildren, Ritchie and Alice. I hope they don't bother you. They have a lot of energy, the little ones. Oh, your father and I are babysitting, so I brought some toys for them from home. But they found this cute big stuffed fly upstairs in your room. I told them to play nicely with it because it looked old."

Garland couldn't hide his confusion. "Stuffed Fly?"

"Oh yes, very interesting looking. A cute little raggedy doll that looks like a large fly wearing gym shorts."

"Oh no! Not that doll! Excuse me, I'm sorry." He started up the stairs.

"If they break the doll, don't worry. I have a friend who has a doll hospital," she yelled to Garland as he raced up the stairs. "I'll pay if they damage it!"

Garland heard laughter in a spare room next to his on the second floor. He cautiously opened the door. What he saw both terrified and amused him.

Little Alice pretended to cook on a fake plastic stove. She set a table complete with a plastic steak, plastic beets, and plastic carrots—there were even pink plastic donuts for dessert. She pretended to cook dinner for herself, her twin brother, and the fly doll. Don Julio had his legs pinned against the sides of his body while Ritchie held him like an airplane and said "Zoom! Zoom!" each time he passed Don Julio through the air in front of his face.

Garland observed Julio's face. He wore a pair of sunglasses. An artificial smile was frozen across his face, and his compound eyes were wider than usual. Every time Ritchie yelled "Zoom," Julio looked at Garland. Finally, a high-pitched voiced that sounded like a robot came out of the smiling but irritated fly.

"The battery on the talking fly doll is running low. Beep! Is time to put the fly doll away. Beep! Battery is low and fly doll is tired. Be-e-e-e-p!"

The young lawyer contained his laughter. "Listen, kids, my name is Garland. This doll is special. It gets tired and grumpy very fast. I need to put him away for a while and recharge his batteries." He tried to gently remove Don Julio from the little boy's hands.

Ritchie would not let go of Julio right away. "Hey, mister, can I pull his wings off first?"

Don Julio responded in his high-pitched robotic voice. "Listen, you little bastard! Beep! How would you like it if I pulled your eyebrows off one hair at a time, eh? Beep!"

"He said bad words! He's mean! I'm going to tell my grandma on him!" The little boy jumped, then flung Don Julio on the floor and kicked him.

"Oh shit, my back, b-beep."

"Listen, big guy, the little fly doll is a *really* old doll. You have to be gentle with him. As I explained, when his batteries get worn down, he turns mean." He picked up Don Julio from the floor and stuffed him in his pocket. "Listen, your sister made a nice dinner. Why don't you guys eat those yummy-looking donuts?"

Alice smiled. "Would you like to eat dinner with us? We have lots of food."

He was exhausted. Julio was complaining about not being fed. Children, particularly other people's children, held no interest for him. The last thing in the world he wanted to do was "play house" with his father's girlfriend's grandchildren. But he also wanted to find out if Don Julio had said anything strange to them.

"Just a minute." He put Julio in a closet. Garland ran into his room, changed out of his business suit and put on sweats, then ran downstairs. Betty had brought over a tray of sandwiches, and he grabbed a salami sandwich. He ran back upstairs and gave the sandwich to Don Julio.

"Julio, here's dinner."

"Ay Dios mío, what is this garbage food? Haven't I have been punished enough? Used as an airplane? That little kid nearly broke my exoskeleton, and now you hand me a stale salami sandwich?"

Garland could not contain his sarcasm. "So sorry! But the local supermarket was fresh out of Beluga caviar. Just eat the salami. I'll get you some better food tomorrow. Right now, I have to distract these kids so they forget about a talking fly they think is a doll." He handed Julio the box from Teo. "I think your new wardrobe is in here." Garland left his bedroom and returned to the spare room where the children were playing.

He sat down on the floor with Ritchie, Alice, and a series of worn out stuffed animals. Alice poured water from a leaky plastic teapot and asked him if he wanted cream and sugar. Ritchie played with a stuffed bunny that he used as a substitute airplane. Garland smiled as Ritchie said "Zoom! Zoom!" each time the rabbit sailed through the air. Then he threw the stuffed animal down, ran over to the dinner table set for three, and made believe he was eating a plastic steak.

Garland sat cross-legged on the floor and pretended to cut a fake steak with a miniature knife and fork. "Mmm, delicious," he said. "But it needs a little salt."

CHAPTER TWENTY-ONE

Zoraida's Boarding House
Straight Street
Paterson, New Jersey

There was no happier man than Fergal Gonzalez. He deposited his ten-thousand-dollar check in a local bank, then he and Señor Pepe took a taxi to a gourmet food store a few towns over from Paterson. Fergal promised Señor Pepe the best meal he would ever have. He decided to spend no less than five hundred dollars on groceries, and he would stock the refrigerator in his boarding house room with food that he considered special treats: filet mignons, jumbo shrimp, lobster tails, and fancy desserts. For Señor Pepe? A ten-pound bag of salted roasted cashews, star fruit, mangos, and a wedge of Jarlsberg cheese. Tonight was special. Fergal would prepare the feast of all feasts for his friend and personal advisor, Señor Pepe. They would dine and listen to music all night long. It was the happiest the old war veteran had been in years.

He boiled the fresh-caught shrimp on the stove and prepared a cocktail sauce of ketchup, horseradish, and a dash of jalapeno juice. In another pot, Fergal cooked jasmine rice. In a pressure cooker he prepared gandules. Twin South African lobster tails were lovingly placed in a broiler with seasoning, as bachata music played in the background from an old CD player. Señor Pepe sat on a chair enjoying a bowl of cashews with large slices of mango on top. His paws moved rapidly as he shoved pieces of nuts and mango into his face. Señor Pepe's cheeks puffed out and looked as though they were about to burst. Fergal smiled. He saw that Señor Pepe was truly enjoying himself.

"Señor Pepe, don't get yourself sick by eating so much. We have plenty of food now, and we'll have more in the future. No need to eat so fast, my little friend." He gently stroked the squirrel on the head.

Without warning the music stopped, and the temperature in the room dropped from a comfortable level to an Arctic chill. As

Fergal exhaled, he saw his own frosty breath. The squirrel stopped eating and looked up at Fergal. Señor Pepe stretched his neck upward in order to see around Fergal's shoulders. In a series of rapid movements, the squirrel looked back and forth, first at Fergal and then behind him. Señor Pepe released a high-pitched squeak to let Fergal know that someone or something stood behind him.

The color on the old man's face drained. "Ah, Señor Pepe, they are here again today, aren't they? The children."

Overcome with feelings of pain and sadness, Fergal turned around to see a small group of children. He recognized the faces of little boys and little girls. He used to give them candy at P.S. 578. The little boy in front of the group, Evan, was especially fond of Turron, a nougat candy sent to Fergal from his cousin in Spain. Evan would always smile and thank him for the delicious candy. Fergal loved Evan because no matter what time of the year, little Evan had plump rosy cheeks and a mop of curly blond hair that always fell across his forehead.

The dark-skinned Dominican man knew the little boy was over thirty years dead. And the children who stood alongside of Evan? Nothing more than shadows of past lives.

No longer flesh and blood, their youth had come to an abrupt end. Pale faces. Eyes sunken into their heads like large black marbles. Some children were bald and some had bits and pieces of hair still clinging to their scalps. White skin covered their bones, and the children were as living corpses.

They were dead children of P.S. 578.

Fergal's eyes filled with tears. "What do you want? There was nothing I could have done."

Evan said nothing at first but nodded as though he were agreeing with him. Then slowly he spoke to Fergal.

"Mr. G." He pointed to some old boxes piled neatly in a corner. "Please help us. You know what you have to do."

"I don't know what to do. I swear, I swear," he sobbed. Fergal dropped to his knees on the hard wooden floor and placed his head in his hands, covering his face. His chest heaved in and out. He could barely breathe because he was so overwhelmed with sadness.

Evan approached and placed his hand on Fergal's shoulder. "It's okay, Mr. G." Fergal looked up and studied the sad face of the little boy who had died in the Passaic County Hospital so long ago. Because he came from a poor family, he was placed in a ward of the hospital reserved for the indigent. Fergal remembered visiting him as he lay dying from cancer. He'd brought him Turron, but the little boy was too sick to enjoy it. Evan gave Fergal a sympathetic look.

Suddenly Evan and his troupe of ghostly children turned their heads to look in a different direction. The sad looks on their dead faces turned to sheer terror. They ran and hid behind Fergal.

"Oh no," whispered the Evan. "She's coming. Please, you must help us."

Fergal composed himself and looked around. He stood up. The children stood behind him. A black mist formed above Fergal's head, and in the center of the mist he saw a set of huge fangs and the body of a large spider. The spider danced in the air directly above his head. It taunted him.

"Leave them alone!"

"You can't tell me what to do, old man," the spider rasped. "Besides, who would believe you? You are insane," the spider whispered. "No one would believe the words of a man in and out of mental institutions. The spirits of the children belong to me."

Without warning, Señor Pepe jumped from his chair and stood on his hind legs. He clawed at the air as he tried to defend Fergal, releasing a high-pitched screech. The spider flew backward into the dark mist, then the image vanished along with the spirits of the children. The room temperature warmed up and the lively bachata music filled the room again.

The retired janitor made the sign of the cross. Fergal caught his breath as Señor Pepe jumped on his shoulder. The squirrel nuzzled him.

"Thank you, Señor Pepe. Thank you." He looked over at the box of old papers. "Perhaps it is not too late. I will do something. I will."

CHAPTER TWENTY-TWO

Garland's alarm clock went off at six thirty in the morning. It had been a late night. The morning had come way too soon for him. Don Julio was ranting and raving in English and in Spanish as he paced back and forth across Garland's dresser.

"Look at me! What was Teo thinking? You need to get him on the phone immediately. I need appropriate clothing. And I want some eggs. Make me a Mexican omelet or a tortilla or something. But first I need some bicarbonate. That salami sandwich from last night is bothering my stomach."

Garland reached over and slapped to top of the old alarm clock to stop it from buzzing. He sat up in bed and looked over at the angry fly, who was hunched over and pacing back and forth.

Apparently, Teo had not been clear with the seamstress that the clothing he needed was for a male. Don Julio was wearing a floral, button-down housecoat with large pockets. He wore a wide-brimmed straw hat with a large sunflower attached to the front. Instead of cowboy boots, Don Julio had a pair of ballet slippers covered in pink rhinestones.

Upon seeing Don Julio in his new clothing, Garland hopped out of bed and started laughing.

"You look like a queen bee. Actually, more like an old drag queen. Nice hat. Do you have a matching purse and a set of pearls? Your moustache adds a nice touch."

"This is not funny! I am humiliated! And that salami you gave me last night made me sick to my stomach. Get me some bicarbonate! Then make me a tortilla and a fresh cup of Nescafé."

"Calm down, Julio. One thing at a time. I'll call Teo and tell him that you need man clothes."

"Tell him to make it quick. I can't investigate a crime dressed like my grandmother."

The look on Garland's face changed. "I'm sorry, Julio, you are going to have to stay here. You're too large to hide under my collar. I can't carry you around anymore."

"What? You can't leave me here alone. What if Isabel finds me? She'll kill me. At least you and Teo can protect me…to a certain extent."

"Julio, she doesn't know you're alive."

"Incorrect. She *knows* I'm alive. That's why I keep growing. She just hasn't found me yet. And the Blood Moon is coming. We are running out of time."

The last thing Garland wanted to do was carry around Julio. "How about if you move in with Teo?"

"He is too busy. He is preparing."

"For what?"

"For the battle that's coming, the battle between Isabel and him. We have to help him."

"Look, I keep telling you. I'll help you with the lawsuit against the town, the school, or whoever I have to take on to make this situation right. I'll help you look for Julio Lopez's killer to the extent the law permits. But those people I met the other day at Edward Williams? They're involved in stuff that is beyond me. Quite frankly, the fact that you're here is confusing enough, even now. I still don't really understand any of this, Julio. I don't think I can protect you even if I want to."

"Did you ever think that all of this means something?"

"What?"

"I was led to you. I think this all means something."

Garland sat down on the edge of his bed. "Like what? The world is coming to an end? The apocalypse?"

"No, not necessarily. I meant, Garlando, that you and I were destined to meet. Fix what was broken by bad people a long time ago." The fly put two of his six legs on his hips and started walking around like a cowboy who had ridden in the saddle for too many hours. "Like John Wayne would say, 'This here is a reckoning, partner.'"

"You watch too many American western movies." Garland brushed his hands through his hair. "I don't know. For me this has been a descent into madness. Julio, I'm just trying to get by day to day. I'll tell you what. Alright, you can stay here as long as you don't get too much bigger. You start getting dog sized, we're done here. Deal?"

"Deal." He extended a leg and shook Garland's hand. "Now my Nescafé, please, con azucar."

"I'll make you some coffee and then I have to get to work. We have some witness interviews on the environmental case involving Julio Lopez."

CHAPTER TWENTY-THREE

Garland ran into a nearby coffee shop and grabbed a bagel. After the first bite, he quickly determined that it was stale. No matter. He had to eat something because his stomach was growling. He rushed down the Newark city streets to get to The People's Clinic for their interview with a grandmother who had lost a child to cancer at P.S. 578.

The hurried young lawyer raced through the door. A wave of guilt passed over him because he knew that he was later than he should've been. Showing up on time for anything was always a problem for him unless he had a court appearance. As he passed through the waiting room where the legal clinic's clients sat, many conversations were going on all at once. The waiting room of The People's Clinic had a full house. Out of the corner of his eye, he thought he saw a client with a familiar face...a familiar face carrying a squirrel in his armpit.

Oh no. Not this guy again. I bet he wants to sue another restaurant owner, Garland thought. *No time for him right now.*

Ina stood outside the conference room talking to Pete O'Connell, whom she fondly called "Petey." The pair spoke in hushed tones. As Garland rushed over, Ina shook her head.

"Well, well, well. Nice of you to show up in a timely manner."

"I'm sorry. My father had some company late last night and suffice it to say, it was a long, tiring visit from unexpected relatives."

"I understand, dearest. I was mostly just trying to annoy you. Ask my friend Petey how annoying I can be, particularly when I am on trial."

Pete laughed. "Yes, my girl was a real prima donna. But one of the finest trial lawyers I ever worked with in the Prosecutor's Office."

"Oh stop, you silly boy. Anyway, Garland, you have a very interesting witness in the conference room. Her name is Letty Johnson. Her grandson, Earl Johnson, was a little boy who went to school with Liliana."

"So I guess when you say 'was,' he didn't make it."

Pete interjected. "Yes, Mr. Attorney, you guess right. Mrs. Johnson's grandson was one of the children in Liliana's class who never made it to the next grade."

Garland looked through the conference room window glass. He saw an African-American woman with short, curly gray hair and long red fingernails. Her hands were folded and rested on the conference table. Well-dressed, she appeared to be in her early 70s.

"That, Mr. Attorney, is Earl Johnson's grandmother. And the late Julio Lopez's former secretary."

"Really? And how did you find her?"

"Liliana remembered her. It seems that Liliana and Earl were friends at P.S. 578. Grandma Johnson used to walk him to school every day."

"That's a hell of a coincidence."

"Yes, it is. But she may be able to provide information on what happened to the water at P.S. 578." He turned to Garland. "Let's get to it, shall we? We haven't got all day. This afternoon we have an appointment at Green Fields Manor."

"A nursing home? Why?"

"Because that is the current residence of Dr. Josiah Meadowloc, the coroner who did the autopsy on Julio Lopez."

"How did you get *that* information?"

Pete smiled. "I have my ways. But we have to work fast here. The good doctor isn't getting any younger while we stand here."

Garland looked at Ina. "He really is amazing, your friend Petey."

Pete bristled. "You, sir, are not permitted to call me Petey. Only the lady of the house is allowed to do that," he said as he pointed at Ina.

Garland gave a slight bow. "My humble apologies. No offense meant, hope there was none taken. Listen, I saw the squirrel guy out there again. Is he suing another restaurant over a tuna fish sandwich?"

"No worries, my darling," purred Ina. "I'll handle the squirrel man. You both take care of that nice lady in the conference room."

* * * *

Ina returned to the waiting room, took Mr. Gonzales and Señor Pepe into her office, and shut the door. Garland and O'Connell opened the door to the conference room where Letty Johnson sat. Liliana had been speaking with her, taking a lot of notes. Mrs. Johnson stood up when Garland and O'Connell entered the room. As she rose to her feet, Letty Johnson extended a hand to Pete and Garland as they introduced themselves. She seemed tense yet determined.

"Thank you for seeing me. This has been a long time coming."

Letty Johnson wore a tailored suit and carried an expensive purse. With sad eyes, she turned to Liliana. "You have grown into such a beautiful young woman. And a lawyer, my, my, how impressive! Little Earl wanted to be a lawyer. He always liked to argue with me, especially when it came time to go to bed or take a bath. He was a feisty little fellow, but he died before he even had a chance. And that is why I am here." Letty Johnson's eyes teared up a little as she spoke of her late grandson.

"Mrs. Johnson, what can you tell us about the water in P.S. 578?" Garland stood in quiet observation as O'Connell got right to the point.

She sat down and composed herself. "Mr. O'Connell, all I can tell you is that my former boss, Julio Lopez, was onto something. I believe he was killed before whatever it was he found could be exposed."

"Did you ever discuss this with the police?"

She nodded. "Yes, in 1988. I met with a Detective Claiborne… Klagdorn? Don't remember his name exactly. And it went nowhere. He said that it was a suicide, and my boss was found dead surrounded by bags of cocaine. He told me I should just let it go." Her voice grew louder. "I knew that young man. He never touched drugs of any kind."

Garland interjected. "You know, Mrs. Johnson, we are looking at a civil matter, not a criminal one."

"I know. Liliana explained it to me. But I think criminals are at the end of this. When my boss started looking into the water in that school, that's when he mysteriously died. That can't be a coincidence."

"Talk to me about the water again, Mrs. Johnson," O'Connell requested. "What do you know?"

"Personally? I know nothing. I can tell you that it mostly happened to Mrs. Smith's second grade class. Oddly, other children got sick, but three-quarters of Mrs. Smith's class died."

"Really?"

"And if they didn't die in second grade, they came down with cancer later on." She sighed. "They all used to drink from the water fountain right outside of the class. Liliana was one of the few survivors. Other children who didn't get sick probably moved away before they drank too much water. Just guessing here."

"But why the water? Not the air or something else?"

"The Riverwood Water Authority had problems years ago. They were pumping water from the Passaic River right into the public water system. That river was contaminated with hexavalent chromium and some chemical called PCBs." Mrs. Johnson shook her head. "With the industrial garbage people dumped in that river over decades, we're all lucky the river doesn't glow in the dark."

"You think that Passaic River water was pumped into P.S. 578?" Garland asked.

"Yeah, and I think Julio Lopez figured that out. He was looking into it after Mrs. Ramos and Lili came into the office. One day, out of the blue, a box was dropped off at his office and left on the front door of the law firm after hours. No return address on the box. Nothing."

"What was in the box?"

"Engineering reports, memos from city officials. I was there when Julio opened the box. When he looked at the papers, I thought his eyes were going to pop out of his head. He said 'Jesus Christ!' and went into his office."

O'Connell looked excited. "Mrs. Johnson, we can really use those records. Where are they now?"

The woman's face grew angry. "The day after Julio was found dead, his office was broken into. The burglars took two things: a Leading Edge Model D Computer and the box of reports. Everything else was left intact, including five hundred dollars in petty cash. The break-in was oddly specific."

Pete nodded. "No way were they looking for money. They wanted to see what the lawyer knew."

Garland nodded in agreement. "This information is helpful. There was something in those records. Something that either the school or the Riverwood Water Authority didn't want Julio to see."

Liliana gently touched Letty's shoulder. "How are Earl's mom and dad taking all of this? It must be difficult for his parents to bring up their son's death again."

"No, it isn't difficult for them at all. His parents were never really in his life. Earl's mother died on the Paterson streets. My son never came to see his only boy. Don't know where he lives anymore. Heard from a cousin that he may have gone south, Georgia or Florida. But I raised that child from an infant and laid his coffin in his grave. So it's really only been difficult for *me*." She wiped a tear from her eye. "I don't want to think my grandson, those other children, and Julio died for nothing."

O'Connell reached for her hand. "I promise you. They did not. We will get to the bottom of this." O'Connell turned to the lawyers. "Won't we, counselors?"

Garland nodded. "Yes. We will. Can you excuse me for one minute? I have to make a phone call." With that statement, Garland quietly left the conference room and moved into a hallway. He pulled out his cell phone and hit the button for Teo on speed dial. After a few seconds, Garland heard a familiar Cuban voice at the other end of the phone.

"Quien es?"

"Teo, it's me. We have to talk. I am on my way to see Dr. Meadowloc."

"Who is that?"

"He's the coroner who did your nephew's autopsy. He's in a nursing home, so he must be in pretty bad shape. The name of the place is Green Fields Manor."

"I will meet you there."

"No, don't. I'm going with a former police detective. He works for The People's Clinic. It would be too awkward if you came and started asking questions. Let's figure out something later."

Garland could hear on the other side of the cell phone, the old santero was smiling as he said, "Yes, I will figure something out."

CHAPTER TWENTY-FOUR

Green Fields Manor
Hackensack, New Jersey

O'Connell and Garland pulled into the parking lot of Green Fields Manor in O'Connell's Cadillac 2018 XT5. As he sat in the Cadillac's soft leathery interior, he figured that O'Connell had a financially comfortable retirement. The vehicle was a far cry from his own cramped Ford Fiesta.

"Ready to go in?" O'Connell asked.

"Sure."

"I'm not. I hate these places. My mother-in-law is in one of these old people homes. When you get to my age, you worry. Nobody wants to end up here if you've led a productive life. Let's face it. You go from being young, virile, and eating steak, to turning into a dried-out corn husk that can barely swallow mashed peas. Personally, if I get to that point, I'd rather somebody put a bullet in my head."

Garland felt his stomach turn. "Are you always so cheerful?"

"Of course I am. That's what keeps me alive. Being cheerful. Come on, Gary, let's go and get this over with."

"It's Garland. But I give up."

The pair entered Green Fields Manor and stopped at the security desk. When they asked to see Dr. Meadowloc, the guard asked them if they were family members. Without breaking stride, O'Connell flashed a badge and the guard immediately gave him access to Dr. Meadowloc's ward in the nursing home. Both men stopped at the nurses' station and asked to be directed to Dr. Meadowloc's room.

"Gentlemen, I'm afraid that you won't find Dr. Meadowloc a great conversationalist anymore. He is very much nearing the end of his life, and he fades in and out of consciousness. You can try to talk to him, but he probably won't respond. He's had several strokes and he's about ninety-five years old. I don't think you'll get much out of him," the nurse stated.

"Thank you, ma'am, I don't think we'll be very long. I promise we will be most respectful of Dr. Meadowloc."

"He is in room 101B. It's a private room."

As Garland walked down the hallway to Dr. Meadowloc's room, he was keenly aware of the smell of bleach and alcohol and other unpleasant smells he didn't want to think about. He suddenly was overcome with the feeling that Pete O'Connell was probably right. A bullet in the head was a better way to go than having people change your adult diaper. This was no way to live. Garland respected the people who worked in this place because they were probably doing the work of the angels for minimum wage and very little gratitude.

O'Connell gently tapped on the door as he entered Dr. Meadowloc's room to announce their arrival. It didn't really matter. Meadowloc would not have known the difference.

There in the hospital bed lay a shriveled old man on his back in a fetal position, dressed in a hospital gown. His eyes were closed and his mouth frozen open. The man looked like a small dead bird in rigor mortis. He was hooked up to a heart monitor. Though his heartbeat was steady, with every breath he took, the investigator and the lawyer heard an audible wheeze. The man lying in the bed clung to life by a thread. Dr. Meadowloc was unconscious with no ability to interact with the world around him.

"I think this is going to be a waste of time, Pete."

"Well, let me give it a shot anyway. I mean, we're already here, right?" said O'Connell. He turned to the elderly man in the bed. "Dr. Meadowloc? Dr. Meadowloc?" he yelled. "Can you hear me, sir? Can you hear me?"

The man lying in the bed continued to keep his eyes closed and made a gurgling sound. No response.

"This is going nowhere," Garland whispered. "He's half dead. We should just leave."

"Yeah, you're right. This guy is out of it. Nothing to do here."

Garland and O'Connell turned and left the room. Out of the corner of his eye, Garland noticed a maintenance man who looked strangely familiar. As he studied the figure, he realized that Teo Lopez was pushing a mop across the floor. Teo winked at him as he continued cleaning the floor in front of him. Garland turned to O'Connell. He needed to distract him.

"Okay, okay, so what's our next mission? I'm thinking we need to get the environmental records on the school, right?" Garland pushed Pete down the hallway of Green Fields Manor in the opposite direction of Teo, the fake maintenance man.

"Makes sense." McConnell nodded,

"Yes," Garland confirmed, "that seems the right way to go. I think we should probably get the environmental records, maybe lunch, and meet with Ina to discuss going forward."

* * * *

Teo was a quiet observer of people. His timing was perfect. The nursing station was busy and no one would notice an old maintenance man working his way toward the room of Dr. Meadowloc. He glanced down the hallway. This seemed like the perfect time. He continued mopping the hall floor, then gently tapped on the door to see if Dr. Meadowloc was awake.

Like O'Connell and Garland before him, he saw the frail, unconscious man who had long ago performed the autopsy on his nephew. He could hardly believe that this shell of a human was once a practicing physician. He looked at the clipboard at the foot of the man's bed to be sure it was Josiah Meadowloc. Teo quietly shut the door. He propped the mop up against the wall and pushed the bucket out of his way. He closed his eyes and raised his hands, then began to chant quietly in Spanish and Yoruba. With each word, Dr. Meadowloc's body began to twitch. His head turned to the right and the left, but his eyes remained closed. As Teo's chanting grew more intense, a smoke-like form in the shape of a floating ball peeled away from Dr. Meadowloc's body.

The phantasm floated in the air above the body lying in the bed.

"Appear in pleasing form and speak truthfully! I command it!" Teo ordered.

The smoke-like ball assumed the human form of a middle-aged Dr. Meadowloc. The man who had lain shriveled in the bed was now a robust forty-something figure, albeit somewhat transparent. The figure looked back at the shriveled ninety-five-year-old body on the bed and then looked at Teo.

"What is this? And who are you?" Dr. Meadowloc asked sternly.

"This, Dr. Meadowloc, is your astral form. Your earthly form is lying on that bed over there. My name is Teofil Lopez. And I have summoned you here to get answers. This could possibly be a time of redemption for you if you tell me the truth."

"What do you mean, redemption? I don't need to be redeemed. Why, I'm not even dead yet."

"Take a look at your body on the bed there. How much time do you think you have left? From my humble estimation, you'll be buried in the dirt pretty soon."

"So what do you want?"

"You did the autopsy on my nephew, Julio Lopez. He was murdered."

"I did a lot of autopsies in my day. I don't recall that one."

"Liar! Think hard. You were the one who said that my nephew died from a cocaine overdose. My nephew never did any drugs. But he was looking into the Riverwood Water Authority."

"Oh yes," the spirit sighed. "I do remember that one. It was very unfortunate. All I know is that I received the body of that young man literally covered in cocaine."

"Now, good doctor, it is time to seek your redemption. Who forced you to lie about the autopsy?"

Dr. Meadowloc hesitated. "It wasn't just the cocaine that killed him. I had discovered a blow to the back of the head. He had been knocked unconscious first, and then the drugs were forced into him. But I was approached and told to leave that information out of my report." The spirit shook his head. "I was paid well for altering my report."

"You were paid well to conspire with murderers!" Teo hissed. The santero tried to control his anger, but Teo felt his strength fading. He would be unable to control Dr. Meadowloc's astral form much longer. He needed an answer, so he persisted.

"Who paid you?"

Someone gently knocked at the door.

Before the spirit could answer, Dr. Meadowloc's form faded. It became a blurry smoke-like ball again, then quickly dove back into the body lying on the bed. Dr. Meadowloc jolted. He moaned, then his fragile body began to shake. The heart monitor beeped at a rapid rate. His heartbeat changed from a steady rhythm into a wild tachycardia. Dr. Meadowloc's eyes popped open as he gasped for air. He looked over at Teo, who stood at the foot of his bed, calm and unemotional.

Then came another knock on the door. "Hello? Can I come in and change the bedsheets?" a friendly voice inquired.

Teo responded by quickly opening the door. "Thank God you came! I was just mopping the floor and I saw that his heart rate is increasing. I don't know what's happening! I think he needs help!"

The nurse's aide ran for the charge nurse and the doctor on staff. Teo immediately stepped out of the room. He watched from the hallway as the medical staff rushed in with a defibrillator and paddles in an effort to save Meadowloc's life. After the first shock, his heart began to beat. He noticed that Meadowloc still had him in his line of sight. It seemed to take all the dying man's strength, but he was able to weakly utter the words "school, Van Marcherz." The santero, disguised as a maintenance man, nodded. Teo's eyes returned to the heart monitor; its steady beeping became a long, steady sound. A second attempt by the medical staff to shock his heart and bring him back to life had no effect.

Josiah Meadowloc was dead. Teo made the sign of the cross as he watched the spirit of the dead man drift toward the ceiling. In spite of the fact that he detested what Meadowloc had done, he blessed the soul of the late coroner. He wondered if the dead man's spirit would be welcomed into heaven or sent to roast in hell's furnaces. Either way, it was not his decision.

The old man had given him the answer he needed.

*　　*　　*　　*

Pete and Garland picked up lunch and returned to The People's Clinic. Upon their arrival, they found that Ina had been waiting for them. She gestured them toward the Clinic's main conference room.

"Welcome back. How did you make out at the nursing home? Actually, before you tell me that, we have something to tell you."

"I'm afraid to ask who the 'we' is?"

"Come in and you'll find out."

Pete and Garland entered the room and saw Liliana, Fergal Gonzalez, and Señor Pepe seated at the conference room table. Señor Pepe peered out from Gonzalez's armpit. Garland gestured to Liliana to step out of the conference room and join him in the hallway.

"Here we go again. Are you kidding me? He's back? Now what does he want?" Garland asked.

"Keep your voice down." Liliana grabbed Garland's hand. "Look, he's a little psychotic. Apparently, he and Señor Pepe had a big party last night. I don't know if he's taking his meds. I think he has been drinking. I don't know. He smells like booze, but he's different. But he is talking about a box of records."

"What? Elvis popped out of his grave and gave him some autographed copies of 'Jailhouse Rock'?"

"Stop making stupid jokes! He was a janitor at P.S. 578."

"What? You mean Squirrel Man has the environmental records from thirty years ago?"

"I think so. I don't know." She shook her head. "We have to talk to him. He doesn't look good. I'm worried that he's on the brink of a complete psychotic break."

"Alright." Garland entered the room and looked at Gonzalez and Señor Pepe.

Something was different. Garland had to look twice. Gonzalez wasn't the disheveled man he had seen in the recent past. He wore a suit and tie and was clean-shaven with a military-style haircut. He looked years younger. This was not the same dirty man with the scraggly beard and ragged clothes he'd convinced to accept ten thousand dollars on a case Garland knew he couldn't win. Gonzalez had completely cleaned himself up. Garland watched the expression on Liliana's face as she looked at the "new and improved" Fergal Gonzalez. It was one of sympathy.

The man's eyes were full of fear. Gonzalez's hands suffered from pill-rolling tremors caused by decades of taking anti-psychotic medication. The only thing familiar about Fergal Gonzalez was the presence of his "financial consultant," Señor Pepe. The squirrel's fuzzy head and beady eyes poked out from beneath Gonzalez's armpit. On a chair next to Gonzalez was an old broken box held together with tape and filled with papers that had yellowed with age.

"Mr. Gonzalez, I understand that you have information concerning the water system of P.S. 578."

Gonzalez nodded. "I don't know what I have. I know that the children told me to come. My memory is not so good anymore. But I have these papers. The children told me about them."

Liliana sat down next to him and gently placed her hand on his shoulder. "I know this is difficult for you, but we need you to answer a few questions. Mr. Gonzalez, what are these papers? Where did you get them?"

His eyes started to fill up and his voice wavered. "The children told me about them. You see, the little ones kept dying. I went to many funerals. So sad, so sad. You know, I was a janitor at P.S. 578. I was in and out of those offices and classrooms for years."

"And then what happened?" Garland asked.

His voice quavered. "In 1988, the children told me about the papers. They said I would find a bunch of letters that looked kind of important. One day when I was emptying garbage in Mr. Van Marcherz's office, I saw some papers. They looked like they came from the government or something. I put the papers in two boxes." He turned to look at Liliana.

"Mr. Gonzalez, there is only one box here. Where is the other?"

"I left it at a lawyer's office, hoping he would do something, but I never heard from him."

"Do you remember who the lawyer was?"

"Some guy in Paterson. But I heard he died." Gonzalez turned to look at Liliana. "Remember Mrs. Smith's class? She had that old water fountain right next to your classroom. I remember you, Ms. Liliana. You drank out of that fountain. And I remember how sick you were."

Liliana put her head down. "And I remember you, too, Mr. Gonzalez. You used to give us candy. You gave it to me and my friend, Evan. Evan died."

"That water, that water had a terrible smell to it. It looked clear but it smelled like rotten eggs."

Garland took the box away from Gonzalez and placed it on the conference table. He started looking at the yellow papers. As his fingers ran through the papers, he pulled a random sheet and began to read it. His eyes widened. His heart raced. "Ms. Ramos, can you step out of the room for a minute?"

"Sure." The two left the conference room.

Out in the hallway, Garland showed her the paper in his hand. "Liliana, this is huge. The death of that lawyer, the water."

"Enlighten me."

"Look at this." He handed her the paper. "This is a letter from the Department of Environmental Protection in 1986. It was written to the principal of the school, Robert Van Marcherz. Unbelievable. This guy was put on notice that the water system needed a filter in 1986. They were pumping water directly from the Passaic River into the school's water system, and without the filter, the water was dangerous. Jesus, look what that water was contaminated with. Hexavalent chromium, PCBs. These things are carcinogenic. I mean, look at this stuff." His eyes met hers. "I'm so sorry. No wonder people got sick and died."

Garland's mind raced. *Teo and Don Julio were right. Teo's nephew was onto this cover-up, and that's why they killed him.*

"Liliana, this is much bigger than I thought. There are things I have to explain to you. Right now, we have a real problem. Our strongest witness is sitting in the conference room talking to a squirrel."

"I think we have a really good case here. Fergal maybe crazy, but he isn't stupid. Even if the people who wrote these papers are dead, we have an official government record."

"We need to get back in there and figure out what else he knows."

The two returned to the conference room and found the atmosphere somewhat lighter. Pete and Gonzalez were engaged in a conversation. Whatever they were discussing, it appeared to make Gonzalez less anxious.

"Fergal, look who returned. Our attorneys are back." Pete smiled. "Did you know that Fergal and I were in Vietnam at the same time? Probably passed each other on night patrols."

"They gave me a Purple Heart for being shot at," Gonzalez announced proudly.

"Me too, Fergal. You know what? My man Fergal got into a bit of a scrap with Principal Van Marcherz. Tell her about it, brother."

Gonzalez shook his head. "Van Marcherz was a bum. I told him that the children came to me. I told him that I was worried about the water. He threatened me. So I hit him with a mop, and next thing you know, I am fired and in a mental institution."

Pete slapped him on the back. "No worries, my friend. I would have done the same thing to Van Marcherz. Except I would have slammed him on the back of the head with my Beretta." Pete looked at the squirrel, who was still poking his head out from under Gonzalez's armpit. "Isn't that right, Señor Pepe?"

The squirrel squeaked in response.

Gonzalez smiled. "Señor Pepe agrees."

CHAPTER TWENTY-FIVE

Village du St. Moritz
Luxury Retirement Community
St. Petersburg, Florida

In order to reopen the investigation into the death of Julio Lopez, Pete O'Connell would also have to look into the circumstances surrounding the environmental problems of P.S. 578. The two events were related. He knew that he needed to start digging into the past. Most of police work is about people and evidence; on a thirty-year-old case, this would be a difficult task. Witnesses die, the living ones don't want to get involved or their memories have faded, and documents get lost or destroyed.

Ina agreed to send Pete to St. Petersburg, Florida to pay a visit to Detective Ted Klagborn, the retired detective who had handled—and closed—the homicide investigation of Julio Lopez.

Prior to flying out, he had done a little background research into his retired colleague. What he found was most curious.

For a man living off a public pension of eighty thousand dollars a year, the retired detective owned a million-dollar condominium right on the Vinoy Resort and Golf Club in St. Petersburg. He drove a brand new Mercedes E class sedan, which he upgraded yearly. Klagborn had recently returned from several vacations—a month in Aruba, a month in Sardinia, and a mere three weeks in a villa on the isle of Santorini. When O'Connell made the phone call to set up the appointment, Klagborn bragged that he had just blown five thousand dollars at a Texas Hold 'em poker table at the Venetian Casino in Las Vegas.

It didn't make much sense. O'Connell knew a cop could have a comfortable retirement, particularly if he had been working side businesses while simultaneously making sound financial investments. But Klagborn? It seemed he was doing a little too well for being a thirty-year retiree. He wished that he could have looked at his bank records, but without a subpoena and an active investigation into Klagborn as a suspect, this wasn't possible.

Pete prided himself on being able to sell snow to polar bears, but he was about to stir up trouble from a long-dead event. Klagborn had already told him that the case was closed and that he had no further or different information. He was amazed that Klagborn was willing to speak to him at all.

*   *   *   *

He picked up a comfortable sedan at an Enterprise rental car service. Klagborn lived in what he called a small cottage in the Snell Isle section of St. Petersburg on the Vinoy Golf Club. O'Connell knew that the "cottage" was, in fact, a luxury condominium which backed up to the golf course. From St. Pete-Clearwater International Airport, it was a fifteen-minute drive without traffic to Klagborn's house. But for whatever reason, traffic was backed up on Coffee Pot Boulevard, and a fifteen-minute ride turned into forty-five minutes with frequent traffic stops.

He pulled up in front of an elegant condo on Northeast Boulevard. The investigator was a little uncomfortable about this interview. He may be implicating another cop in wrongdoing, and he hated that thought. But O'Connell knew he had a job to do, and that was that. He had been around long enough to know that the blue brotherhood was always true, even at times when it shouldn't be.

He rang the doorbell to Klagborn's condo. Sounds rang out like the peals of Westminster Abbey announcing the New Year. A small, thin man peered through a clear glass triangle on an ornate stained-glass door. O'Connell flashed his badge. The man nodded and smiled. O'Connell heard a series of sliding bolts and locks before the door opened fully.

"Detective Klagborn?"

"Used to be. Now I'm just Mr. Klagborn. Please come in. Call me Ted."

Theodore Klagborn stood about five foot five. He was a slight man with a voice that should have belonged to a man over six feet tall rather than a man who weighed a hundred and ten pounds soaking wet. He was about the same age as O'Connell, but a much less physically fit version with salt-and-pepper hair. Standing in the doorway of Klagborn's house, O'Connell had a straight view into a large kitchen where he saw a tall, long-legged woman dressed in a black mini skirt with a matching tank top and platform sandals. She hovered over several pots that were boiling away on the stove, flipping back long bleached blond locks each time she stirred a pot or wiped down a kitchen counter.

She looked between thirty-five and forty, a far cry from Klagborn's tired-looking sixty-eight.

O'Connell looked at Klagborn and smiled. "Remind me to get the name of your maid service."

Klagborn laughed. "Oh, that's actually Arelia, my wife. Adorable, isn't she?"

"She's lovely. How long—"

"Only five years. I was a widower, you know. A man gets lonely. We met online, one of those internet things. A short courtship, then a quick trip to the courthouse. She was a model in Venezuela. So I made her my wife."

And I bet she needed to get out of Venezuela, so she found herself a stupid rich old white guy. Pretty smart girl. Klagborn must be sucking down Viagra by the gallon to keep this girl happy, he thought to himself.

The blond came out of the kitchen and smiled. "Hello. Lunch will be ready shortly." With a polite nod, she returned to the stove.

"Nice girl, Ted. Best of luck to both of you. Listen, I don't want to take up too much of your time."

"Oh please, Pete. I'm retired. All I have is time. Shall we have a little taste before lunch?"

"And why not? A little scotch on the rocks would be great, if it isn't too much trouble."

"Wonderful. Let's get started then, shall we? Arelia, my love!" he yelled to her in the kitchen. "We men would like a little scotch, which we will take in the sunroom."

O'Connell watched Arelia's reaction. "Yes, my darling, right awa-a-y." He observed that the tone of her voice was both sweet and sarcastic.

O'Connell was directed to a small sitting room. It was bright and sunny, lots of chrome and glass tables reminiscent of a 1970s décor with a modern touch. He found himself comfortable on a wicker couch with overstuffed, large velvet pillows. Part of O'Connell was impressed by Klagborn's living quarters.

"I must admit, Pete, I was a bit surprised to hear that the murder investigation I closed thirty years ago has been reopened. It was an open and shut case, really. Case closed."

"Total transparency, Ted. I work for The People's Clinic in Newark, where they basically provide free legal services for the poor—"

"Right, one of those liberal outfits run by do-gooders..."

O'Connell ignored the insult and played into his ego. "What can I say, Teddy? I'm retired and it's a paycheck. But just so you know, the homicide investigation hasn't been reopened, not yet, anyway. But that's the problem. It isn't so open and shut. We believe that we have evidence suggesting that Julio Lopez was onto a fraud involving the municipality, and he was killed."

O'Connell noticed a very small twitch in Klagborn's paper thin upper lip. For decades, O'Connell had been a patient student of human behavior. He studied witnesses and criminals, their eyes, their facial expressions, and their head movements. Movement, the body's immediate reaction to words or situations, meant a person was either telling the truth or lying. He kept a passive yet steady gaze at Klagborn.

"You see, we obtained some records indicating that there were some environmental problems that may have caused a cancer cluster at P.S. 578."

O'Connell looked at Klagborn's lip...*twitch*...*twitch*...*twitch*. His lips tightened and then he replied, "You don't say."

"Wish I didn't have to say, really."

"So are you reopening the homicide?"

"Not yet, but—"

"As far as I am concerned, this is a closed matter. When I find a man covered head to toe in cocaine, lying dead in a pool of blood, well that's the end of my investigation. He overdosed. Plain and simple. The coroner, Dr. Meadowloc, thought so."

Nobody mentioned finding his body in a pool of blood, he thought to himself. *In fact, this is the first I'm hearing of it.*

"Yeah, Dr. Meadowloc. Tried to talk to him, but the old boy has one foot in the grave and the other on a banana peel. He lives at Green Fields nursing home. And he's in a coma."

"Oh. Too bad."

"Yeah, right. So you never looked for any suspects, right? Who was first on the scene in the Lopez homicide?"

"I was with a couple of uniforms. I was off duty when the call came in, but when I heard it was Lopez, I decided to lead the investigation myself."

"Why?"

"Well, I knew of him. He was the local ambulance chaser, always representing people against the police and the county. He was a young guy, a young guy with a big mouth."

"Doesn't sound like you liked him very much."

"None of us did."

"But he certainly didn't deserve to be murdered."

"It was suicide. He wasn't murdered. Oh look, here comes our scotch."

Arelia entered the room holding a large sterling silver serving tray. She rested it atop a glass-top table, much to her husband's annoyance. O'Connell watched as she turned to her husband and gently handed him the first glass. Klagborn bristled.

"Watch that glass table. I just bought that for you. What's wrong with you? Where are your manners, Arelia? Serve my friend here first."

"I am sorry. Mr. O'Connell, may I serve you?"

O'Connell looked at Mrs. Klagborn. He looked at her tanned arms and noticed what appeared to be finger marks, like someone had grabbed her arm and twisted it. O'Connell looked at Arelia, then looked back at Klagborn.

"Arelia, did you bump into something? What happened to your arm?"

O'Connell watched Klagborn's upper lip...*twitch...twitch... twitch.*

There was an unsettling nonverbal exchange between O'Connell and Arelia. He knew the expression of women who had suffered from domestic violence. Then she spoke. "I was cleaning and then I, how do you say it in English," she stammered trying to find the correct translation, "I bumped, yes, I bumped into the wall. It is nothing, really."

O'Connell glared at Klagborn, trying to contain his disgust. "Amazing how a wall can just jump out in front of you." He reached for the scotch. O'Connell shook his head. "So, where were we? Yes. How did he wind up in the basement of P.S. 578? If it was a 'suicide,' why did he decide to douse himself in cocaine in the basement of an elementary school? You know, the elementary school where half the second grade class died of cancer, and the county tried to cover up its water problem. Isn't that where you found the body back in '88?" O'Connell watched as Klagborn's eyes shifted to the left to avoid direct contact with his own.

"Yeah, that's right, I think that's where I found the body. Look, it was the eighties. Murders in Passaic County were...I mean Jesus Christ, it was a zoo. Bodies were dropping on the streets back then like bird shit falling from the sky. I don't know what you're expecting me to say. What are you looking for?"

"The truth, that's all." He drank the entire glass of scotch in one gulp. "We've just discovered that P.S. 578 probably covered up some of its environmental problems in order to save money. The savings came at the cost of children's lives. But hey, it was an inner city school and no one probably gave a damn anyway."

"So what does this have to do with me?"

"Nothing, really. But you handled the murder case of Julio Lopez, and he was investigating the Riverwood Water Authority. And look what happened. The poor bastard turns up dead. I just thought that you may have had a hunch that perhaps Julio Lopez's death wasn't a suicide. I was just looking for information, that's all."

"Sorry my friend, I have told you all I know." He yelled to his wife in the kitchen. "Arelia, where's our lunch?" O'Connell noticed that Klagborn's friendly demeanor was fading fast. He felt sure that his poor Venezuelan wife would be taking the brunt of Klagborn's hostility once O'Connell walked out the door.

"You know, Ted, I have some other people to see while I'm in St. Petersburg, so I think I just may pass on lunch, if you don't mind."

"You sure? We have plenty of food." The tone of Klagborn's voice sounded almost relieved. "Arelia makes a mean Cuban sandwich but just Venezuelan style."

"Sounds delicious, but I am afraid that I'm going to have to go."

"Let me show you to the door." Klagborn quickly rose to his feet and made idle chatter about his latest golf game and his next planned vacation. O'Connell politely responded about his own plans, which involved a trip to Disneyland with grandchildren. As O'Connell stood in the doorway, Klagborn made one final statement.

"Pete, you and I both know that as cops we see things that we shouldn't—and don't see things that we should. I think you should let the whole Lopez thing go. It's been over thirty years. Why do you want to resurrect something that's dead?"

O'Connell smiled. "Well, what's that old saying? The dead travel fast? Or was it Stephen King who wrote, 'Sometimes they come back.' But thanks for the scotch."

Klagborn placed his hand on O'Connell's arm. "You really should let this one go, brother."

"Can't make you any promises. This is a civil matter at this point. But who knows where my investigation may take me? You know how investigations go. Take care, my friend. I must come back for that sandwich sometime." The two retired detectives shook hands, and Klagborn closed the door behind O'Connell.

* * * *

When he was sure his visitor was in his car and far away, Klagborn raced over to a small table and picked up a cell phone. He frantically dialed a number, his palms dripping with perspiration.

When a male voice at the other end of the phone answered, Klagborn grit his teeth.

"Hello. Yeah, it's me. You told me that I would never be caught up in this. Now I got some retired cop chasing me down in Florida. Keep me out of this mess. I am not going down alone on this. No matter how much you pay me!"

He hung up. Then he ran into a nearby bathroom and grabbed a towel to dry his hands. As he walked toward the kitchen he began yelling, "Arelia! It's after one o'clock already. What the hell is taking you so long? I'm starving."

CHAPTER TWENTY-SIX

Home of Nicholas Nowell
Fairlawn, New Jersey

Everything in Garland's life could be summed up in one word—stress.

    When Garland arrived home, he immediately went upstairs to the small room where Don Julio lived. Trying to manage the life of the uncooperative fly made his palms sweat. He was very concerned about the fly's increasing size and his ability to keep him hidden from prying eyes.

    Work was also eating away at him. He was working for free, living in his father's house, and living off the twenty thousand dollars he had received from selling his ex-fiancée's ring. The money was running out. It was actually *costing* him to volunteer at The People's Clinic. As if this weren't enough, now it appeared that the newly discovered evidence implicated Liliana's old school not only in a massive toxic tort case, but the reopening of a thirty-year-old homicide. Garland was both fascinated and terrified at the same time. When he opened the door to the room where he hid Don Julio, he was amused by what he saw.

    His father's girlfriend had left a rundown Barbie doll camper in the vacant bedroom on the second floor. Don Julio had removed the doll furniture from the camper and arranged it on a large sunny windowsill. He opened a tiny sun umbrella with the word "CinZano" written all over it. He put together a makeshift picnic table. Sitting on the table was a bottle cap carefully filled with a mixture of water and honey. A large black fly had its shiny head partially stuck inside the bottle cap. The fly made buzzing noises while Julio sipped a clear fluid from a pink plastic Barbie doll martini glass.

    It was *Saturday Night Fever* revisited.

    Julio was dressed in a white three-piece suit with a black shirt. His feet were covered in white platform shoes. A small gold chain with a map of Cuba dangled from his neck. He sat crossed-legged in a portable camping chair. The look on the fly's face was one of joy.

"Julio, nice suit. Trying out for Disco King tonight? John Travolta would be proud."

Don Julio waved a leg at him. "Please don't be jealous. I look good, eh? I introduce to you Miss Yvette. She is from the Camargue, a beautiful marshland near Arles, France. A most talented lady! She is fluent in French, Spanish, and *Domesticus,* which is the universal fly language. A virtual linguist, who knew?"

"Jesus Christ, you're going to kill me." He slapped his palm against his head. It left a red mark on his forehead. "You're flirting with some strange French fly. Is this what you do when I go to work? What if she's a carrier of disease?"

The black fly, who had been gently sucking down the fluid in the bottle cap through an appendage called a "proboscis," stopped what it was doing. It rose up in the air and dove straight for Garland's neck and bit him.

"Ouch, dammit!" He started blindly swatting the air. After buzzing around Garland's head, the black fly flew out of the room.

"Look what you did!" Don Julio threw down the martini glass. A few drops of clear liquid spilled out of the little plastic glass as it bounced across the windowsill. "You insulted her. You called her a disease carrier and now she left."

"Who cares? Your little crepe suzette bit me!"

Julio began to pace. The sound of his platform shoes made little clicks each time he took a step on the wooden windowsill.

"Why do you hate me?"

"I don't hate you."

"You are killing my sex life." He threw himself back in a chair. "She was a Blandford Fly, straight out of the marshlands of the Camargue, smuggled in with a piece of candy tucked in a vintage Chanel suit. And she was no ordinary housefly. I have been giving her honey and water all morning, sweet talking her until you came along. And I was just about to make love to her until you pissed her off and made her fly away." He flew out of the chair and hovered in front of Garland's face.

"Why don't you find yourself a girlfriend? What about that nice young lawyer at The People's Clinic? Maybe you need some love, eh?"

Garland smiled and spoke softly. "Liliana, her name is Liliana."

"Yes, very good, amigo. Now why don't you take up with her and leave me to amuse myself?"

Garland sat down. "Julio, we need to talk. Teo was right."

"Teo always thinks he's right about everything."

"No, listen to me. A client came in to the office. He was an older guy who was a janitor at P.S. 578. He had papers dating back to 1988." Garland leaned forward. "Julio, they knew. Those bastards knew. The school and the Riverwood Water Authority pumped contaminated water directly into the school's water system without a filter. They were warned, but to save money, they did it anyway. Now we have the documents to prove it. And I think Teo's nephew died for it."

"You think that Teo's nephew *did* know about the poisoned water?"

"Yes. A copy of the documents was dropped off at his law firm anonymously back in 1988. Then suddenly Teo's nephew dies. His death was written off as a suicide. But the next day Julio Lopez's office was burglarized. The only thing taken was a computer and a copy of the box of documents now in our possession. The documents? Memoranda and letters warning the principal about the contamination of the water pumped into to P.S. 578."

Julio made the sign of the cross with all his legs but the two he stood upon. "Does Teo know this? You know he will seek revenge. He has to."

"Julio, this isn't a blood feud. And the revenge we will seek will be through the court system when we sue the school, the principal, and any government agency that knew about this and did nothing. Then we'll approach the county Prosecutor's Office and talk about reopening the homicide investigation."

"I wish I were in human form. I would curse the killers myself. They would wake up with warts, boils, and disease. We have no time for the courts."

"What are you talking about?"

"Amigo, the Blood Moon is coming. We must act quickly."

"Is this about that little meeting we had at the college? Because I want to be clear—I don't want to be part of whatever club they belong to, Julio. Not interested. They can do their Voodoo, magic, witchcraft without me."

"They don't need you for the work they do. We just have to resolve this case before the Blood Moon or else."

"Or else what?"

"That's the problem. I don't know what. Isabel is dangerous. She would have no problem killing you. Her powers will be strongest at the Blood Moon, which is three days from now."

"I thought she was a giant spider? What is she going to do? Wrap me in her web and suck the blood out of me?"

"You never know."

He sighed. "Julio, look, I don't have time for this right now. Let's talk later. I'm going out tonight."

"Where are you going?"

"Out."

"Who's going with you?"

"No one."

"What time will you be home?"

"Don't know."

Julio began twirling his moustache. "You have a date with a woman tonight, yes?"

"None of your business."

"It's that young lawyer, isn't it? Ms. Liliana?"

"See you later, Julio. I have to take a shower and then I'm out of here." He winked at the fly. "That style suit is over forty years old. My father wore a suit like that. A little old fashioned, don't you think?"

"This suit is a classic. You are just jealous because only a special kind of man can wear it."

Garland laughed. "But you aren't a man, are you?"

Julio twirled his moustache again. "No, amigo, not yet."

*   *   *   *

Garland felt nervous. It had only been several weeks since he had met Liliana. Everything around him was moving at a rapid pace. To occupy lonely nights, he had his share of Bumble, Tinder, and Match.com after he and Sissy Blackwood had broken up. Garland was sick of uncomfortable online conversations, and women who misrepresented their age by posting a picture that was fifteen years younger than they were in real life.

But Liliana intrigued him. She was real. A thoughtful and intelligent woman, yet in many ways her persona was simple and uncomplicated. What impressed him about Liliana was how kindhearted she was. She treated The People's Clinic's clients as though they were wealthy executives employed by a multi-million-dollar corporation rather than poor people who could not afford to hire legal counsel. Liliana cared deeply for the indigent people she served.

Thoughts of Liliana made Garland's heart soften. He found himself wanting to protect her from something, though he didn't know what that something was. At work, he gave her quick affectionate glances over the water cooler when she wasn't looking in his direction. Garland enjoyed the limited time they spent together, whether it was collaborating with Liliana on cases or chatting with her over a sandwich during lunch. They had dinner once in a great while, but these were business dinners usually in the presence of investigators or other colleagues at The People's Clinic.

Years ago, he learned that a man should never play where he works. But for some reason with Liliana he would make the exception. It took him quite a bit of time to finally get up the nerve to ask her out on an official date. Garland was pleasantly surprised when she said yes.

*   *   *   *

The last few weeks at The People's Clinic had been exhausting with long nights and broken sleep. This had been going on for a month.

At one point, Liliana asked Ina if she could work at home for a few days, from Wednesday to Friday. Ina agreed as long as she had no court appearances and could respond to emails. Liliana found that when she worked from home, she was able to clear her head from interruptions by telephones that never stopped ringing.

Besides dealing with the office's landlord-tenant issues and the run-of-the-mill juvenile drug possession cases, Liliana devoted the lion's share of her day to researching the organizational structures of the public entities possibly involved in the 1988 cover-up at P.S. 578. The box of documents had proven to be most helpful in explaining how the contaminated water got into the school, then eventually into the bloodstreams of its students.

What she read was both sad and shocking.

Prior to his tenure as the school's principal, Van Marcherz had been a physical education teacher and head of the sports program. Memoranda provided by the former janitor showed Van Marcherz lamenting to the past principal about the lack of sufficient athletic equipment. He didn't seem to understand that the bottled water needed for the schoolchildren was more important than new basketballs. Bottled water had been provided to P.S. 578 since 1975. No one ever asked why.

Principal Van Marcherz had been contacted by the New Jersey Department of Environmental Protection to alert him of the need for proper water filtration in P.S. 578. Contaminants from the Passaic River water caused by industrial pollution since the early 1900s had not been addressed by the government or the polluters. The water was dangerous, yet through old pipes it had made its way into P.S. 578. Letters written by various government authorities explained that a filter would be needed to prevent ingestion of contaminants in the school's drinking water. He had been *warned*.

Van Marcherz simply chose to ignore the warnings, then paid a private environmental company to test limited water samples. Of course, Van Marcherz received the answer he wanted: the water met acceptable standards and therefore, no filtration system was needed. With the money saved by not filtering the water, Van Marcherz diverted money toward his own pet projects.

As she read each document, her heart ached. Memories of her childhood made her suffer. She recalled the days after a chemotherapy infusion when she thought she would never stop throwing up. She remembered holding her mother's hand as they walked up to her classmates' caskets. It seemed like she and her mother attended a funeral every other week for years. What upset her the most was the vivid memory of Mr. Gonzalez removing the desks from Mrs. Smith's classroom each time a child died.

She tried not to let sadness get to her. She carried with her so much guilt. Why did she survive and not the other children? Why was she special? When she found herself getting emotional, she spoke with Ina. Her mentor comforted her like a mother. Then matter-of-factly, Ina explained that the best way of getting over horrible things in life was to get past them and live well.

"Money cannot make up for death or illness, dearest. It can't. Lives are lost, medical illness interferes with your ability to do certain things in your life. It's time you can never get back," she stated. "Even Napoleon, the little corporal, once said, 'Land I can regain, but time never'. But your revenge will come in a different way. You will take them to court and take every dime from these people," Ina ordered. "The only thing that hurts companies and people who engage in heinous acts is a good stab to their bank accounts. Bleeding dollar bills and bad publicity hurts them, dearest. Success is the best revenge, as is making the future better for others."

She lit up a cigarette. A smoke ring formed around her head like a halo surrounding a saint, and she grinned. "Now let's go get the bastards."

Liliana drafted a civil complaint that would make heads spin at the government agencies. It was a masterpiece of legal writing. And she made sure that Van Marcherz's name, the man largely responsible for this whole mess, was prominently displayed as the first defendant in the caption of the complaint. She saved the complaint on her computer, then emailed it to Ina for final approval before they would electronically file in Passaic County Court.

Ina was right. Success would be her revenge.

Glancing down at the cellphone on her desk, she saw that it was nearly eight thirty. She realized she had to get ready because Garland would be at her front door any minute. Time to end her work day. Time for some fun.

She ran into the bathroom to freshen her makeup. A buzzer rang and the concierge announced the arrival of Garland Nowell. Her heart fluttered a bit, and she wasn't sure why. After all, she saw him every day, five days a week. Why was she suddenly struck with butterflies in her stomach? It was only dinner. Deep inside she knew the truth. She had romantic feelings.

The doorbell rang. Liliana fluffed her hair and prepared to greet Garland with a big smile as she opened the door.

A tall man wearing a large black Amish-style hat stood in her doorway. His hair was shoulder length with blond and gray streaks. His face was thin and angular with a sharp aquiline nose. Were it not for the skin covering his face, he could have been a walking skeleton. His eyes were deep, hollow, and empty. A scarf was tied around his bony neck. He wore a black shirt and a long black leather trench coat.

Liliana noticed that his left shoulder had a large lump that became more prominent as he leaned over her. The ambient light in the hallway of her condominium was soft, but she was aware that the lump on the man's shoulder was not only large, but it also *moved*.

Liliana stood back. "Yes?"

The man smiled, displaying large spaces between cigarette-stained teeth. "You are near perfect. You must be the lawyer. The one working on the case of P.S. 578."

She wasted no time. "What I do is none of your business." Then it clicked—she had seen him before. "You...I saw you outside on the street. Who the hell are you?"

"A friend, or perhaps even sooner...a lover." He raised a hand and tried to touch her cheek. She slapped his hand and tried to slam the door in his face.

"Get away from me!"

The dark shadow that had been moving back and forth moved closer into the light. The last thing Liliana saw before blacking out was a set of large fangs lunging toward her throat.

* * * *

Garland was running late. By the time he had parked his car in a Newark garage near Liliana's condominium and made it over to her building, it was nearly nine o'clock. Liliana lived in a newly developed building, which was formerly Hahne and Co. The building had been established as a department store in 1858 and had barely survived the Newark riots during the sixties before it closed in 1987. A developer with an imagination created a mixed use building on the property with apartments, dry cleaners, and an organic food store. Garland walked up to a rotund security guard, who glanced back and forth between his cellphone and a glossy fishing magazine. For the most part he was oblivious to his surroundings as people walked in and out of the Hahne complex.

Garland tapped on the desk. "Hi. Good evening. Apartment 7A. Liliana Ramos. I'm expected."

The rotund, disinterested African-American security guard looked at Garland then pointed to a log book. "Sign in and I will announce you. Name?"

"Garland Nowell."

The man's eyes widened. "What? Show me some identification."

"Why?"

The guard grew indignant. "Because, sir, you were just here. I just let you up to her apartment."

Garland's heart raced. "Here, take it." He reached in his wallet and threw his driver's license at the guard. "You need to let me up to that apartment. I need to see if she's okay. *I'm* Garland Nowell."

The guard looked at the license, then looked back at Garland. He picked up a two-way radio. "Eddie, you need to get off break and cover the desk." The expression on the guard's face changed. "Come with me."

The two men rushed into the elevator. Garland grew more and more tense as a robotic voice announced the elevator's arrival at each individual floor. When the elevator doors finally opened on the seventh floor, Garland bolted out of the elevator. Without thinking, he ran off to the right.

"Wrong way, sir. Apartment 7A is on the left side of the building."

Garland turned in the direction of Liliana's apartment. Though he was moving fast, the security guard jumped ahead of him and put his arm up to block Garland from moving in any closer. For someone who was overweight, Garland noticed that the security guard was light on his feet.

"Stop. Her door is open. You don't know who's behind that door. Let me go in first, sir," he stated as he unholstered a gun.

"You're carrying?"

"Yeah, I'm an off-duty Newark cop."

"Good to know. What's your name?"

"Tumbler, Officer Otto Tumbler."

The freshly painted door to Liliana's apartment was open ever so slightly. Officer Tumbler put his index finger to his lips to silence Garland. He gently pushed the door open wide with his fingertips as he drew his gun. Officer Tumbler called out, "Ms. Ramos, you in here? Hello? Ms. Ramos?"

The security guard passed over the threshold and entered the dining room. He called out again for Liliana. "Ms. Ramos? You alright? Hello?" The men searched the apartment. He turned to Garland. "She's not here."

"Officer, something is wrong. We had a date tonight."

"Okay, man, I understand. I need to call this in." Tumbler pulled out his cell phone and called 911.

Garland was in shock. He feared the worst. "The guy who claimed he was me. What did he look like?"

"The fake Garland Nowell? Tall, skinny, large black hat and trench coat. You were kind of creepy looking. Don't go anywhere. The police will want to talk to you."

"Officer, does this place have security cameras?"

"Yes. Let's go take a look, Mr. Nowell."

The two men left the apartment and took the elevator to the basement. They entered a small office packed with computers and security equipment.

"The days of the old camcorders and videotapes are over. We keep everything digital. We should see something." He sat down in front of a keyboard and typed in the date and time. A computer screen opened up and ran the recorded footage from eight o'clock to nine o'clock.

At 8:40, Garland saw what he feared. His heart raced.

The digital footage showed a tall figure with a black brimmed hat and black trench coat entering the building. The figure approached the security desk. Both men watched as a disinterested security officer directed the figure to sign his name in the logbook without looking up.

Officer Tumbler paused the footage and pointed to the screen. "What the hell is on his shoulder? I don't remember seeing that thing when he came in."

Garland hesitated. "Gee, I don't know. Kinda looks like a big rubber spider. That guy must be some kind of a weirdo." He laughed nervously. "I mean, what kind of a jerk walks around dressed in black with a huge rubber spider on his shoulder, right?"

Officer Tumbler shrugged. "Takes all kinds, my friend. Let's look at the rest of the footage."

The men watched as the figure turned the corner and entered the elevator. The footage in the elevator showed the individual with his head down and the brim of his hat covering his face.

"See that right there? That guy knows he's being watched on camera, that's why he's got his head down," said Officer Tumbler. A voice came over his two-way radio. He picked it up and began talking. "Okay, okay. I have the guy right here. No, he isn't the one who kidnapped her. He's her, um, boyfriend, I guess."

Garland swallowed. *Boyfriend? I'll go with that. But kidnapped? My God. What have I gotten her into?* he thought. *I have to get to Teo.*

"Yeah, I'm her boyfriend. Finish the recording."

Both men watched as the black hat knocked on her door. They saw a brief exchange as Liliana attempted to push him away and slam the door in his face. Then without warning, the "rubber" spider jumped from the black hat's shoulder and lunged at Liliana. After making contact with Liliana, she dropped to the floor. The black hat bent down and scooped her up. The spider moved back onto the black hat's shoulder. Carrying Liliana in his arms, he moved quickly to the nearest fire exit and left the seventh floor.

The recording ended. The next frame on the recording was black-and-white static.

"Are you kidding me?" Garland exclaimed. "That's it? There has to be more!"

"Look, this place was only built last year. The building manager hasn't set up the cameras in the fire exits yet. But there are police officers scouring the building inside and out. If she's in the area, we'll find her. We have cameras in the parking garage and surrounding areas. There has to be something."

"I hope so before it's too late."

Tumbler quickly began adjusting his surveillance equipment. "Here's the footage from the parking garage." He paused, then asked, "She have any family?"

"Not that I know of. I can't believe this is happening."

"You know the black hat?"

"Never saw him before in my life. Who does this kind of stuff?"

"Whoever it is knows about you and her. Remember, he identified himself as Garland Nowell to get to her. Are you involved with drugs? Any bad people who have it in for you?"

"No, no. Nothing like that. Liliana and I work together at The People's Free Legal Clinic here in Newark. It's a legal aid clinic for the poor."

"She do any criminal defense?"

"Minor stuff. Not drug kingpins. But she and I are working on an environmental case that may have serious repercussions for a local municipality."

Officer Tumbler looked thoughtful as he spoke. "Maybe somebody on the other side of that case wants to stop the litigation. You'd better be careful." Officer Tumbler looked at the screen. "Okay, here's the footage of the garage."

Another computer screen popped up. The screen showed the black hat carrying an unconscious Liliana in his arms. He starting walking toward a big white van. Without warning he stopped in his tracks. Slowly he turned. The scarf around his neck covered his nose and mouth. Empty, dead-looking eyes looked into the camera, and then the screen went from completely black to static.

"What about the license plate on the van? What about the van?"

Tumbler returned to the keyboard and hit multiple buttons. "I don't understand this. This is a brand new system. There shouldn't be any breaks in the footage. The recorded footage between the time black hat looked at the camera and entered the van isn't here. Just static. I got nothing. He's gone."

Garland slammed his fist on the table in frustration. "I have to go."

"You need to stay and be interviewed by the police."

"If they want to talk, they can call me." Garland threw his business card on the desk. "I'm leaving. You know where to find me."

CHAPTER TWENTY-SEVEN

Garland drove back to his house and picked up clothes and Don Julio. He tossed the Barbie doll-sized fly in the back seat of his Ford Fiesta. He had already called Teo to let him know that he would be having two houseguests on the couch overnight.

While Garland was drowning in his own thoughts, he noticed that the usually chatty fly was strangely quiet. He sniffed the air and smelled the familiar scent of tobacco. As he looked in the rearview mirror, he saw that Julio was puffing away on a small cigar. He shook his head. Don Julio had changed out of his white disco suit and now wore a guayabera shirt, shorts, and a Panama hat.

"You okay back there? Where did you get the cigar?"

"While your father was out with his woman, I raided his carton of cigarettes and…borrowed…a few pieces of tobacco." He waved the tiny cigar in the air. "Not quite a Cohiba, but it was the best I could do with your cheap American tobacco. And listen to me. I have a very bad feeling about all of this, very bad."

"That makes two of us. Whoever this Isabel is, she has Liliana."

"Isabel couldn't have done it alone."

"She didn't, I saw it on the recording the security officer showed me. Do you know anybody who wears a big black hat and trench coat? Maybe somebody from that bunch of witches or a magician from Edward Williams College?"

"No, amigo, despite what you may think, they are not bad people. As far as the universe goes, they are keeping the balance of good."

"So what can we do? The police don't know where to start looking and neither do I."

"Teo is a psychic. Perhaps he can sense where she is."

"Yeah, great. I have to rely on santeros, witches, and a talking fly. I thought my life was depressing before I met you. Now look at it."

"But you are not alone in this. You have me."

"How are you going to fight an Amazonian spider the size of a dinner plate?"

214

"I fight because I have faith." The fly flicked his cigar ashes on the back seat of Garland's car to irritate him. "Do you believe in God?"

"No. I'm an atheist."

"Ay Dios mío! Do you believe in love?"

"No. Well, maybe, I don't know."

"Take my advice. You need to believe in something. Because if you do not, it could kill you."

CHAPTER TWENTY-EIGHT

Home of Teofil Lopez
Ocean Grove, New Jersey

By the time Garland and Don Julio arrived at Teo's house, the old santero had salmon fillets, rice and beans, and a chopped avocado salad waiting for them. He opened the door. When he saw Garland, he reached out and embraced him.

"Please, Garland. Don't worry. We'll find her. Now come in and relax. Eat."

Garland's eyes pleaded with Teo. "The Newark police keep calling me. I don't think they can even find her. For all I know, she could be dead."

"I feel that she is not dead, not yet. Be strong. We will do what no one else can. This is a much larger battle than you think."

They sat around a comfortable dining room table. Teo prepared a small plate for Don Julio, who had brought a tiny knife, fork, and spoon from the Barbie doll camper. The table was quiet as Teo passed food around. Not a word was spoken until Don Julio broke the silence.

"Damn, I've seen more life in a morgue." He looked at Teo. "What's the plan? We have to do something and do it fast. By the way, the salmon steak is seasoned well, but it is a little too dry."

"You are never content." Teo shook his head. Looking directly at Garland, he took a deep breath. "Isabel's time in this world is fading. She needs a new life force. That is why she took your woman. She needs a new body."

Garland dropped his fork. "And how is she going to get one?"

"The dangerous ritual of *anima mutatis mutanda*—soul switching. Isabel removes the soul of your woman and places it inside the spider. Isabel then takes over Liliana's body, her knowledge, and her life. Liliana's spirit becomes trapped inside the spider. That is what I did to Isabel many years ago. For her, it was meant to be a one-way

trip into the Amazon. That kind of soul switching can be reversed."
He sighed. "But then there is the other kind."

"And what would that be?"

"She takes over Liliana's body without soul switching. The spider dies but first she has to—"

"Kill Liliana." Garland finished the sentence. "I won't let that happen. I would rather die first. So what do we do?"

"Before Dr. Meadowloc, the man who lied on my nephew's autopsy, died," he said, clenching a fist, "the old man muttered two words: 'school' and 'Van Marcherz.' That is where we start."

"So are you suggesting that we pay a little visit to Principal Van Marcherz?" asked Don Julio.

"We don't," stated Garland. "But I know who can."

CHAPTER TWENTY-NINE

Bomb Shelter
Basement of P.S. 578

The air around her was cold but still had the musty smell of moss and dampness. Her head pounded and she felt feverish. The right side of her neck throbbed. The young woman wanted to reach out and touch it but quickly realized that her hands were tied behind her back, and her feet were bound at the ankles. She heard a familiar buzzing sound, and there was the slightest trickle of warm air circulating around her feet.

Sounds like the old heater in my office, she thought. *Where the hell am I?*

She opened her eyes and saw nothing but darkness. She struggled with the ropes tying her hands and feet, but it was no use. Wherever she was, she was trapped. She resigned herself, at least temporarily, to sit quietly until she could figure a way out of this prison.

In the distance, she heard footsteps and a man's voice softly humming. She screamed, "Help! Help! Someone help me, please!"

Something silently lowered itself from the ceiling. In complete darkness, Liliana saw nothing until a large set of glowing red, almond-shaped eyes stared back at her. Then she heard the raspy voice of an old woman.

"No use in screaming, my dear. We are far below in a sub-basement, a bomb shelter from the 1940s. No one can hear you."

"Who are you and what do you want from me?" she whispered weakly.

The voice laughed. "Patience, patience. You'll find out soon enough. Ah, my Tredd is here."

The person responsible for the humming and footsteps she had heard entered the dark room. Wearing his dark trench coat and wide-brimmed hat, he flipped a switch on the wall. Several incandescent bulbs dangling from the ceiling illuminated the room.

"Hmm, interesting. Surprised those even worked. After all, how many years has it been since they have been turned on, dear? Fifty years, perhaps?"

"Much longer than that, my love," the spider replied. "I am thinking more like seventy-four years. After all, this building was constructed in 1945. This bomb shelter was probably built back then."

The spider dangling in front of Liliana severed itself from its silk line and scurried across the cement floor. It climbed up one of Tredd's legs, then across his chest, and settled comfortably onto the man's left shoulder. Liliana watched as the man with the spider draped across his shoulder walked over to her. He knelt down and smiled at Liliana, who sat upon the cold cement floor with her back against a wall.

Liliana's mind raced. She wondered if she was hallucinating. She was tied up in a basement listening to an enormous talking spider. But since she knew she was going nowhere anytime soon, she tried to get information. "What do you want from me?"

"It's complicated, miss." The man removed his hat and tilted his head. "You see, you should be thrilled to be a sacrifice in part of a much larger plan."

"What you are talking about. What plan?"

Liliana watched as the spider turned its eyes to the man and spoke. "She doesn't need to know more. She just needs to be kept alive until the night of the Blood Moon."

"Yes, yes, my dear. Perhaps I have said too much. Hungry? Would you like something to eat, Miss Ramos?"

"Go to hell." She spat in his face. "No. I want you to set me free."

Without reacting, he wiped the spit from his cheek. "Hell, now that's a familiar place to me. You know, Miss Ramos, the venom of the spider Theraphosa Blondi isn't as venomous as some other spiders and snakes. But by looking at your neck, and based on the swelling and the inflammation surrounding the bite mark, you appear to be allergic to the venom. If my Maria Isabel attacked you again, you would probably die."

"So what's your point? If you want to kill me, just do it."

"No!" the spider hissed as her jaws opened and closed. "We won't kill you now. We have to wait for the Blood Moon. And then you will die. No one knows you are here, Miss Ramos. And no one will ever find you. But *I* am actually hoping someone comes looking for you."

"And who would that be?" Liliana asked.

"The man who put me in the body of this spider. If he comes looking for you, I will be offering two sacrifices for the price of one. And my rewards will be greater than you can imagine."

*   *   *   *

The following morning at The People's Clinic, plans were being made. Garland had reached out to Ina, but by the time he arrived at work, the police had already been there.

Garland was panic-stricken. He looked in Ina's office and saw her sitting at her desk reviewing papers. Garland caught her attention and stood in the doorway. His heart raced.

"Ina—"

She looked over the top of her reading glasses. "This is not your fault, Garland. Now come in, sit down, and talk to me."

He threw himself in a chair. "I feel like it is. If I had only been on time for our date. Maybe I could have prevented this from happening."

"Look, I spoke to the police. We went through her files to see if there was a defendant or a case that could have provoked the kidnapping. There was nothing. A bunch of landlord-tenant matters, that infamous squirrel case, juvenile possession of marijuana—absolutely nothing special, except—"

He finished her sentence. "P.S. 578. The environmental case."

"Yes. O'Connell had a talk with Newark police. They think they may have a partial on the license plate on the van as it entered the garage, but the security cameras in that garage are worthless." Ina sat back and her chair and raised an eyebrow. "You know, they told me the man who kidnapped her signed his name as Garland Nowell.

OF GODS, FLIES, AND DESPERATE LAWYERS

Whoever this is, they know who you are. Are you involved in any-thing, how shall I say this politely, unsavory? Drugs? Gambling? A jealous woman, perhaps? Is there some dark, exciting part of your life no one knows about?"

A talking fly, a santero who wants revenge for the death of his nephew, and a social club of witches, he thought to himself. *Nothing strange here.*

"No, Ina. My life is pretty boring. No excitement here."

"Didn't think you did, but I had to ask."

"This has to do with the P.S. 578 case."

"I think that is exactly right. And I think we keep pursuing the case while the police do their job."

Garland nodded. "What's next?"

"Liliana emailed me a copy of the complaint before all of this happened. I'm reading it and making edits. Then I want the damn thing filed with the courts immediately. And I want press coverage. We need to get this out in the open."

"What would you have me do?"

She passed him a draft of the complaint, The People's Clinic versus Van Marcherz, The Board of Education of Passaic County et al. "Start reading. Work with O'Connell and make sure we have the evidence to back up what we're alleging. We are going to sue some pretty powerful people. When you take a shot at these kinds of ani-mals, you shoot to kill, not wound. We need to win."

"Message received."

Ina rose from her desk. She pulled up a chair next to Garland. "I know you're upset. Liliana is a like a daughter to me. I feel the same way."

"If they find this bastard, I will kill him if he hurts her."

"Now, now, patience, Garland. Liliana is a very strong young woman. She survived cancer, she was an immigrant, and she put herself through college and law school as a scholarship student. She's tough. If anyone can survive this, it's her. But time is of the essence with any kidnapping. And I don't want to have to defend you on a homicide charge. Now let's get to work on P.S. 578. Liliana would want it this way."

CHAPTER THIRTY

Zoraida's Boarding House
Straight Street
Paterson, New Jersey

After a visit to his psychiatrist, Dr. Eahrbern, Fergal received a renewal for his medication. Looking to pass the day, Fergal and Señor Pepe sat in St. Michael's Park feeding the local pigeon population. He had purchased a large sack of loose dried corn. With a silly smile across his face, he sprinkled the corn around the park bench where he and his companion sat. The local pigeons swarmed him, much to the annoyance of the other people in the park who found the birds dirty and noisy.

An elderly senior citizen living at Zoraida's Boarding House yelled over to Fergal.

"Why do you feed those feathered rats, boy?"

"None of your damn business, Lola. Those birds are my friends!" he shouted back.

"You crazy imbecile, wasting your time, feeding dirty birds! You and the squirrel belong in a mental hospital!"

"Tell me something I don't know!"

Fergal laughed as he emptied the bag of loose corn on the pavement. More hungry birds flew in, much to the annoyance of Lola, and surrounded him. He looked at Lola, then pointed to a tree across the park.

"Look over there, you old bat. There's a nice tree for you to hang in upside down. Ha!" He found another small bag of corn in his pocket. He flung a handful of corn in Lola's direction so the birds would fly over to her and peck at her feet.

It was January and thirty degrees, but the frigid air didn't bother Fergal or his pet squirrel. Since receiving the settlement in his civil rights case, Fergal had been enjoying life, spending money on things he wanted. His most recent purchase was a very expensive ski jacket at Nordstrom's. It kept him and Señor Pepe quite warm. The squirrel hid inside the jacket, periodically poking his head out, sniffing the cold air before returning to the warm fold of Fergal's armpit.

Fergal spoke to Señor Pepe. "You like my new jacket, Señor Pepe? It is made by a Mr. Burberry and it was reduced from $1200 to $800."

The squirrel responded with a squeak. Fergal reached into a pocket and pulled out a few cashew nuts and fed them to Señor Pepe, then glanced down at the Invicta watch he had purchased at Walmart. "We have to go now."

Darkness came in quickly, and sitting in a park in the City of Paterson after dark could be dangerous. At exactly five o'clock, Fergal walked to Tranquility House, a local soup kitchen near his rooming house, for dinner. He indulged in a free meal of overcooked rubbery chicken, tasteless canned green beans, and instant mashed potatoes covered in a greasy gravy. Señor Pepe and Fergal agreed to pass up the tasteless chocolate pudding served by Tranquility House because a much finer dessert waited for them at home.

The day before, Fergal had picked up a cherry pie and eclairs at a gourmet French bakery. Fergal was sixty-eight and knew that he was borderline diabetic. The last thing he needed was sugar of any kind, but he couldn't resist the temptation of large succulent cherries floating inside a light, flaky pastry crust. He had consulted with Señor Pepe and, as expected, the squirrel agreed with him: cheating on his diet once in a while wasn't a terrible thing.

He put his key in the lock and opened the door to his room at the boarding house. Señor Pepe jumped out of his armpit and headed straight for a small kitchen table. He sat up on his hind legs and looked back at Fergal.

"Now wait a minute, Señor Pepe. We will get to the pie. I can only move so fast, you see."

He hung up his new coat in a closet, whistling "La Vida Es Un Carnaval" by Celia Cruz. He turned his back on the squirrel and removed a large white box from the refrigerator. After cutting off the red-and-white bakery string, he removed the cherry pie and lovingly placed it on a large dish. With each note he whistled, the squirrel barked and squeaked in response. It was a strange musical duet between a man and his squirrel.

Then without warning, the squirrel stopped making noise. Fergal stopped whistling. It was as though time had come to a standstill. The air in his room became frigid, and when he exhaled, he could see his breath.

It was happening…again.

For no reason, Fergal was overcome with sadness—the kind of sadness a person feels when someone receives news of a death. He placed his hands on the sides of his head. Visions of his past flooded his brain. Like a terrible movie, Fergal saw flashes of the most horrible events in his life with every smell, temperature, and emotion that accompanied each incident.

As he walked back in time, he felt the heat in the jungles of Vietnam, a simple soldier carrying an M16. In the next flash, he smelled the sickeningly sweet aroma of floral arrangements as he stood alongside his mother's coffin in a funeral parlor. Then a chill came over him as he felt the coldness of his infant son's lifeless body. His son had died from Sudden Infant Death Syndrome just after he came home from war.

The memories broke his heart. Throughout life, death had been a companion he knew all too well. And it was here once again.

He found his voice. "I know you are here. What do you want?" Then he turned around to face them.

The children of P.S. 578 were back. They stood like pale little soldiers in front of him. Evan stepped forward from the back of the group. "Mr. G, we still need your help."

"I gave them the documents like you wanted. I know I should have done that years ago." He sighed. "What is it this time?"

"Our friend, Liliana, she's hurt and needs our help."

"Who hurt her?"

"A bad man. A bad man who lives in the school. He took her."

He shook his head. "I don't understand. Nobody lives in the school."

The little boy smiled and shook his head. "Nuh-uh. The bad man does. He lives in the school. Way down deep."

"What can I do?" Fergal bent down and looked into the eyes of the dead child. "What is his name?"

The little ghost boy stretched his arms out to hug Fergal. "You need to help her before the bad man hurts her, and the moon changes its color to blood. If the moon changes to blood, she's gone forever." Fergal wrapped his arms around Evan.

"And when does that happen?"

"Tomorrow," he whispered.

"What do I do?"

Before the little ghost boy answered, he, along with the other children, vanished. Señor Pepe jumped off the table, scurried over to Fergal, and hopped on his shoulder. The squirrel nuzzled his ear, and Fergal gently patted his head.

"We have work to do, Señor Pepe," he sighed. "But right now, we will just eat some pie."

CHAPTER THIRTY-ONE

The Day of the Blood Moon
Home of Teofil Lopez
Ocean Grove, New Jersey
9:00 a.m.

The old santero created a temple dedicated to Yemaya in his house. The walls of the temple room were painted in blue and white. Her altar contained elements from the ocean, seashells, dried starfish, and seahorses. A sopera was placed on the altar filled with salt water. In the center of these water symbols stood a tall statue of a tan woman with long, flowing red hair. She was surrounded by a bottle of white wine, seven pennies, seven blue-and-white carnations, and seven statues of dolphins. Seven blue candles had been burning for seven days, next to a large raw aquamarine stone.

There were other statues on his altar, such as La Caridad del Cobre and Kwan Yin, but it was to the Great Yoruba, Mother of Oceans, that Teo had dedicated his life's work. As one of her children, he would now call upon the goddess for justice…in this world and the next.

Teo had been drawn to the sea since he was a young boy. As a child, he would stand on the beach and speak to the ocean. Water was his friend. As he stood on the shoreline, he would tell the ocean how beautiful it was. After a time, a motherly voice would answer him and thank him for his kind words.

When he was ten years old, he'd swum too far out. An undertow pulled him out to sea. Teo remembered his mother's face as she stood helplessly on the beach, crying, watching her little boy being dragged beneath the waves.

When his body had reached near unconsciousness, he heard the same motherly voice that had always spoken to him on the beach.

"My beautiful son, have faith. You are one of my children and I have you in my arms."

Teo remembered gentle yet strong arms lifting him above the waves. Water was forced out of his lungs, and once he regained consciousness, he found himself riding the crest of a wave until he was gently deposited on the beach at his mother's feet. That was the strength of Yemaya, the Mother of the Sea. She had saved his life. Now he would save the life of someone else—Liliana.

But he knew what he would be facing was deadly. He would humbly beseech the goddess's help the way he had when he rode the crest of a wave back to shore as a child. He closed his eyes and let his mind drift back to the beach he had played upon as a child.

The doorbell rang and his meditation was broken. Teo got up, opened the door slightly, and saw Garland outside of the door holding a suitcase.

"Teo, let me in. We have to talk."

"Yes. We do. Time is short. Please come in and sit down."

Teo escorted him to the living room and asked him to sit down. Garland placed the small suitcase on a coffee table and unzipped its sides. He pulled up the flap, and out popped Don Julio.

The fly had grown larger. He was now two and a half feet tall, and though he was still wearing his guayabera. The pants were too short, the jacket was too small, and his feet poked though his shoes again. Once again, he had outgrown his clothing. And as usual, Don Julio was extremely upset.

"Look at the me! This is Maria Isabel's work! That lousy, rotten spider. When I get her, I will pull her legs off one at a time and enjoy every minute of it!"

"Calm down, Julio. This is all going to be over shortly. I will get you some new clothing."

The fly looked back at Teo. "Do you have tools in your garage? I need tools."

Teo looked curious. "Yes. Why? Do you need to fix something?"

"Yes." The fly then left the room and flew out of the house, headed for Teo's garage. Garland looked at Teo.

"Should we follow him?"

"No, let him play in the garage. I need to speak with you."

"We have to find Liliana, Teo. The police are looking but have no leads. She could be dead by now."

"I feel that she isn't dead. But I do feel that she is being kept alive for a purpose, and once that purpose is over, she *will* die. Everything will happen tonight."

"How can we find her?"

"Did you file that lawsuit yet?"

"No, not yet. It's being finalized. Then it will be filed electronically and then served on the parties today, probably P.S. 578's lawyers. Why?"

Teo paced a bit. "Can you serve it on Principal Van Marcherz directly?"

"Yeah, I can have Investigator O'Connell do that. Why?"

"It will be interesting to see if Van Marcherz has any reaction to the lawsuit."

"So what will that do?"

"I think it will be telling about many things." He took a deep breath. "Do you believe in heaven and hell? Good and evil? Dimensions to other worlds?"

Garland threw himself back in a chair. "Why not? I have a two-foot fly dressed in a men's suit, and now he's out in a garage trying to build something. So yeah, I do believe. I believe there are things in this world that I will never understand and things in this world that should never be tampered with, like the occult. Teo, I'm sorry to say this, but I wish I never met you or the fly."

"Or Liliana?"

"Well, I wouldn't go that far."

"But how do you say it, you are all in now. There is no turning back. And now you must stand and fight with us if you want to save your woman."

"So what would you have me do?"

"You and Don Julio will come with me tonight to find Liliana and destroy the witch Maria Isabel. We will have help from others. But this fight truly belongs to us."

"Great. How are we even going to find the witch?"

"My friend, I think that she is trying to find us. I think Liliana was taken by Isabel and her accomplice not only for her soul, but to lure me out of hiding. But I am ready. We will know before the moon rises."

Garland stood up. "Whatever it takes, I will stand…"

Before he could finish the sentence, both men heard loud crashes coming from outside. Teo and Garland ran through the kitchen and to the back yard. Teo had a very large Victorian carriage house in the back of his property that he had converted into a garage for his car and tools. The garage doors were closed, but through the top of the glass windows the two men saw sparks flying. They looked at each other.

"What the hell do you think Julio is doing in there?"

"I don't know. But let's get in there quickly before he burns down my house."

Teo lifted the garage door. He saw the fly struggling with a small table saw as he was cutting through a big aluminum garbage can. In the small amount of time he had been in the garage, he had wreaked havoc. Most of Teo's tools were scattered across the floor. Julio cut several holes in garbage can, and he laid the pieces on the floor of the garage. Some pieces were round while others were square or rectangular. He had knocked over another garbage can, pulled out the garbage, opened the garbage bag, and removed an empty soup can.

"Julio, what are you doing? You spilled my trash all over the place. Why have you cut holes in my garbage can?"

The fly was unapologetic. "Tonight we enter a battle with a witch. Do you two think I'm an idiot? I'm going in with protection. I am making body armor out of your garbage can. It will resemble the armor used by King Arthur and the Knights of the Round Table. Look at this. I am almost done with the breastplate." Don Julio picked up two round pieces of metal tied together by leather shoelaces. He placed it over his head. It looked like a sign for advertising the opening of a new store or restaurant.

"I decided to leave more room in the back so that I could achieve maximum flight speed."

Teo placed his hand over his mouth. Garland smiled. The two men tried not to laugh. Garland pointed to the soup can. "What are you going to do with that?"

Don Julio walked over and grabbed the empty Campbell's Soup can. He placed it on his head. "A helmet, once I clean it and cut holes in it for my eyes." A droplet of soup fell near his mouth, and he sucked it up. "Cream of tomato. Not bad."

Teo could no longer contain himself. He laughed loudly. "My friend, I ate that can of soup last week. You are eating last week's soup." Don Julio started to yell at Teo, but the soup can fell completely over his head and muffled the fly's words. The weight of the can was too much and made Don Julio fall flat on his back.

Garland shrugged. "Be happy, Teo. At least he's recycling. You know, I feel like I'm in a bad science fiction film. If we survive this mess tonight, what are you going to do with the Campbell's Soup warrior?"

"I have no idea." He turned to Garland. "But you should go home now. Have the lawsuit filed and delivered today. Much will be revealed shortly."

"But how?"

"You will find out probably before I do. Now go home and wait."

*   *   *   *

Garland returned to The People's Clinic around three o'clock. Ina's secretary had the complaint ready for filing with the Passaic County Court. Garland reviewed the papers quickly and signed them. The secretary worked rapidly. She scanned the papers and then uploaded them to the court. After she had printed them out, she handed Garland a copy.

Ina and O'Connell sat in the conference room. Garland saw that they were talking quietly, but he needed to interrupt them.

"Ina, I want this hand delivered today."

"Any particular reason why?" She smiled, seeming to know the answer.

"It's just something that needs to be done, Ina. Liliana would have wanted us to do this."

She nodded. "I understand. The papers are ready?"

"Yes."

"Investigator O'Connell, I know that you usually go home around now, but would you mind a little overtime?"

He stretched back in his chair. "Since I am the investigator on the case, I can't serve the complaint. But I can go with someone who can."

"Let me guess. You have a friend in the Passaic County Sheriff's Department."

O'Connell grinned from ear to ear. "How did you guess?"

* * * *

P.S. 578
Passaic, New Jersey
Office of Robert Van Marcherz
3:45 p.m.

O'Connell and Sheriff J. Harry Smith pulled up in front of P.S. 578. The school day had ended and children were being released from school through the main doors of the elementary school. It was a cold day. The two investigators parked across the street with their car motors running, waiting for the crowd of buses, parents, and children to thin out. Once they saw the crowds dissipate, O'Connell and Smith moved in.

O'Connell rang a bell. A female voice from inside the school asked the men to identify themselves. Smith explained that they were from the Sheriff's Office. The voice then told them to place their faces in front of a small glass window. Lights flashed and then the door buzzed and opened to permit their entry into P.S. 578. As they passed over the threshold, they saw a sign with an arrow pointing in the direction of Principal Van Marcherz's office. They followed the sign, and it led them to the office of Van Marcherz's administrative assistant. O'Connell smiled to himself as he looked at her.

That old girl's wearing too much face powder. And that red lipstick on that wrinkled white skin? Makes her look like Dracula's grandmother, he thought. *And Jesus Christ, it's as hot as hell in here.*

"Gentlemen, I'm Mrs. Ford, Principal Van Marcherz's assistant. Here are your photo identification badges. You may take off your coats, and you can hang them in that janitor's closet right behind you."

O'Connell looked at Smith. "Janitor's closet? You want me to hang my coat next to the janitor's cleaning supplies?"

Mrs. Ford giggled. "Oh, please don't be offended. It's just that we're renovating the teachers' lounge and various coat rooms. There just isn't a lot of space right now. So unfortunately, we're trying to make do. The janitor was kind enough to move his supplies elsewhere so that we could hang our coats in his closet. It's very roomy. Once you open the door, you'll see. Hats and gloves belong on the upper shelves."

"Okay. We understand your space problems, don't we, Harry?" O'Connell winked. He watched as Harry shrugged in response, disinterested in the entire conversation. He was simply there to serve the papers on the school's principal and then collect on O'Connell's promise of a beer when they were finished.

"I'm good. I'll just keep my coat on, if you don't mind."

O'Connell was roasting in his thick down jacket. He removed his coat and opened the door to the janitor's closet. He was surprised. The old secretary with the terrible makeup was right. It was a big walk-in closet, and it had several coats hanging in it. There was one particular coat that immediately caught his attention, and for a moment he couldn't take his eyes off it.

It was a long black leather coat.

Perhaps this wouldn't have been cause for alarm, except a wide-brimmed Amish-looking black hat sat upon the shelf above the long black leather trench coat. O'Connell had a keen eye for detail and recalled the film footage from the security camera. He had used his law enforcement connections to view the footage at a local police station. He remembered that the man who abducted Liliana Ramos wore a long black trench coat and large black hat. He felt blood rushing to his face, but he would keep the information to himself—for now. He must remain calm.

Mrs. Ford announced to Principal Van Marcherz that there were two police officers waiting outside for him. O'Connell heard an audible "What?" and then the shuffling of papers before Van Marcherz appeared in the doorway. When he entered the room, O'Connell noted that the good principal appeared to be flustered.

"Good afternoon, gentlemen, how can I help you?"

O'Connell smiled back. "Unfortunately, we have to give you something. Harry, please give Mr. Van Marcherz the papers."

Sheriff J. Harry Smith anded him the complaint captioned The People's Clinic versus Robert Van Marcherz, Public School 578 et al. "Sorry, my friend," Harry stated flatly. "Nothing personal."

"Of course." Van Marcherz took the papers. O'Connell noticed that as he started reading the first few pages, his face grew red. He glanced up at O'Connell.

"I have no idea what this is about. We pride ourselves in being environmentally conscious. I must forward these on to our school attorneys at Williams and Fisk. Big firm in Newark. Ivy League lawyers. Quite an impressive bunch, really. They should be able to handle this easily."

O'Connell gave him a devilish Irish grin. "Oh, I'm sure. But, uh, on a completely different note, I really just *love* this black leather trench coat I saw in your closet. It's fantastic. Where did you get it?"

"The long black leather coat?"

"Yes, and it kind of looked like there was a hat that matched it. Very cool. Very *avant-garde*. Where did you buy it?"

Van Marcherz looked nonplussed. "Oh, that's not mine. But I know the coat. It belongs to my son. He's a janitor at the school."

"Oh. It's a great look. Do you know where he purchased it? I'd like to buy one for myself."

"When I see him, I'll ask him. I have to get back to these contracts I was reviewing. Well, is there anything else, gentlemen? If not, Mrs. Ford, please escort them to the door. Thank you for coming." Van Marcherz went back to his office and closed the door.

O'Connell looked at Mrs. Ford. "No need to show us out. We know the way."

She smiled and nodded. The two men walked away. As O'Connell headed out the door, he noticed a very old fallout shelter sign. He knew many old buildings in Passaic still had fallout shelters from the 1950s and 60s buried deep in the bowels of their buildings. He had a hunch. The coat, the hat, and an old bomb shelter. Maybe Liliana was closer than he thought. He called Garland.

CHAPTER THIRTY-TWO

The Night of the Blood Moon

Garland picked up the phone at The People's Clinic. He wrote down all the information O'Connell gave him. O'Connell told him to provide the information to the local police. Garland decided to get on the phone with Teo first.

"The lawsuit was filed this afternoon," he told Teo. "O'Connell served the papers. While he was at the school, he saw a long black trench coat and hat. Turns out it belongs to Van Marcherz's son, who's a janitor in the school. The school has an old bomb shelter. I think that's enough for a search warrant."

"Perhaps, but if we have the police move in too quickly, this psychopath son of Van Marcherz could kill her. Tredd Van Marcherz, I remember that kid. Heavy drug use, was arrested several times for torturing animals. Probably a product of his environment, I guess. We go back to the school at midnight. Then we call the police."

"Sorry, I can't wait that long."

"Garland, listen to me. You have to wait. You have no idea what you are going to walk into, but I do. No, it's too soon. We have to wait for the moon to be at its zenith, its peak. That happens at midnight."

"Change of subject. How's Julio?"

"Getting larger. But after tonight, who knows? He finished modifying his suit of armor and now he is working on a weapon. He's been welding."

"That would almost be funny if someone's life wasn't at stake. Teo, I'm going in. I can't wait until midnight. I'll meet you at the school." He hung up the phone.

* * * *

Teo shook his head. He knew this was a mistake and he couldn't stop Garland, but at least he could try to get him some help. He picked up the phone and called Dr. Nettlebrook.

A charming British accent answered the phone. "Good evening, my dear friend."

"Hello, Brogan. We must begin the process now."

"Yes, yes of course. The Cone of Power to stop darkness from entering this world."

"It has become more complicated. We believe that the operator is conducting a soul switching ceremony and has taken a hostage to be used as a sacrifice. I am going in to interrupt the ritual. I also believe this same person is responsible for the 1988 murder of my nephew."

"I see. This has gotten a bit more complicated, but nevertheless, we shall move forward quickly. I have spoken with the young chaos magician, Mr. Stremnik. He has identified the sigil. It belongs to a demon named Betel. The sigil will be used to bring this creature into this world in exchange for a human soul. The blackest of magic, ugly work, really. But all of us are prepared to help stop this. We already have enough hell on earth. We don't need any more."

"Understood."

"This is dangerous work, my friend."

"I am prepared to accept whatever fate the orishas have chosen for me."

"Teofil, I've always had the highest respect for you. We shall begin to work in our own various disciplines to raise the Cone of Power tonight. You know, the last time I did this was back in England in 1940. We stopped one devil once."

"You prevented Hitler from entering England. He was a devil of special kind. Thank you, my friend."

"Not at all, Teofil. After I hang up with you, I shall call all the parties involved and tell them to begin their magical work immediately. Be safe."

"Good night, my friend." Teo hung up the phone.

CHAPTER THIRTY-THREE

The Magicians
8:00 p.m.
A cottage in Ridgewood, New Jersey

Leopold Stremnik had just guzzled down two Red Bulls and a box of licorice when he received the call from Dr. Nettlebrook telling him to begin his magical ritual of protection. The nineteen-year-old chaos magician ran to his room. He turned on four laptop computers, entered passwords for each computer, and put on a headset. He dialed numbers on his cell phone.

"Let's see, it's ten o'clock in New York," he said out loud. "That means my boy should be sound asleep in his crib in Cairo at four in the morning." The computer beeped and the sleepy face of a young Arabic man popped up. "Good morning, Aledin, wakey wakey time!"

"Oh man, this couldn't wait? It's four o'clock in the morning here. What's the matter? You got old ladies chasing you down the street again? Did you screw up another love spell?" With the last remark, the young man rolled over and pulled a pillow over his head.

"No, my brother. This is serious business. We got a nut trying to bring a demon to earth. We need to raise a Cone of Power. I need some of that Sufi magic of yours. Nettlebrook called me."

The young man sat up. "Nettlebrook? Then this is serious. I'm in."

The computer beeped again. A lovely round-faced old lady with wisps of gray and cellophane-blue eyes popped up on the computer screen. Leopold smiled. "Hello, Grandma Vivian, sorry to bother you."

"Merry meet, y'all!" she stated with a Georgia drawl. "And it is no bother, darling. Brogan called. My entire coven is here. The Firestorm Witches of the South are ready to work. Who else are we waiting for?"

The computer beeped again. On another computer screen, a young man with white skin, heavy black eyeliner, and a blue-black mohawk appeared on the screen. "London calling. Heard we're in a bit of a crisis across the pond, right? The Temple of the Sacred Star is here and ready to work. The good doctor called and told us."

"Nigel, did you get the copy of the sigil I sent you?" asked Leopold.

"Yes, I received it. We know who it is. It's one of the lesser demons who's trying to make entry into this world. This needs to be stopped. Tonight. Are we all online? I see Grandmother Vivian, Aledin, and where is Shmuel?"

The computer beeped again. "Hello? Not late, am I? Dr. Nettlebrook called me. A solitary Kabbalist is ready to work."

"What time is it there?"

"The time is five o'clock in the morning on Friday in Tel Aviv."

"Shalom, my brother. Okay, everyone is here. Let's get this party started."

* * * *

The Home of Izilda Montague
The Ritual Room overlooking Weequahic Park
Newark, New Jersey
10:00 p.m.
The drums beat loudly.
Pa-pa-rum-pa.
Pa-pa-rum-pa.
Pa-pa-rum-pa.
Izilda Montague received the call from Dr. Nettlebrook. It was time to begin the magical work on the evening of the Blood Moon.

Women wearing white turbans in long flowing white skirts whirled around an altar decorated with the offerings of rum, flowers, and fresh coconuts. The drummers seated played the same beats over and over again.
Pa-pa-rum-pa.
Pa-pa-rum-pa.
Pa-pa-rum-pa.

Izilda was a Mamba, a Voodoo priestess. The religious paths she and Teo had chosen were both similar yet very different. Both had the capacity for doing good or evil. But tonight was a night to do great good and prevent a sinister evil from passing into the mortal world.

First, she would ask Papa Legba, the Keeper of the Paths, for his blessing to begin the work. If he agreed that her desire was worthy, he would send a loa, a Haitian god, to block the evil magic or guide her as to how she could do it. As the drumming grew more intense, she whirled around the altar and looked at one of her priestesses. The young woman's eyes rolled back in her head, and her body began to twist and contort. She began speaking in Yoruba and French. Papa Legba had answered. A loa was coming, and he had mounted one of Izilda's priestesses-in-training, Yvette, a young Creole woman from Mississippi. The drumming stopped as the woman entered a trance.

"Keep drumming and don't stop until I tell you!" Izilda ordered. "Yvette, be prepared to receive the loa! Praise to Papa Legba!"

The drummers pounded harder, and the drumbeats resonated off the walls of the room.

Pa-pa-pa-rum-pa.

Pa-pa-pa-rum-pa.

Pa-pa-pa-rum-pa.

The young woman's body twisted and writhed. Her turban fell off. Her legs grew longer, and her torso and arms stretched. Her fingers became long and her fingernails became claws. Yvette was only five foot three, but she shot up to over six feet tall. Her delicate facial features became more masculine, and her caramel skin turned grayish white. A lengthy scar that looked like a railroad track appeared across her left cheek. The young woman's eyes sank back in her head, leaving two empty black sockets with tiny red pupils. She dropped her chin to her chest and raised her head slowly. Long black wavy hair shot out from her head. The hair moved and flowed with a life of its own because it was comprised entirely of pencil-thin black garden snakes. The spirit looked directly into Izilda's eyes.

Gone was the young lady with the pure white dress. In her place stood a male figure with a skeleton face and body. He wore a black tuxedo with a silk top hat. From the breast pocket of the tuxedo, he pulled a pair of hexagonal sunglasses and put them on. The spirit leaned on a walking stick that had a small crystal skull on top. He smiled at Izilda with missing teeth. The spirit looked like a dead rock star from the seventies brought back to life as a zombie. Drummers and priestesses were wide-eyed as they witnessed Yvette's transformation. Their faces were somewhere between awe and sheer terror as he spoke.

"Hello Sister, Papa Legba sent me. I was hoping to have sex with a mortal tonight, but instead I was sent to pick up a soul." He walked over to Izilda and pointed a single claw. "Is it you? Ha! You know, we can have a quickie before my bitch of a wife Maman Brigitte shows up. After all, I have this nice young body. Let me use it. What do you say? Shall we make love?"

It was Baron Samedi, Lord of the Graveyard, a foul-mouthed spirit of the dead. He was the husband of another powerful death spirit, Maman Brigitte. The couple would often fight because Baron Samedi had a penchant for chasing after mortal women. The baron eyed Izilda's body like a hungry dog who had just found a raw sirloin steak. "Hmmm, mademoiselle," he said.

In the Voodoo tradition, Baron Samedi was capable of healing or destruction. Izilda took a deep breath and bowed before the death specter. He was not a loa to be played with because he was temperamental. If he was offended by the person who summoned him, he would kill the Voodoo priest. Yet he had the capacity for saving a life if he felt like it. It all depended on his mood.

"Good evening, my Lord Baron Samedi. Please accept my humble offering." Izilda puffed away on a cigar and blew the smoke in his face.

He inhaled the smoke through the bony opening in his skull where a nose would have been, then exhaled it through his rib cage. As a gentleman would, he then doffed his top hat in response for the favor. "Hmmm, thanks. I like a good cigar in the evening. By the way, your mama, my Lady Mavis, sends her greetings from the other side," he hissed.

"Please send her my love."

"I am not your messenger boy! You asked Papa Legba for help. He sent me. Here I am. So what the hell do you want?"

"Dark magic is being worked because of the Blood Moon."

He snickered. "So I have heard, so I have heard. Someone wants to come over from the eternal furnaces."

"Lord Baron, that spirit does not belong with the living."

"So you want to stick me with this idiot? I have enough crazy spirits in the land of the dead. I don't go near the hellish ones," he stated as he admired his claws.

"But my Lord Baron Samedi, you are an escort of the dead. Can you not escort the spirit—"

"Escort the spirit back to hell? No!" he shouted. "I work in cemeteries. I keep the dead from becoming zombies, and I have on occasion saved someone *from* me. But I don't go near the devil's furnaces. It isn't my territory." He rubbed his bony chin thoughtfully. "Although there was this one time, I did push a soul through the Gates of Hell. I hated that guy. He was a complete asshole."

Izilda prostrated herself before the great Voodoo lord of the dead. "Great Baron Samedi, most brilliant of all the spirits, I beseech you to help me save a life tonight."

He sighed. "One will die this night. That's all I can tell you. I will escort that person into the Land of the Dead personally, if that makes you feel any better."

Izilda raised her head. "And who will that be?"

"None of your damn business! That is my choice."

"Will you not help me prevent the entry of evil into the living world?" She blew more cigar smoke in his direction. Izilda knew the Baron of Death loved cigar smoke.

"I'll think about it." He inhaled the smoke, and Izilda watched again as the smoke exited his empty rib cage where a heart and lungs would have been in a living person. "Hmmm, nice." He rubbed his claws together. "Okay, you convinced me. I will help you, but then you, my dear, will owe the Great Baron Samedi. More smoke, please."

Izilda took a deep breath and puffed a large cloud of cigar smoke in his direction.

The baron never specified the terms of the bargain. He could ask her for routine sexual rendezvous, cigars, rum, and a drum party every Saturday night in his honor. Or Baron Samedi could take her life and make her his permanent consort in the Land of the Voodoo Dead.

"If you help block the evil coming to this world from Hell, I will do as you ask, Lord Baron Samedi."

"Very well then," the skeleton grinned. "We have an agreement." With those words, the spirit faded. The body of the young girl reformed and dropped to the ground. She appeared to be semi-conscious and her clothes were ripped to shreds.

"Get Yvette some water and some food," Izilda said as she wondered what the rest of the night would bring. "And a new dress."

* * * *

It was closing in on nine thirty. Nurse Bridgette Leere was finishing up notes on her patient's chart. Flowercross West, the name of the floor for cancer patients, was unusually quiet. Many of the sicker patients had passed away, and the few left on the ward were resting comfortably in their beds. For the most part, the ward was virtually empty, and the hospital floor was quiet.

She heard the familiar sounds of footsteps that she had heard time and time again.

He's back, she thought.

"Good evening, Dr. Quietus."

A tall, thin gentleman, mid-forties with slightly graying hair, a long face, and black round horn-rimmed glasses stood in front of the nurses' station. He fumbled with his clipboard and looked awkward. His lab coat had several coffee stains on it.

"Doctor, I think you need to send that lab coat to the dry cleaners."

"Oh yes, yes I know. By the way, Bea, you look very nice this evening, as...as usual. I-I-I was hoping that we can have a cup of coffee tonight, after you're off work, I mean," he stammered. "You know, you can call me Alfred."

"Alfred, I received a call from Brogan Nettlebrook."

"Oh, oh is he the guy who knows about, um, me? I mean me and you?"

"Yes. And he needs our help tonight. Something is going down. Big time."

He adjusted his eyeglasses. "He needs *my* help?"

Bea pushed a wisp of blond hair off her face. "Yes, I think he needs all the help he can get. I'm leaving early. It's slow and the floor has coverage. Will you go with me tonight?"

Alfred adjusted his glasses. "Yes, I'll go if you think it is appropriate."

* * * *

Viktor Einarsson finished his conversation with Brogan Nettlebrook. He agreed that he would help with the night's ritual work, but he would do it alone and in his own way. He hated working magic in groups. He was a tall, strong man and felt stronger alone. It was just his way.

He owned a small Cape Cod house in Ridgefield Park, a working-class town in northern New Jersey. Viktor had built a room over his garage, and it was in that room he kept an altar dedicated to Odin, Thor, and the other Norse gods. It was a simple altar, a meticulous piece of polished wood from the stump of a large oak tree he had cut down in his yard. Upon the altar were hand-carved statues of Odin and his wife Frigg nestled between dried oak leaves. Next to that was a brass chalice and an athame, a ceremonial knife.

To begin his work, Viktor would meditate on the runes, small stones with an ancient Germanic alphabet carved into them. The rune stones were used since the time of the Vikings to foretell the future, answer questions about the present, and warn of events yet to come. There was a special hiding place within the oak altar where he had hidden his rune stones. As he slid the statue of Odin across the top of the altar, a small drawer popped open. Viktor reached into the tree stump and removed a small handmade leather pouch. Inside the pouch were Viktor's precious rune stones, which he had created from clay. He removed two of the rune stones, Tiawaz, the rune of victory and Algiz, the rune of protection, and placed them upon the altar.

A prayer to Odin the All Father opened the ceremony. He cleared his mind and thought of clear forests on a moonlit night. He focused on the runes and envisioned sending victory and protection to whoever needed it. Closing his eyes, Viktor prayed to Odin for wisdom, strength, and the ability to send that energy to those in danger tonight. The runes began to glow. He smiled. Odin had answered.

* * * *

James Yao had just finished a conference call. Immediately afterward Dr. Nettlebrook called requiring his services. He agreed to help, even though he was exhausted. But at least he was where he wanted to be, far away from New York City noise.

Yao had just sealed an important deal resulting in another million-dollar contract. At the end of the day, it would make him richer than he already was. The import/export dealer had an apartment on the Upper East Side of Manhattan but preferred to spend his time alone on his fifty-five acre estate in Suffern, New York. Yao named his estate "High Ground" because of its location in the Ramapo Mountains. Alone at High Ground, he had the perfect place to practice Gu, the art of poison magic.

Because it was January, it was too cold for the forty-year-old magician to work outside. Yao retreated to his occult library with over ten thousand books, many of which were priceless. He removed a rare copy of Plutarch's *Moralia*. When the book was lifted up, the entire bookshelf slid backward, permitting him to enter a secret chamber he had built behind the bookcase.

The chamber was an altar room dedicated to ancient Chinese gods. It was his sacred space, a place where he prayed and worked the magic taught to him by his family. He bowed respectfully as he entered. He went behind a black lacquer screen and disrobed. He removed his expensive business suit and put on a floor-length black-and-red silk robe. When he was finished, Yao moved slowly and deliberately toward a small but ornate red-and-gold-painted niche, carved into the wall of his temple room.

In the niche was an arrangement of black-and-white photographs, old color Polaroids, and daguerreotype pictures from the 1800s. Yao had arranged pictures of his deceased family members in a large oval inside the niche. He bowed again and placed flowers and fresh fruit before the photographs of his ancestors as he asked for their blessing.

After a few minutes, he left the altar of his ancestors and turned his attention to the four enormous stone statues on the other side of the room.

Yao had stone statues created to honor four powerful Chinese gods. In the center stood the Jade Emperor, the god who had created mankind from Yangtze River clay. To the right of the Jade Emperor stood Guanyin, the Goddess of Mercy. On the left was Yan Wang, the Lord of Death and the Underworld, and finally to the left of Yan Wang was Caishen, the Lord of Wealth.

He bowed before the Lord of Death. From the base of the statue, he removed a large cauldron with a lid that opened in two halves. The magician placed the cauldron on a large pedestal and opened the lid of the cauldron on one side. Yao backed away from the cauldron and turned his attention to three small cages covered with a black velvet cloth near the pedestal. He removed the cover from the first cage. Inside the cage was a black mamba, one of the world's most poisonous snakes. At first the snake was quite active. It hissed and slithered around the inside of the cage. Yao raised his hand over the cage. The snake closed its eyes and did not move. He reached into the cage and removed the black mamba. He placed the snake inside the cauldron and shut the lid.

He went to the second cage. Inside that cage was a black Arabian fat-tailed scorpion. The scorpion was active and ready to attack with its tail. Once again Yao waved his hand over the cage and the arachnid went limp, appearing almost dead. Yao picked up the scorpion and dumped it into the cauldron where he had placed the black mamba.

Finally, he returned to the last covered box where a black widow had built a large web. The spider attempted to jump from its web onto him. Yao waved his hand over it and the spider dropped to the bottom of the cage. He reached in and picked up the spider and placed it in the cauldron with the others.

When all three creatures were in the cauldron, he locked the top of the container. He placed the cauldron before the feet of the statue of Yan Wang. Yao waved his hands over the cauldron. The statue's eyes began to glow until the entire statue was engulfed in a bright yellow light. Yan Wang became more human in appearance. Then the god spoke to Yao.

"You bring me an offering, Master Yao. That is good."

"I am humbled that you accept my offer, Lord Wang. Tonight I engage in an action. I wish to create a most deadly poison, my lord."

"I see. The snake, the spider, and the scorpion are three deadly creatures with three of the most deadly poisons. Who will win the battle? I do love a gamble. Especially where death is involved." The statue smiled. "Do you wish my blessing?"

He bowed. "Yes, my lord."

"Then one must die this night."

"So be it. For the greater good."

The statue of Yan Wang returned to stone. Yao placed his hands over the cauldron and yelled, "Arise and fight!" The closed cauldron began to vibrate and shake as the creatures inside fought for their lives. Wild sounds and hissing came from the cauldron for nearly fifteen minutes. Yao closed his eyes and kept his hands on top of the cauldron. Finally all became silent.

Then the cauldron glowed an eerie green color. As Yao stood there, he kept his eyes closed until he heard the voice of Lord Wang in his mind.

Master Yao, the spider has defeated the snake and the scorpion. Her poison and spirit will be the most venomous of all. Well done!

His eyes turned skyward. "Thank you, my Lord Wang."

* * * *

Father Elias Hearn had just settled down with a cup of Darjeeling accompanied by a fresh lemon wedge. He sensed the evening would not be a quiet one. It was the Night of the Blood Moon when forces both good and evil would collide. As he was about to sip his tea, the phone rang in the rectory at St. Morand's. He knew who was calling.

"Good evening, Brogan," he said. "I was expecting your call."

"I thought you might. Tonight is the night."

"Yes, I know. I felt it. Tonight I will say a mass asking for St. Michael to intercede."

"Thank you."

"And you will do your Kabbalistic work?"

"Of course. I keep out the evil spirits who want to enter the realm of the living."

"Have you named and identified it?"

"Yes."

"Don't tell me his name. We can't give it more energy than it deserves."

"I agree. Elias, I am truly worried."

"So am I. But we have the power of good behind our work. We can defeat it. Best of luck to you tonight, Brogan. God bless. It's time." He hung up the telephone.

*　*　*　*

Nettlebrook tried to keep the faith. He knew Elias Hearn was no ordinary priest. He had been touched by angels and his prayers to Archangel Michael were more powerful than those of most priests. As a Catholic priest, he was a formidable adversary against evil. Brogan Nettlebrook was not exactly a weak man either. He knew and understood the mystical workings of Kabbalistic magic. He could banish demons, summon angels, and communicate with spirits in different worlds. He had seen many things in his ninety plus years, and very little bothered or shocked him.

But for whatever reason, tonight he felt something that he had not known in many years—fear.

CHAPTER THIRTY-FOUR

The Reckoning
Bomb Shelter of P.S. 578
Passaic, New Jersey

Garland changed his mind and decided not to call the police right away. He arrived at P.S. 578. He parked his car and ran across the school's empty parking lot to try to enter the school. He went to the back entrance and pulled on the door handle. No good. He tried to pry open a window. It was locked from the inside. His heart sank. The school was surrounded by security cameras. If he smashed the window or broke the door lock, alarms would sound and the police would be there in seconds. Little blinking red lights indicated that the cameras were working and they were pointed directly at him. He immediately moved out of their range. He hoped he wasn't already recorded.

Garland was no hero. He was just a guy who was involved in something he didn't understand. He had no idea what he was walking into. His body felt frozen in the icy January air, and he was worried. When he entered that basement, what would he find? Would it be Liliana's cold, dead body? Tonight was about magic, monsters, and blood. Garland leaned against the brick wall. He slammed his fist in frustration, feeling so helpless and out of place.

Out of the corner of his eye he caught a glimpse of something orange, bright, and glowing. He turned his attention skyward and saw its beauty and its majesty.

"The Blood Moon," he whispered.

"It is truly beautiful, isn't it?"

Slowly, he turned around. A glowing figure stood in the shadow of the moon wearing a white short-sleeved shirt and white summer pants. For a minute, he thought he saw a ghost.

"Teo, is that you? You look…look different. You're glowing and you have no coat. Aren't you freezing?"

"No, I am not cold at all. Are you scared? Don't be. A big, strong young man like you. You could probably take an old man like me in a fight." He laughed.

"I doubt that. Teo, I'm terrified not for my life; if I die, so be it. I'm terrified that I can't save her."

"Trust that she is still alive. I feel it."

"How do we win? I'm not a sorcerer, a santero, or anything like that. I'm not that guy. And besides, who is on our side these days? Those people at the college? You have some guy who prays to Norse gods, a kid who uses a computer to do magic spells, a Voodoo lady, a Catholic priest, a Chinese magician who can't decide if he's good or evil. And then there's that strange nurse. I have no idea what she does. We can't win. We're all too different."

Teo stood unmoved. "Yes, many different branches, but all growing out of the same tree. All powerful in different ways. Oh, and you forgot about the talking fly."

"Yeah, then there's that. Where is he?"

"Here he comes."

In the shadow of the moonlight, a dwarf-sized figure jogged on the pavement. The figure was carrying a small halberd, a two-handed pole weapon from the fourteenth century. When the figure grew closer, Garland tried not to laugh.

Julio the fly had welded together various pieces of metal and created a coat of armor using tin cans. A metal basin from a birdbath made an ornate chest protector. He used an aluminum pot as a helmet. In order to protect his face, he cut two large holes in the front of the pot so that he could see out. His substantial wings poked out from under the armor.

"I am ready for Maria Isabel," he announced.

"You look like a toy I used to have when I was a kid, Robby the Robot. Except Robby was a little better constructed. He didn't have a lobster pot for a head. Oh well, why not? We gotta move. How are we going to deal with *this*?" He pointed to the locked door.

Teo moved forward. "Like this." He touched the door handle and closed his eyes. There was a buzzing sound and the door popped open.

"Teo, what about the cameras?"

Teo muttered something and closed his eyes. The camera lights ceased blinking. The santero looked over at Garland. "Cameras are out, amigo. Now to the bomb shelter."

*　*　*　*

She faded in and out of consciousness. Her captor had given her laudanum, a tincture of ten percent opium mixed with alcohol that Tredd Van Marcherz had created in his basement. He'd found a recipe for laudanum from the Victorian era. Liliana was the subject of his experiment. Searching on the dark web, he found the necessary ingredients. For the past few days, he had been feeding the opium to her and kept her alive by force-feeding her minimum amounts of food. For the ritual of *anima mutatis mutanda,* soul switching, Liliana needed to be kept alive, even if only barely.

Isabel and Tredd worked several rituals trying to open a gateway to hell before they were actually successful in doing so. It was a little harder to break through to the underworld than they thought. Strong walls, some created by magic and some by religion, kept the living world separate from dark beings. However, over time as Isabel's black magic had become infinitely stronger, she and Tredd were finally able to punch a hole from the living world into the depths of hell. They had mastered the magical techniques by using *The Lesser Key of Solomon.*

In history, Solomon was recognized as a king of Israel. Legends speculated that he possessed a magic ring that controlled and identified seventy-two demons. The spirits were later described by medieval scholars and identified by sigils. After reading *The Lesser Key of Solomon*, Tredd determined that hell, not unlike any major human business corporation, had a hierarchy. There were kings, princes, dukes, presidents, and corporals, with the grand emperor of the demons being Satan. Each identified demon had a legion of 6,666 lesser demons beneath their title. It was said that the ring of King Solomon controlled all of the demons, including the devil himself.

Tredd and Isabel sought the intervention of the grand emperor. If they didn't think Satan would respond directly, the pair anticipated they would receive the assistance of either a king or a prince. When the two performed a ritual summoning demons, they were surprised to find that a demon named Betel, an insignificant corporal in the hell's hierarchy, answered their call. According to *The Lesser Key*, Betel had the power to find lost objects, speak all 7,103 languages in the human world, and transfer souls from humans into animals. It was the soul-switching part that they were most interested in. Liliana was the perfect vessel to receive the transfer of Isabel's spirit with Betel's assistance.

Liliana was kept sitting upright tied to a chair. Her legs were numb from being seated in the same position for seventeen hours a day since she had been kidnapped, except for periodic bathroom breaks using an invalid commode located to her right. Tredd untied her, permitted her to perform necessary bodily functions, then tied her up again. He kept a large hunting knife tied to his belt. He periodically waved it in her face as a reminder that she was very close to death. Between the laudanum and being fed minimal amounts of food, Liliana was weak and frail. When Tredd wasn't watching her, the spider was. But at one point she found some courage. She looked at the spider.

"You red-eyed bitch," she whispered. "Why don't you and your boyfriend just kill me and get it over with?"

The spider laughed. "Oh my dear, we will. If we had any mercy we would put your soul into the body I am currently inhabiting and give you a chance for another kind of life." She opened her fangs. "But we have no mercy. So your life as you know it will come to an end."

"Your boyfriend in there killed my mother's lawyer, didn't he? Julio Lopez discovered that P.S. 578 water was being poisoned, and he died for it."

"Too bad. So sad. Does it really matter? That was so many years ago."

"Children died. I got sick. Yeah, it matters. You won't get away with this."

"I am half hoping we won't get away with it. I hope people come looking for you. I really do."

She skittled across the floor from the other side of the room. "I especially hope that the bastard who stuck my spirit in this spider's body comes looking for you. Then I will finally have my revenge."

Liliana shook her head. "Maybe this time someone can transfer your spirit into a cockroach."

*   *   *   *

Teo, Garland, and Julio the fly had a difficult time finding the entrance to the bomb shelter beneath the basement of P.S. 578. Very few people knew this area of the school even existed. It had been closed and sealed up years ago because of problems with asbestos. One small door led to the old shelter. After racing through the school's basement, Garland noticed a small faded bomb shelter sign on a rusty metal door.

"Follow me." Garland opened the door. The stairway was dark, but Teo's glowing body provided enough light to prevent the trio from tripping over the stairs and each other. As they descended the stairwell, the air changed, growing heavy and uncomfortably hot.

"It smells like rotten eggs down here," said Don Julio. "Under normal circumstances, the smell of rotten food doesn't always bother me. But this, this is different. It makes me sick. Can you feel the heat?"

"It isn't the smell of rotten eggs, Julio," Teo said. "It's the smell of sulfur and brimstone. You are smelling the scent of the Underworld, the odor of demons. It will get worse, the closer we get. And of course, you know where the heat comes from."

The trio continued its descent. The air around them grew hotter and hotter and the smell of sulfur grew worse. Garland wiped the sweat from his brow. Finally, they could go no farther. In the distance, they saw one final door. It was the door they needed to pass through before they reached the main room of the bomb shelter itself. Garland took a deep breath. They had reached their destination. Garland looked through a small glass windowpane on the door. What he saw terrified him.

The walls of the room were painted black with inverted pentagrams. A makeshift altar for two bodies had been constructed. Liliana's naked body lay on one table while the large spider that was Dona Isabel rested on another. Tredd wore a long white hooded robe and held something in his hand. His skin was as pale as his robe. He began to chant in Latin. A ring of fire appeared, surrounding him and the altar. Outside the large ring, a smaller ring of fire appeared. It burned with a frightening brightness and spewed the same awful odor.

"Teo, what's going on? This looks like a scene out of a low-budget horror movie."

"This, amigo, is ceremonial magic of the medieval kind. The magician has to stay within the large circle. The demon appears in the smaller circle. He can't step out of the circle when the demon comes. If he does, he dies. That thing he has in his hand? It is a wand that controls the spirit."

"Jesus Christ."

"Let's hope Jesus and many others are with us tonight," Teo whispered.

"So what do we do, Santero Teofil?" Garland asked.

Teo became very serious. "I will call upon the orishas for strength. At the right moment, we break the circle and interrupt the work. And hopefully send her to hell."

"Let me at Isabel," Julio whispered. "I have this axe. I'll chop her legs off one at a time. I'll send her to the devil in pieces, one leg at a time."

"Julio, be patient. Your time will come. Now we must save a girl's life."

Tredd Van Marcherz had transformed. He was no longer just the crazy murderer living in his father's basement. Dressed in his robes and in a hypnotic state, he became something much more powerful, much more dangerous. He was mentally disassociated with everything around him. He had but one mission—to open a pathway from hell to the living world.

In a trance-like state, he walked around inside the flaming circle counterclockwise. In his hand he held a long, slender stick. Each time he passed the smaller circle, he pointed the stick in that direction. Each time he did this, a puff of yellow smoke emerged and the smell of sulfur increased. The flames around the circle grew higher and more intense. Tredd began to chant louder and louder:

Venit obedientes animae viventis!Veni!
Venit obedientes animae viventis!Veni!
Venit obedientes animae viventis! Veni!
Venit obedientes animae viventis!Veni!

"Teo, what is he saying?"

"'Come obedient creature, come.' Didn't you study Latin in law school?"

"Sorry, it wasn't a requirement."

"We have to wait until he summons the demon."

"What?! Are you kidding? No! I am not waiting. That's insane."

"Remember what I told you? The rules of this magic are specific and dangerous. We must wait, amigo."

"Why wait? So he can open a gateway and flood the world with evil? Let's shut this down before it's too late."

Don Julio interrupted. "I think the lawyer has a point."

"No! We need the demon present to take Isabel."

Garland tried to open the door but Teo held him back. Garland grew angry and pushed the santero out of the way. He opened the door and burst into the room. The conjuror's eyes immediately looked at Garland. When their eyes met, Garland was shocked.

Tredd's eyes were no longer normal human eyes with pupils and irises. Instead the eyes of Tredd Van Marcherz were shiny pitch-black ovals. Tredd clung to his conjuror's wand and pointed it at Garland. An unseen force lifted him from the ground and hurled him across the room, slamming his body against the wall. He dropped to the floor, momentarily senseless. In his mind he saw a strange symbol and the face of Viktor Einarsson. He heard Viktor's voice in his head, laughing at him.

C'mon, hotshot. You can do better than that. My grandmother moves faster. Get your ass up and go!

Garland was overcome with a surge of physical strength. He looked at his fingertips and saw small sparks around his fingertips. Seconds later, he was back on his feet and was racing toward Tredd. The magician cocked his head and appeared confused by Garland's quick return to his feet.

Teo and Julio had followed Garland into the room. Teo looked over at the larger Amazonian spider, who size had tripled in size. Once the size of a dinner plate, Isabel was now as large as the altar she had been placed upon. Her flaming-red eyes were as big as saucers.

"Teofil, it has been a long time. And I see you brought Julio with you. I shall enjoy killing you both tonight."

"Not if I kill you first, Maria Isabel de la Fraga!"

Teo placed his hands together, creating a ball of lightning. He cursed and raised his hands a foot apart, creating a bluish-white ball of pure energy between his palms. Pretending he was going to toss the ball of lightning at Isabel, he instead made a quick turn on his heel and flung it in Tredd's face. The movement caught the magician off guard and knocked him to the ground. The wand dropped from his hand. Teo yelled over to Garland.

"Garland, grab that stick!"

Garland was overcome with strange energy that he had never felt before. It was the adrenalin rush of something between a race car driver about to approach the finish line or a lion about to pounce on the prey he had been hunting. Darting to the other side of the room, he picked up the slender hazel stick. The young lawyer quickly noted that the stick had carved sigils and semi-precious stones embedded in it. *Someone went to a lot of trouble to make this.* Garland smiled and looked into Tredd's black eyes.

"Looking for your magic wand, pal?" He snapped the wand into two pieces and threw it on the floor.

At first, the magician was angry and cursed at him in a guttural voice. Then he laughed. "You can't stop him from coming. The portal is already open. It's too late."

"For what?"

Suddenly another voice came into Garland's mind and he saw several faces of people he didn't know, but one voice was familiar.

The voice belonged to the computer kid from Edward Williams, the chaos magician.

Dude, this guy thinks he understands magic, but he doesn't. The spirits are controlling him. He's not controlling the spirits. Take back the power!

Garland had no idea how to take back the power, because he had no idea what that meant. There was no time to analyze the messages. But when he looked across the room and saw Liliana semi-conscious, something struck him. Without her, this whole "magical operation" would fail. There was no soul to take if she was gone. He knew he had to get to her. Then he heard another familiar yet strange voice in his head. It was the voice of Father Hearn.

Words are powerful. Use them, my son. Contemplate St. Ives. The patron saint of attorneys.

"Contemplate. No time to do that," he said aloud.

* * * *

Isabela had grown bigger and stronger. She jumped in the air and landed on the ground in front of Teo. Her fangs were giant metal knives. She lunged forward repeatedly, trying to attack Teo with them. But Teo was agile. He dodged each strike as he prepared to hit her with another blast of lightning from his hands.

"Maria Isabel de la Fraga, there was a time when you were a beautiful, sensible woman. What happened?"

"You happened, you bastard! You refused to walk the dark path with me. You and the fly!"

Teo laughed. "I think you are too sensitive." With that remark, he shot a lightning blast at Isabel, knocking her backward. Don Julio flew over and hovered in the air above Isabel.

"Hola, Isabel! Long time no see!" He swung his axe and only managed to slice into one of her legs. She screamed, then lifted another leg and kicked the fly. He tumbled around in the air and lost his metal helmet but flew back in her direction with his axe raised. She turned and swatted him away with a leg, sending him hurling into a wall. He hit his head and fell into unconsciousness. She returned her attention to Teo.

Across the room Garland and Tredd wrestled. Garland finally pinned him down on the floor and continued punching him in the face over and over again, bloodying his nose and splitting his eyebrow open. Blood flowed from Tredd's face until the weakening man had a sudden burst of energy. Tredd pushed Garland off him, turning his attention away from his opponent. The bleeding man was more interested in what was happening within the smaller circle he had drawn with salt. Sparks flew and smoke rose within the circle. Flames began to rise.

"My Lord Betel arrives!" he yelled. "Lord Betel, come!"

Garland found his opportunity. While Tredd was focused on welcoming the demon into the room, Garland ran over to the table where Liliana lay. He loosened her restraints. Scooping her up in his arms and tenderly kissing her. She opened her eyes slightly and whispered, "Garland? Is that you?"

"Yes, my love. Hold on just a little bit longer. I'm going to get us out of here." He looked across the room and saw Teo battling Isabel. Don Julio struggled to get back on his feet. Teo looked back at Garland and Liliana. One of Isabel's pincers scratched his arm, tearing his shirt and drawing blood.

"Take the girl and go! Now!"

Garland looked at the beautiful woman he held in his arms and spoke to her. "Look, I'm going to put you down against the wall for a minute. It's going to be okay."

She smiled. "I know. You have to go and fight, Garland. Your friends. They need you."

"Here, take this." He gently placed her down and gave her his coat. "We'll have time later, I hope."

"We will." She smiled weakly. "Now get over there and kill that spider."

The walls of the room vibrated as the heat increased. For a minute, all eyes were drawn to the smaller circle where Tredd stood with his arms upraised awaiting the arrival of one of hell's minions.

"Arise into the living world, Lord Betel! Arise and take our most precious offering!"

Garland watched with wonder. Flames shot up from the small circle and scorched the ceiling. As the flames grew smaller, the smoke dissipated. In the center of the ring stood a small, thin man wearing a suit. He looked about fifty years old and had salt-and-pepper hair. Large black horn-rimmed glasses hid small piggish eyes. Standing casually with his arms behind his back, his double-breasted pinstripe suit was outdated and worn.

Rather than a minion from hell, the man looked more like a tired law professor.

Isabel flew across the floor and ran over to him. "Lord Betel. We have the human for the soul switching."

"Where is my sacrifice?" Once he opened his mouth, any thought of this man being normal was gone. The voice coming from the demon was deep and guttural. "A soul switched for a soul and a servant to do my bidding. That was our communication."

Isabel whipped around. "My Lord Betel, we have a pleasant surprise for you. I have three souls for you in addition to the woman I shall offer to you. There is an old man, a young man, and a creature that is half human. They will make wonderful additions to the Underworld as your servants."

"Excellent." The little man gave a smile that was largely composed of his elongated teeth, like those belonging to a wolf. "Your generosity is not unnoticed. Lovely Isabel, will you not let me step out of the circle to allow me to give you a proper thanks?" He opened his arms to her as though he wished to embrace her.

"No, Lord Betel. It is best that you stay within the confines of the circle and we bring the soul to you. Now, will you keep your promise and switch my soul into the body of the young woman?"

He released a deep guttural laugh. "Yes, yes, I did make that promise. And for every promise there is a price to pay. I am a demon of my word. Let us begin. Master Tredd, are you ready? Bring me the girl."

Garland looked over at his group and assessed what was happening. He tried to figure out who could fight and who couldn't. He saw that Teo kept his eyes on Isabel. Julio desperately tried to shake off being thrown against a wall. Tredd levitated off the ground and floated over to where Liliana lay. Garland jumped in front of him. With the demon present, Tredd's strength increased. With a single push, Tredd hurled Garland halfway across the room.

"Well done!" hissed the demon. "Bring the girl to me."

"Yes, Lord Betel." He scooped up Liliana, who used her last ounce of her strength to scratch his face.

"Lie still!"

Garland picked himself up and ran toward Tredd. As he passed by, he quickly glanced at Teo, whose facial features stretched and shifted. Suddenly Garland heard another voice in his head. The voice was musical and familiar to him. He had heard it once before on the beach. It was the Goddess of the Sea, Yemaya.

I am coming! Keep the demon talking for a little bit longer.

Garland walked over and stood outside the smaller circle where Betel waited. The words of Father Hearn and the chaos magician seemed to make sense. He would try to take back the power…with words.

"It seems to me, Lord Betel, that you would need a much stronger spirit than this puny girl. I mean, your servant over here, Master Tredd, probably hasn't fed her properly or even drugged her."

"What game are you playing, mortal?" The demon was clearly annoyed and displayed his disgust by showing his fangs and hissing.

"Well, I mean, look. You are about to place the spirit of the spider in the young woman here, yes?"

"That was the deal, yes."

"And in doing so Isabel, as a living, breathing woman, becomes your entry into the human world, correct?"

"Yes."

"And just so we're clear, you made the deal with Isabel and the conjuror holding the woman so that they can be *your* servants, correct?"

"Yes! Yes! And your point is?"

"Well, I don't know how to say this, but I think you have been… well, used by these two and made a fool of. I mean, let's face it. It took a lot of energy from these two," he said, pointing to the spider and her magician, "to bring you here from hell and then offer you a defective sacrifice. I mean, you are a Lord of Hell, right? Or just a rank and file soldier?"

"I am a Lord of Hell! Show me respect!"

"Oh, I am, I am, Lord Betel. In fact, I am trying to show you even more respect than your two so-called servants. As a Lord of Hell, your sacrifice should be...*must* be perfect."

The demon placed a three-fingered hand on his chin. "I agree. So what are you going to offer me?"

"Me."

"No!" The spider skittered across the floor and stood outside the circle. "I do not want that body!"

"But I would be a willing servant. That female sacrifice? She isn't interested in serving anyone, let alone you. Is not a willing servant better than an unwilling one? And your contract would be fulfilled. You see, I know a little bit about contract law, unlike these two." He pointed to the spider and Tredd.

Julio, now fully awake, ran over to Garland. "Stop! You can't do this. You can't take her poisonous soul into your body. I won't let you!"

Garland's eyes flared red. "Let it go, Julio."

"Lord Betel, you promised!" Isabel screamed. "I am supposed to be a woman. Tredd is to be my lover and *my* servant."

"Silence!" Betel roared. "I don't give a damn about your love life! I promised I would soul switch and you promised me a sacrifice. Once I switch out your soul into this fine specimen of a man, I have fulfilled my end of the bargain. Look at his body. He has a fine body. Take it or leave it."

"Bastard demon!" Tredd screamed. "I'll send you back to hell!"

Betel laughed. "With what? Your broken magic wand? Think you'll get any other help from the Underworld from anyone other than me?"

The room began to vibrate again. Water in the shape of a snake appeared and slid across the floor. The snake circled the floor outside the salt ring surrounding the demon.

"What magic is this?" Betel demanded.

Garland saw the demon glaring at him with red eyes. "Isn't me, Lord Betel. I think it's that someone else."

She's here. It's Yemaya. Thank you, Goddess.

Tredd threw Liliana to the floor. From under his robe, he pulled out a knife and lunged at Garland. Garland screamed as the knife sliced into his shoulder. As he dropped to the ground shouting in pain, a long watery hand pulled the knife from his shoulder and flung it to the ground. The long water snake that had been circling the demon changed into a large fist and punched Tredd in the face, knocking him to the ground. Garland grabbed his bleeding shoulder and ran to Liliana.

Inside the circle where Betel stood, the salt ring spread a little wider. The demon looked confused as the floor opened and flames shot up, striking the ceiling. Something was coming, rising from the bowels of the earth.

"Who is doing this? Is it you, witch?"

"No!" screeched Isabel. "I am not!"

"A few friends are to join us. I hope you don't mind," stated the goddess sweetly.

Across the room where Teo once stood was the radiant sea goddess, Yemaya. A globe of water encircled her, and she stood poised with a silver machete in the shape of a sliver of the moon. Her red hair gently drifted in the breeze as her energy lit up the room. Her skin was bronze, her eyes were hypnotic, glistening seas of green. With an inscrutable smile, she took in her surroundings.

Julio's armor clanked as he ran over and bowed before Yemaya. "My lady."

She smiled and nodded. "Sir Fly."

"Julio Javier Hortachea de Lopez, at your service."

The smaller demon looked terrified as the tips of long curling ram's horns started to rise from the fiery hole in the floor. Slowly, a green-faced creature with long white hair appeared. His features were half human, half reptilian with large yellow eyes. When he fully emerged from the ground, he towered over the smaller demon in the circle. At the end of his webbed hands were bear claws that dripped blood. His lips were also covered in blood. Evidently he had just finished eating something or someone. The creature's body was enormous and muscular, but his feet were small like that of a goat. It was amazing that such small feet supported such a large, heavy body.

Yemaya addressed him. "Furzoune, Lord of a Thousand Lies, Eater of Dead Souls, Finder of Treasure, and Teacher of the Politics of both Heaven and Hell."

The creature smiled and bowed. "Beautiful goddess."

"May I ask why you are here, Furzoune?"

"Betel had no authority to enter the human world. Hell is not unlike human corporations such as Standard Oil, IBM, Eastern Airlines, or even Lehman Brothers. There are rules, you know. Switching souls was never within his authority. We have structure. We have protocols that Betel violated." To emphasize his anger, he ran a bloody claw down Betel's jacket and ripped one side of it in half. "Moreover, he is no 'Lord of Hell.' Betel is a nobody, a soldier demon; envision, if you will, the devil's file clerk. Corporal demons have absolutely no authority to make blood contracts with mortals without the permission of a higher-ranking demon such as me. Apparently Betel didn't get the memorandum." He ran a claw down the other side of Betel's suit and ripped the rest of the suit jacket from his skinny body.

Betel shivered. "It-it was a mistake, Lord Furzoune." With that statement, Furzoune released a high-pitched scream that caused Betel to whimper and cover his ears.

"Betel exceeded his authority. That being said, Goddess, Betel was promised a soul, and I am here to collect. Now who will it be? You know what happens when a hellish promise is broken." He grinned. "I can cause chaos in the living world."

"And in terms of power, I outrank you!" She struck her silver machete on the floor, and the demons stumbled within the circle. "And I am sure you do not wish to see my husband Orula come to your domain, demon!"

"No, no please, Goddess," he said, bowing. "I meant no offense."

"However, I am willing to fulfill the bargain and provide you with a soul. Let's make it interesting, shall we?"

She pointed her machete toward a closed door. When the door swung open, Fergal Gonzalez walked in surrounded by the ghosts of the children of P.S. 578. Señor Pepe sat perched on his shoulder like a parrot on the shoulder of a pirate. Yemaya drifted over to Tredd Van Marcherz.

"See who's here? Look at them," she hissed. "Go on. *Look* at them. Look at those children your father permitted to die. Feel their pain!" She waved her machete over the top of his head.

First, Van Marcherz felt dizzy. Then he was overcome with the nausea. He clutched his stomach. His hair fell out in clumps. Pinholes in his arms began to bleed as he felt the pain of a hundred needles jabbed into his arms. As he lay on the ground, he feebly tried to whisper a magical incantation against the goddess. It was of no use. And through all the pain, he saw the faces of the dead children staring at him. Little Evan, the leader of the group, pointed at Tredd.

"You are a very bad man," he whispered.

"No, please, I didn't do this to you. My father ignored the water problems! Please! Go haunt him! Take his soul!"

From the back of the crowd, another figure appeared. It was the ghost of Teo's nephew, Julio Lopez. The specter of the murdered lawyer stood in front of Tredd. The goddess smiled.

"Remember me?" he inquired as he bent down in front of Tredd. "I never forgot your face. You are the man who killed me in that basement all those years ago."

"Please," Tredd begged. "Go after my father. This is all his fault. He used to beat me when I was a kid. He told me to kill you. I have mental problems. Isabel, help me!"

"Oh, save yourself! I have my own problems," she hissed.

"Isabel?" he whispered. "I love you. Don't abandon me, please."

"Stop it. Do you really think I ever loved you? You're weak."

Across the room, Furzoune, still confined within the magical circle along with Betel, had been sadistically enjoying Tredd's humiliation. As Betel continued to cower beneath him, he called over to the goddess.

"This is amusing. Love is so fickle, isn't it? Goddess, I would like to have that soul of the magician. The spider is right. He is weak,

275

but more important, he is malleable. I can easily beat him into sub-
mission and make him my slave."

Yemaya looked thoughtful. "No, no. That would be too easy."
She looked at the spider. "I have something better in mind."

Señor Pepe jumped off Fergal's shoulder. The little squirrel
hopped over to where the huge spider stood ready to attack. Señor
Pepe stood up on his hind legs and sniffed the air nervously. Isabel
laughed.

"That's all you have? You've got to be kidding me. A squirrel?
You are sending a rat to kill me? Hardly a fair fight, don't you think?"
She lunged forward. Her jaws snapped at the squirrel. Her deadly
blades missed Señor Pepe by millimeters.

"No, Isabel, this will be a fair fight," the goddess announced as
she turned to Garland and smiled. "Mr. Yao sends you his warmest
regards."

She had barely finished the statement when Señor Pepe began
to grow in size. His body flattened out and extra angular legs poked
through his sides. The squirrel's face and body began to change until
it became a mirror image of Isabel. Señor Pepe had become a spider,
much larger than Isabel with the same deadly pincers, but with the
additional weapon of a scorpion's tail.

Isabel assumed an attack position, but the squirrel-spider moved
faster. Pepe's scorpion tail stung Isabel in the middle of her back. She
screamed. Julio, now conscious, came running over with his axe and
buried it in her back. Isabel rotated her head, then sliced through his
armor with her jaw. He was bleeding, but Julio managed to make
sure the axe remained securely lodged in her back.

Suddenly the Amazonian spider's legs wobbled. She moved
from side to side briefly before collapsing in a disgusting heap. Yao's
black magic poison worked. Isabel was finally dead from the scorpion's sting. A smoky form rose from the spider's body and took a
solid form in the shape of a woman. Isabel appeared as the woman
she had been so many decades ago. In her youth, she had actually
been quite beautiful, with long black hair, large sensuous eyes, and
full lips. Right now, she looked terrified and could not look directly
at Yemaya.

"Maria Isabel de la Fraga, you have offended the orishas. Your actions and those of the magician you have trained resulted in the spilling of innocent blood. I no longer consider you one of my children, and I am under no obligation to protect you. I shall turn you over to one of my brothers, the great Baron Samedi."

Loud rock music began to play. From across the room, Liliana and Garland looked at each other.

"Garland, that song."

"Yeah, I hear it."

"Is that 'Highway to Hell' by AC/DC?"

"Yes, it is. I wonder who's coming to visit now. I don't think I can take any more surprises," Garland stated flatly.

In a mushroom cloud of purple smoke, Baron Samedi appeared in a dramatic purple satin tuxedo with a black beaver top hat and a black velvet cape. He had braided his snake-like hair into dreadlocks to give himself a neater, cleaner appearance. A lavender handkerchief was tucked in his breast pocket, and he carried his walking stick. Ever the gentleman, he looked as though he were about to attend an opera. When he saw Yemaya, he bowed in an effusive manner.

"My Lady of the Sea, I was told to come by a mortal. How can I help?"

"I have a recently deceased soul for you."

"Oh good. Where do I send her?"

"Wherever you like, but may I make a suggestion?" Yemaya pointed her machete in the direction of the two demons trapped in the magic circle.

"Certainly."

Baron Samedi jumped up in the air and grabbed Isabel in his skeletal arms. He sniffed her hair and her breasts. He stroked her hair and tried to kiss her. Isabel turned her face away and squirmed in his arms.

"Let go of me! You smell like a cemetery."

"I am the Master of Cemeteries. Hmmm, I love the smell of the newly dead. Such a pity," he said as he continued to stroke her hair. "We have no time to get to know each other—"

"Let go of me!"

"But our love cannot be. We are so different. I mean, I am an ardent lover, well-read, a traveler. You and I are intellectual opposites. I am an intellectual and you're the opposite. Don't be upset. You're just not my type. Oh well!" He turned to the demons, who looked excited at the prospect of receiving a soul. "Furzoune, old friend, how are you? Long time no see. Last time we saw each other was when I pushed that soul through Hell's Gate and ran away. Sorry about that."

"Think nothing of it."

"What was that guy's name again?"

"Don't remember. He was a forgettable soul. Had a bad toupee, as I recall. His political speeches didn't make sense and he wouldn't stop talking about himself. Found the need to keep telling me how great he was," Furzoune responded. "Do me a favor. No more politicians. This soul is not a politician, right?"

"Nah, just a dried out old witch to add to your collection. Here, Furzoune catch!"

The death specter threw a screaming Isabel into the arms of Furzoune while everyone in the room watched. Furzoune caught her in mid-air. When she landed in his arms, she had changed from a beautiful young woman into a hideous old hag. Her skin was like an old leather saddlebag and her hair was a yellowish gray. Furzoune licked the side of her wrinkled face with a long serpentine tongue.

"Such fun we shall have, Isabel. You will be my personal pet. I think I will call you Lizzie." The demon looked at Yemaya. "Goddess, I consider our contract fulfilled."

Isabel looked at Yemaya pleadingly. "Goddess, please, I do not belong in hell."

"Isabel, you opened the portal. You brought hell to the earth and succeeded. You have received exactly what you asked for. Now go!"

The demons nodded respectfully at Yemaya. A fiery chasm opened in the cement floor of the bomb shelter. Furzoune spun around in a circle as he began his descent back into hell carrying the screaming ancient Isabel in his arms. As he descended, he grabbed a whimpering Betel by his ripped suit and dragged him along with him. Baron Samedi tipped his hat toward the goddess and vanished. When the demons were completely out of sight, the cement floor closed up. The floor was left as though nothing had never been there.

Yemaya moved to Don Julio. "Don Julio, my time in this body is short. You have served honorably. I can restore you to the man you once were, but you will be mortal. What do you desire?"

"Great goddess, I would like to remain a fly, maybe part-time, just a much smaller version. I like the earth and don't want to leave it so fast. I can help that young lawyer. I can teach him our ways. That is all I really want. But since flies have a short lifespan—"

"I understand." She smiled and nodded. Then her attention was drawn to the children and Teo's nephew. She used her machete to cut open a door way into a cement wall, and a wonderful comforting light shone through to the room. Like a gentle wave on a peaceful ocean, she floated over to the little boy in front of the other children.

"Such a brave little boy you are! What's your name, child?"

"Evan, ma'am."

"Can you lead the children through that door toward the light?"

"Yes, ma'am." Evan turned and smiled at Fergal. "Goodbye!"

The goddess pointed in the direction of the doorway. "Very good. Now, on the other side of that door you will find people who love you and angels waiting to greet you. Hurry up now!"

Everyone watched as the children, led by Evan, laughed and smiled as they skipped and ran toward the light. Julio Lopez followed slowly behind the children. Then he turned and looked at the goddess.

"Thank Teo. He never gave up on me." Once he passed into the lighted doorway, the door closed, and the wall, like the cement floor, looked untouched.

Fergal ran across the room to the tiny body of Señor Pepe, who had changed back from a spider into a squirrel. Señor Pepe was unconscious but still breathing. Fergal scooped him up.

The goddess looked at Fergal. "Do not worry, my son, your little friend just needs time to recover."

Fergal nodded politely. He cradled Señor Pepe in his arms and exited the room.

Yemaya turned to Garland, who brought Liliana to her feet. The couple bowed respectfully. The goddess gently kissed Garland on the forehead. "I must leave you now. From the bottom of my heart, I thank you."

With her work done, Yemaya, the Goddess of the Sea, vanished.

The body of Teofil Lopez collapsed on the floor. Gone was the robust body and dark hair. He was thin and frail-looking, every inch an eighty-year-old man. Garland knelt on the floor.

"Teo! Teo! Talk to me!" He quickly checked for a pulse. It was weak. Teofil Lopez was dying. Garland picked up his head. He heard human voices and radio communications off in the distance.

He yelled. "Help! We need help here! A man is injured!"

Uniformed police officers raced in the door with guns drawn. Behind them, wearing a Kevlar vest, was O'Connell. He directed a woman in a nurse's uniform to go to Liliana. The nurse ran over to her carrying a blanket.

"Hi there, sweetie. My name is Bea. I'm a nurse. This is Dr. Quietus. We need to take you to a hospital."

"Okay," Liliana answer weakly. "Listen, that man over there needs your help more than me." She pointed to Teo. "And that other guy with the robe, he's the one who kidnapped me."

Bea gave her a savage smile. "Oh, you mean that man?"

Across the floor, Tredd Van Marcherz lay on his stomach.

"Oops, my bad," said O'Connell as he slammed Van Marcherz's head on the cement floor. While he was down, another police officer cuffed him, yanking his shoulders back off the ground. Both men pulled Van Marcherz to his feet, and he was quickly escorted out of the room to a waiting police cruiser.

Bea turned to look for Dr. Quietus and called over to him. "Alfred, I think you're up."

Dr. Quietus ran over to Garland, who cradled Teo in his arms. "Doctor, he's weak."

The doctor looked at him with kind eyes and took his pulse. "Let's get him into an ambulance. I'll get a stretcher." He walked away.

Teo opened his eyes. "Garland, thank you for helping me find my nephew's killer," he whispered. "Now he will face justice."

"He will. I didn't do anything. I think we owe Julio some gratitude."

A large fly landed on Teo. Garland smiled. "Look who's back in fat fly form."

"Hello, my people," said Don Julio. "Teo, man, you don't look so good."

Teo looked into Garland's eyes. "Garland, the energy of the Yemaya was powerful. It has weakened my body. But that is okay. I will be seeing the goddess shortly."

"No, no, you just need to get to a hospital. You're going to be fine. You aren't ready for the guy with the top hat."

Teo smiled. "Baron Samedi of the Graveyard? He's not so bad. A bit of a ladies' man, but he's okay."

"You are not going anywhere. Look, here comes the doctor with a stretcher. We're going to take you to the hospital."

Dr. Quietus and a paramedic lifted up the frail santero and placed him on the stretcher. He looked at Garland. "Why don't you meet us at the hospital?"

"Yes, if I could."

"Very well. We should go."

* * * *

Dr. Quietus told the paramedics that he would ride in the back with his patient, and if he needed assistance, he would call. He directed the paramedic to start an intravenous solution and attached Teo to a cardiac monitor. After the paramedic was finished, Dr. Quietus explained that Teo had been his patient for many years and that he wanted to have a private word with him. The paramedic agreed, and he left to sit in the front passenger's seat of the ambulance with the driver.

When Dr. Quietus knew they were alone, he spoke with Teo. "How are you, Mr. Lopez?"

"I have had better days," he whispered. "I know you have come for me. I hope I have lived a good enough life to enter a peaceful place. Shall I call you Monsieur Ankou? Have you come for my soul? I know that back in Breton, France, you collect souls in a four-wheeled cart drawn by horses, but these are modern times, right? You use ambulances instead?" He chuckled.

"Ah, *mon ami, we* must keep up with the current society, *oui?*" When Dr. Quietus spoke this time, he had a notable French accent. "I didn't know you recognized me. You, my dear friend, have lived an exemplary life on earth. Therefore, a man like you has nothing to worry about in the afterlife. Be at peace."

"That is good to know." Teo smiled and drifted off into a deep sleep. Just as the ambulance pulled up in front of Passaic General Hospital, Teo's heart stopped beating.

CHAPTER THIRTY-FIVE

It was an unusually warm, sunny day in February, a peculiar day for a funeral. The service at St. Morand's was quick. Father Hearn presided over the Mass of the Christian Burial, and though the church was packed, Garland quickly learned that Teofil Rodrigo Lopez had no relatives.

Much to his surprise, a curious document was dropped off at The People's Clinic a week earlier. Before all the madness occurred on the night of the Blood Moon, a thick envelope had been sent to Director Ina Furnstein's attention. There were specific instructions that the document was not to be opened until after the death of Teofil Lopez. It was his Last Will and Testament. The will left his entire estate to Garland Nowell with burial demands. Teo asked that, upon his death, he was to be cremated. When spring arrived on the first warm day, Teo wanted his ashes to be thrown into the ocean with seven new pennies.

The will also authorized Garland to throw a huge repast at Los Tres Gatos restaurant, complete with all of Teo's favorite foods—pork and clams, rice and beans, platanos maduros, and chuletas. He further demanded that Garland place a large statue of Yemaya in the center of the feast, as he wished her to preside over the repast in his memory.

Garland and Liliana sat on a bright orange crushed velvet couch in front of elaborate matching velvet drapes with cornices. Tres Gatos was packed with mourners, and Garland looked at the crowd with both confusion and amusement.

"Who are all these people, Garland?" asked Liliana. "I thought he had no family."

"He doesn't. Most of his family is deceased. These are all people to whom he'd given spiritual guidance or financial assistance over the years. Looks like he helped a lot of people."

She put her arm around him. "Teo was a good man, an amazing man. I'm so sorry."

"Thank you. It's so weird. I feel kind of lost without him. I guess these people must feel like us."

"Well, I am not at all like you, Mr. Nowell."

A well-dressed James Yao stood in a doorway, and he actually had a smile on his face this time. Garland didn't know what to do, so he just said hello.

"Hi, Mr. Yao. Thank you for coming."

"Think nothing of it. Teo was my friend of many years. And please call me James."

"Sure. You seem much friendlier than when we first met. Perhaps I misjudged you."

"Perhaps I did the same, Nowell. Stupid question, but are we in someone's house?"

"Yes. It belongs to those three guys over there with white aprons running around in the kitchen, the Corazon brothers. And that little old lady behind the stove is their mother, the head chef."

"I'm familiar with these kinds of places. I've eaten in a lot of underground restaurants in Chinatown. Listen, may I ask you another question?"

"Sure."

"I understand that you are Teo's heir."

"James, I had no idea. Apparently, an envelope was delivered to my office a week before the, the—"

"The incident from the other night?" he stated as he winked at Garland.

"Yeah. Teo must have known that he was going to die. I had no idea that he had no family. I had no idea he even liked me that much."

Yao laughed. "Neither did I. Hey, where's the fly?"

Garland pointed across the room to a short, chubby, white-haired man wearing a colorful brocade vest. He had a large whisk broom moustache and wore a pair of fake Dolce and Gabbana sunglasses. Don Julio stood in the center of three young women while slowly sipping a glass of red wine. He was holding court, telling stories and making the young ladies giggle.

James shook his head. "Amazing. I thought he wanted to remain a housefly."

"He did. But apparently he can change back and forth from fly to guy."

"Shapeshifting, Nowell. It's called shapeshifting."

"Whatever. Apparently, as long as he is alive and I own Teo's house, I have to provide a place for him to live. So guess what? If I want to live in the house, I have a new roommate," said Garland sarcastically. "Unless, of course, you want to take him in."

"No, no, Nowell, that's quite all right, he's all yours. Oh look, Izilda has just arrived. I must greet her." James Yao quickly hurried away.

"Yeah, that's right, Yao. Coward! Run away while you still can!"

"Who was he?" Liliana asked innocently.

"A master of Chinese poison magic called Gu."

"Oh boy. Is he the one responsible for changing that squirrel into the other scorpion-spider?"

"Uh-huh. See that woman over there? The one Yao ran to? She's a powerful Voodoo queen. That big tall guy who looks like Thor and looks like he eats nails for breakfast? A laborer by day and Norse magician by night. That kid with the iPad? He's some kind of a chaos magician and a mathematical genius."

"I remember that woman. The nurse who gave me a blanket. And that doctor. What are they?"

"She really is a nurse, but I have no idea what or who she's connected to in the world of magic. That guy in the bad-fitting suit with the white hair talking to the priest that buried Teo? He was a member of some group called the Golden Dawn. He, Teo, and the priest have been friends for many years."

Liliana looked confused and frightened. "So these people all have day jobs? Yet they all know each other and practice different forms of magic?"

"Teo wasn't a magician. He practices Santeria, a religion. But he believed no matter what people's differences were, they could all work together if they worked together for the power of good."

"And the fly?"

"Don Julio? He has no job but to annoy me. He has some role in all of this, but I haven't figured it out. But if it weren't for him," Garland extended a hand and touched her cheek, "we would have never met."

"I know." She kissed him on the cheek. "What about you? What are your magic powers?"

"Liliana, I'm just a guy. The only power I have is to seek the truth in a court of law. That's not magic. That's what you call 'normal,' I guess."

"After the other night, I don't even think I know what normal is anymore."

"That makes two of us," stated Garland. "One day I'm on the verge of insanity and Don Julio the fly lands in my house and asks me if I am going to finish some whiskey. Then he tells me that he needs a lawyer. The next thing you know, I'm involved in all this." He opened his arms to emphasize the point. "I was never much for the mystical myself. I've always just kind of lived day-to-day, just trying to get by."

"There are so many things that I can't figure out."

"Like what?"

"How did O'Connell find us, Garland?"

"As O'Connell headed out the door, he noticed a very old fallout shelter sign. He knew many old buildings in Passaic still had fallout shelters from the 1950s and 60s buried deep in the bowels of their buildings. He had a hunch. The coat, the hat, and an old bomb shelter. Maybe Liliana was closer than he thought. He called Garland."

"Garland, what's going to happen to that homicidal maniac who kidnapped me?"

"He confessed to the murder of that lawyer, Julio Lopez, back in 1988. He also very quickly gave up his father, Robert Van Marcherz. The local police arrested the school principal at his home last night. He's in the county jail along with his son."

"Really?"

"And the son claims that he was under duress and that his father forced him to kill Julio Lopez over the environmental problems at

P.S. 578. Once this hit the newspapers, the insurance companies started reaching out, wanting to talk settlement. We can maybe bring some peace to the children's families."

"Let's hope you're right. Insurance companies may not want to take the word of a crazy guy who practices black magic and falls in love with a big spider."

Garland went on to explain that when the police scanned the area for forensic evidence at the crime scene, the officers found the body of a dead spider the size of a large serving platter. Not even the toughest officers wanted to touch it. They called in local animal control authorities to get rid of the spider's dead carcass. What no one could explain was a tiny little axe sticking out of the spider's abdomen.

Garland and Liliana laughed. Liliana's attention was drawn to several other people entering the room.

"Ina! O'Connell!" She turned to Garland. "Look, Garland, normal people." Liliana left Garland's side and ran over to her favorite investigator and legal mentor. Happy to see them, she embraced them.

"How's my little girl doing?" asked Ina. "That ghastly man didn't touch you, did he?"

"No, thank God it never came to that. He was more in love with a hairy spider."

"If that scumbag laid a finger on you, tell me and I will personally go down to the county jail and finish smashing his head against the pavement again." O'Connell couldn't hide his ear-to-ear grin. "Accidentally smashing his head, of course."

"Absolutely," agreed Liliana.

"And by the way, ladies, I heard this wild story from one of my buddies in the Sheriff's Department. Spider boy claims that his father and the spider told him to kidnap you. He talks to a spider, what a lunatic! Anyway, I hear that after he pleads guilty to the 1988 homicide and your kidnapping, he's going to be dumped in the Vroom Building for the criminally insane in Trenton State Psychiatric Hospital. The word on the street is that he cries all day long about how his lover, the hairy eight-legged one, betrayed him."

Ina raised an eyebrow. "O'Connell, there are no such things as talking spiders. And it's a good thing he's going to be confined to the laughing academy for the rest of his life. The man's insane, of course."

"Of course," said Liliana. She failed to mention that she'd had multiple conversations with the evil spider who was actually an old witch in disguise, and that demons rose from hell to try to steal her soul with the spider's help.

Some things are better left unsaid.

*   *   *   *

When Teo's repast was over, Garland and Liliana walked to his car. Garland was just about to open his car door when he heard a familiar voice.

"Well done, Garlando. Teo would have been proud."

"Julio, I thought you left already."

"No, the Corazon brothers brought out Aguardiente Antiqueno that they picked up from their last trip to Colombia. I couldn't pass it up." He pulled out a bottle from the inside of his jacket and took a swig. "Hey, look who's coming."

Dr. Nettlebrook walked at a hurried pace down the street. "Mr. Nowell, how are you? And of course, the lovely Ms. Ramos. Garland, may I have a word?"

"Sure. But Liliana stays. I have nothing to hide from her. She knows about everything. I told her about your little group of magical friends."

"Ah yes. What did you call us? The Metaphysical Justice League? Harry Potter Club? That's fine. Magical friends. I'm sure Viktor will like that last one."

A large hulking figure stood in the shadows smoking a cigarette. "I don't like it at all." Viktor Einarsson came out from the shadows. "I'm a pagan. I take what I do very seriously. I'm nobody's magical friend. But Nowell, you impressed me the other night. You fought well. You made the All-Father proud."

"Hey, I don't know what I did the other night, I thank you. But I just want to get back to a normal life. Julio can live in the house and do what he wants, be a man or be a housefly. It's all good. For me, this is over."

Dr. Nettlebrook shook his head. "The reluctant magus. I've known a few in my day. Men and women who have gifts, talents, and the ability to master things in the unseen world. You may want to learn how to master certain natural skills that you do not realize you possess."

"Unseen world?" Garland pounded his fist on the hood of his car. "Are you kidding me? Not interested. Truth be told, I want to forget about what happened the Night of the Blood Moon. I saw evil, and yes, it really did have horns and a tail."

"Yes, and you also witnessed the power of good that overcame evil. Please don't forget that."

"True, but I am still not interested in playing with the occult. It's dangerous. It should be left alone."

"I understand. But I do believe you have certain untapped talents. Should you change your mind, here's my card." He handed Garland a red business card with bright gold embossed lettering.

Garland studied the card. He looked at Nettlebrook and shook his head. "I can't believe this. You call yourselves 'The Urban Order of Moonlighting Magi?' Sounds like the name of a bad Las Vegas lounge act."

"Well, truth be told, Mr. Nowell, we all have, let us say, day jobs. In modern times, unless you are independently wealthy, one cannot focus on the occult all day long. The Urban Order of Moonlighting Magi started out in the cities decades ago because it was easier for people who had certain qualities, shall we say, to hide from what you call normal people. We're average citizens by day. But we moonlight—"

"So you guys work part-time, you moonlight to prevent demons from leaving hell?"

"You are over simplifying. It is really so much more complicated than that. I know you are very confused, but let me ask you this, Garland. Do you think it was any coincidence that you met Don Julio and Teofil Lopez?"

"Don't know. Don't care. Nice talking to you." He turned to the fly. "Julio, the house is yours. Good luck and good night." He opened the car door for Liliana. She got into the car and he followed suit. They drove away leaving Don Julio, Viktor, and Dr. Nettlebrook standing in the street.

*   *   *   *

As they drove back to Liliana's apartment, both remained silent until Liliana spoke. "Look, I wouldn't judge you if you wanted work with those guys."

"What, the Moonlighting Magician's Club? Not interested. But looks like since I'm stuck with the fly for a while."

"Maybe Dr. Nettlebrook was right. Maybe you should learn a little bit more. You could have some wonderful ability you don't fully comprehend."

"No, Liliana. I accidentally became involved in this, and now I own a house with a half man, half fly. If the gods were kind, they could have given me something cool like a Hobbit or one of the hot elf maidens from *Lord of the Rings*. Teo, the only man with a little bit of sanity in all of this, died. You were kidnapped by some black magician, and I almost lost you. As far as I'm concerned, this stuff should be left alone."

"So what are you going to do?"

"Tonight? Absolutely nothing but have a drink at your apartment, if you want me there."

Liliana raised her hands and placed them on her temples, pretending she was talking to an invisible spirit. "Yes, yes. I will tell him! The spirits are telling me that you should come over and stay over. The spirits are also telling me that you should make me some scrambled eggs with bacon when you get up in the morning."

Garland smiled. "With or without salsa?"

EPILOGUE

Fergal Gonzalez nursed Señor Pepe back to health. He felt better knowing the children were finally at peace.

Several months after the Night of the Blood Moon, Gonzalez appeared in court with Señor Pepe. He sat quietly in the back of the courtroom and watched Liliana Ramos, Esq., on behalf of The People's Clinic, place the settlement against P.S. 578 on the record. Families who had lost a child because of the contaminated water pumped through the school's pipes received compensation of an undisclosed amount. As Liliana left the courtroom, she stopped to see Fergal and Señor Pepe and was warmly greeted.

With the fees received for The People's Clinic legal work on this matter, they would be able to keep the Clinic's doors open to help the indigent who needed legal representation.

* * * *

Robert Van Marcherz was determined not to go down alone on the homicide charge. He informed the Passaic County Prosecutor how for thirty years, he had paid retired Detective Ted Klagborn and several others, including the late Dr. Meadowloc, hundreds of thousands of dollars to keep their mouths shut about Julio Lopez's murder case.

The police finally arrived at Klagborn's front door to extradite him to New Jersey, but his young Venezuelan wife had taken justice into her own hands. When the police rang the doorbell at the Snell Island cottage to arrest Klagborn, a bruised and bleeding Arelia opened the door and pointed to the man sprawled out on the kitchen floor like a rag doll. After one too many beatings, she attacked Klagborn with his own golf clubs and left him unconscious.

When Klagborn awoke in St. Petersburg's Medical Center, he found that he was handcuffed to a gurney with a police officer seated at his bedside. O'Connell had made sure that he would be treated like any other criminal who required medical treatment before being processed in the criminal justice system.

* * * *

Tredd Van Marcherz was placed in solitary confinement at Trenton State Psychiatric Hospital. Staff claimed that he cried day and night, pining for some woman named Isabel, asking anyone who would listen to explain why she left him.

* * * *

Izilda Montague had a busy morning. She was scheduled to attend a private showing of new designer handbags imported from France. Her executive assistant, twenty-five-year-old Joanie, came running into her office to inform her that there was a man, a very handsome one, waiting to see her.

"Am I scheduled to have lunch with this gentleman?"

"Let me check, Ms. Izilda." Joanie ran back to her desk and returned. "Funny, Ms. Izilda, I'm sorry, I must have just missed this appointment. It's here, but I didn't see it yesterday. How strange! It popped up just now. But you do have a free hour for lunch today, if you want to take it. Man, this guy in the waiting room is hot, with a very slight Italian accent, I think. Jet-black hair, blue eyes, and a dazzling smile! Tall, muscular guy. He's not only attractive, but a real sweetie pants."

Izilda sat back in her executive chair. "Sweetie pants? Really? Or perhaps just another amateur chemist who would like us to help him become to the next Prince Matchabelli or Coco Chanel. Or another scarf designer who thinks that he's the next Hermès. Probably here to make a sales pitch. God, I have so much work today. All I really wanted to do was just eat lunch at my desk today." She sighed. "Does this sweetie pants have a name?"

"Yes, ma'am. He says his name is Count Alexander Baroni de Samedi. I bet he's one of those new Italian shoe designers."

Izilda felt a chill come over her. She knew exactly who it was, and he wasn't a shoe designer. In truth and in fact, he was more of a debt collector.

"Send Mr. Sweetie Pants in. I'll see him. After he enters, close my door."

Art by Christopher Stewart

www.ingramcontent.com/pod-product-compliance
Lightning Source LLC
Chambersburg PA
CBHW051144030726
47504CB00004B/1023